Praise for...

The Better Part of Valor

"Ann Jeffries has done it again! Intrigue, greed, power, and romance all combined to make this a real page turner!"
—J.A. Meinecke, Author of *A Woman To Reckon With*

"Ann Jeffries never disappoints! Once again, she has the reader hooked and wanting more!"
—Bella Fayre, Author of *Maelstroms of the Silent*

"Author Ann Jeffries takes the reader on a ride filled with twists that will leave you wanting more. In this case, she keep[s] your head spinning as you wait for the next novel to be published."
—L. S. Casey, Author of *Alma Mater*

"Once again, Ms. Jeffries captivates the reader with characters and plot that demand complete attention. She weaves a story full of intrigue, but leaves plenty of time for romance. This book is a must read."
—Nancy Engle, Author, *Reunions Can Be Murder*

"Ms Jeffries gives us a story of deep compassion and love combined with suspense, action, and drama. A great read."
—Abraham Lieb, Esq.

Moments to Remember

"Ann Jeffries, once again, puts us on the edge of our seats, delivering a compelling story line, complete with drama, intrigue, and romance! Jeffries takes no prisoners! A must read!"
—Catherine Lowery, Author

An Unguarded Moment

"I love a story that immediately grabs your attention and keeps you involved till the last page. Good read. Highly recommended."

–Gayle A. Hopper, MD

"Ann Jeffries does an excellent job of weaving her characters' stories together and keeping the reader captivated."

–Nancy Engle, Author, *Murder at Mount Joy*

"Ann has a terrific voice for romance—it [is] light, readable and the characters were a lot of fun."

–Kara Cesare, the Richard Curtis Literary Agency

"I loved the story line! A little suspenseful which I like. The story flowed and it felt like I was reading a movie. I enjoyed the book."

–Gina, an avid reader

"An engrossing and sensuous love story that immediately grabs your attention and keeps you involved till the last page."

–Abraham Leib, Esq.

"My overall view is that this is a good, intelligent read! It's the kind of story you never want to end."

–Janice Sims, Author, *This Winter Night*

"I really admire Ann's smooth writing style and the appealing premise of this project."

–Mavis Allen, Associate Senior Editor, Silhouette Books

Touch Me In The Morning

"I could not put my iPad down once I started reading. Loved the characters and story line which kept me guessing what was going to happen next."

–Pauline, an avid reader.

"Ms. Jeffries has given us a love story about two adults who, having experienced some of life's darker moments, fall deeply and passionately in love. Her characters are real life and enable the reader to eagerly ride along with them on their adventure."

–Abraham Leib, Critic.

"I loved this novel; many times finding myself lost in their lives. The author did a fantastic job with character and plot development, and an unpredictable story line."

–Jessica Tilles, best-selling author of *Loving Simone*

"Ann Jeffries puts so much into a book [and] pays special attention to characterization so that by the time you finish reading one of her stories you feel you know the characters. Ms. Jeffries handles the romance between Satarah and Doug with realism and with passion. You really believe they're falling in love. Satarah makes him a part of her big, loving family, a multicultural clan that will steal your heart."

–Janice Sims, best-selling author, *Thief of My Heart*

"I met [Ann Jeffries] and…knew her books would be exciting and full of real life experiences. She is as dynamic as her characters are in the book. As I read, I became a part of the book. She knows life and can take you places you have [never] been. Excellent book."

–Danny Keith

Uncommon Choices

"Ann Jeffries has given us a great adventure story and a terrific love story together with whose characters immediately come alive and involve us in their searing passion and heartbreaking dilemmas."

–Abe Leib, Esq.

Northern Exposures

"Ms. Jeffries never writes a slow read. Her novels are impossible to put down. I can't wait for the next installment of her Wisdom of the Ancestors Series."

–Trisha Moriarty, Author, *The Secrets She Kept*

Another Point of View

"Ann Jeffries has done it again! Once you start reading you won't be able to put the book down!"

–J. A. Meinecke, Author, *A Woman to Reckon With*

"Another home run for Ann Jeffries! Deftly woven plot twists and the pace of the novel is strong and the story intriguing."

–Jessica Tilles, best-selling author, *Loving Simone*

Southern Exposures

"Ann Jeffries definitely has a skill for storytelling. There is vitality and high drama in Southern Exposures. *The author did an excellent job with honing in and focusing on the three main, important characters of which the drama surrounds. I fell in love with the Alexanders. Job well done!"*

– Jessica Tilles, Editor, and Author of *Loving Simone*

"Loved the way [Ann Jeffries] described the activities…I felt as though I was there witnessing everything [that she was] describing. [She] immediately got my attention with the colorful…attention to details. The book is very warm. The characters have to face challenges and each does it in a different way. Loved the focus on loving family—members of the family loving each other and believing in each other."

–Brenda Irons LeCesne, Esq.

"There are a lot of promising plots within the story. I thoroughly enjoyed… this [novel]. I think [Ann Jeffries'] ability [to] create emotion is a true talent. [She] did a great job creating suspense. The [characters'] stories seemed most authentic and entertaining. Language and dialogue [o]ver all…is a strong area for [Ann]."

–Karen R. Thomas, President, Creative Minds Book Group

"I always like a happy ending and being the romantic that I am the ending makes me want the continuation to be available for me to see the two characters Vivian and Benny to have the happy ending like KJ with the respective characters Chuck and Stacy."

–Sharon Jarret-Brown, Aurora Reading Group since 1896

The Better Part of Valor

*Another Family Reunion Novel—In the
Wisdom of the Ancestors Series*

ANN JEFFRIES

ACKNOWLEDGEMENTS

I bow in humble appreciation to:

The Creator

The Ancestors

Jessica Tilles, Editor Extraordinaire

Abe Leib, Esq., for many things

The Carolina Forest Authors Club for all things great and wonderful

My faithful family, friends, and fans for being there

The journey continues and the struggle for literary perfection
shall never end

I remain faithfully yours,
Ann Jeffries

*It is good to be brave, but
it is also good to be careful.
If you are careful, you
will have no need to be brave.*

CHAPTER 1

April, near Camp David, Maryland…

The jarring pain in Dakota Sinclair's left leg was getting worse. That is, if she let herself think about it. She didn't. Of course, she wouldn't. Neither would she marvel at the fine old trees, beautiful forest blooms, the scent of pine, nor the beauty of the azure blue sky. Still, she was always alert to every little change in the environment. Like her pain, if it didn't signal danger, she ignored it. If she didn't, she would have to admit the pain was excruciating, like having a tooth pulled without the benefit of Novocain. There was now no doubt about it. She was in deep trouble. Yet, she fought against the pain, against reality, against the passage of time.

Time was running out.

Moderating her pace to a slower jog, which, for her, was still faster than most professional athletes could boast, she kept pacing her time in her head. She rounded a curve on a rocky, dirt road leading to her cabin. The gravel incline slowed her stride even more. Grimacing at the thought of not being able to run four miles, when six months earlier she could run ten miles without breaking a sweat, she steeled her determination. However, that was then. That was before the fall that landed her in the hospital for a month with compound fractures of her right tibia, left fibula, patella, and in therapy at a convalescence center for another two months. At thirty-five, bones did not mend as quickly as when she was fifteen or even twenty-five, but nothing seemed to be the same anymore. The challenges were not even as great, but the incline she once ran every day, with relative ease, seemed to be fighting her today. Yet, words like 'giving up' or 'failure' were never in her vocabulary.

She pushed herself harder, breathing deeper, calmer, and faster. One more bend in the road, she thought, and then she would be there. Albeit in record time, she expected more of herself. Still, it was a challenge from which she would not shrink. If she could just push herself a little more, then she would be able to mend the broken parts of her life. The parts she had controlled as easily as she controlled her body.

As she breached the crest of the hill, she saw a familiar male figure leaning against a white, custom-made BMW. Designer shades covered his startling, deep-sea blue eyes. His practiced pose alone stopped many women—and men—in their tracks. To call William "Bill" Chandler, Code Name: The Stallion, handsome was a gross understatement. He was awesome. Drop-dead gorgeous, in fact—a Matt Bomer clone. His face and physique graced many high-fashion magazines, billboards, television commercials, and full-length motion pictures. An entrepreneur of high magnitude, his adult movie production company, line of men's clothing, and magazine, *Risqué*, were extremely popular in Europe and Asia, where he was known in high-fashion houses as Chandler. More often, however, his picture in the buff appeared in *Stallion*, his top-of-the-line gay trade magazine that sold above the market and had broken sales and circulation records. His own line of greeting cards, featuring him nude, was giving Hallmark heartburn. Dakota slowed her pace as she neared her cabin to begin the cool down cycle of her twice-daily routine.

Absently checking her specialized wristwatch, she noted, with non-visible concern, she had missed her goal for today by three minutes.

"You're pushing too hard, Dakota." Bill watched her pace in a circle-eight, breathing deeply, with her hands on her hips.

"Too hard? What's your definition of too hard?" She huffed out and then took in air sharply, shook out her limbs, and began to jog in place. She swiveled her head, feeling neck muscles stretch and bones creak. She did not need Bill monitoring her activities, reminding her, yet again, she was not meeting her goals. "I've got work to do."

"Too hard is when you haven't given yourself time to deal with what happened. Your parachute got hung up in the trees on a night helo jump in A-stan and you fell forty feet. No one could have predicted the wind shift at that low altitude. You were badly hurt.

"Too hard," he continued, his New York accent pronounced, "is when you haven't taken time to look at other options." He moved in front of her, blocking her path. "Too hard is when you don't communicate with people who care about you. You haven't answered your satphone since you left rehab months ago AMA, against medical advice."

Dakota glimpsed Bill, stepped away from him, and continued her cool-down cycle, stretching from side to side, with deep-knee bends. She inhaled and bent over, hands resting on her knees, her flat stomach continuing to concave and convex in rapid succession. Whom was she trying to fool? Certainly, not Bill Chandler. His insight was too sharp and he had known her far too long and well. He had seen her at her best and now, she was not anywhere near adequate. No. She had to face facts, but in private and not in front of him or anyone else.

"There are no other options. What happened was my fault. I've jumped hundreds of times, in all kinds of weather, and at night. I trained as a SEAL and survived Basic Underwater Demolition (BUD/S) training. I lost my edge; something a warrior can never do. It's not something anyone can give back to me. I have to do this my way—on my own."

"Without any help, as usual, I see." His voice was devoid of emotion, although a maelstrom brewed inside him. He turned his head toward her and noted the determination etched on her face, along with the beauty... and the pain.

Dakota wiped the sweat from her brow, using the sweatband on her wrist. "You didn't drive all the way up into these mountains to play psychiatrist. What's on the agenda?" She glared at his shade-covered eyes.

Bill lifted the expensive designer shades to the top of his thick, raven-black head of hair and returned her stare. There was no way to soften the blow he was there to deliver. She wouldn't appreciate it if he did. Dakota, Code Name: Wind Breeze, did not abide warm and fuzzy or anything sugarcoated. She'd sooner spit in his eye. "You're off the Mid-East/Arab/Israeli assignments. You will be heading the Southern Africa team for a company called CompuCorrect International."

An expletive slipped from her lips, as she turned her back to him, raised her head to the clear, blue heavens, and slowly paced. She was not afraid of much, but she was afraid this would happen. "That's a desk job. I could phone this in from here."

"That's the word, Dakota." He extended a jump drive toward her. "Unless otherwise advised, you're still on light duty medical leave until further notice. Your new cover dossier is outlined on the drive."

She stared at the small device, as if it were a poisonous snake, before she reluctantly took it from his hand. "I'm going to talk with—"

Slowly, Bill shook his head. "I've already tried, but my legal skills, on your behalf, weren't persuasive. I have to admit I'm not disappointed about it." He studied her carefully. "Take the time, Dakota. You have been at the top, as a team leader, for a long time. Longer than most. You're the best expert on criminals and insurgents in Arab markets. You would be invaluable at HQ. Maybe it's time to evaluate what you want to do with the rest of your life. From now on, answer your damn satphone."

Dakota had no response. His statement cut her deep in every muscle and sinew of her body. She turned and walked up the grassy area toward her cabin. As she closed the door, she heard Bill's car roar to life and speed away. Anger gripped her, as she flung the jump drive across the room into a chair, and then paced the open-concept living quarters. The cabin—a two-thousand-square-foot, A-frame, post-and-beam structure, with an open loft bedroom situated on a wide catwalk, and two baths—could only be described as fashion challenged. It was rustic in its interior design and sparsely furnished, yet it did not look like anyone's home. Then again, it had never been intended to be a home. It was just a place to hang her hat when she was IC (in country). Most of her life was lived OCONUS— outside of the continental United States—in places a lot less comfortable or hospitable than this.

Finally, she stopped pacing, sat on the single sofa, and cupped her face in her hands, resting her elbows on her thighs, reflecting on her past. Because she had nowhere else to go, she went to college year-round. She was recruited in her senior year when she was twenty-one. *Where had the time gone?* she wondered. Washed up at thirty-five. Next stop would be out the door. Then what?

CHAPTER 2

Well, you've won—for now—Mr. Ambassador," Craig Newhart, family law attorney, said in his usually slow, deliberate way. A whiff of Boston still lingered in the way he spoke. His family was thick as thieves with the Kennedys of Hyannis Port and other old, established, wealthy families. He was also a college friend of the New England region.

Jefferson Logan leaned back in his overstuffed, executive chair. The fine, rich leather creaked pleasantly with his movements. He learned to listen, not only to the words a person spoke, but also between the lines to the inflection in the voice and the body language. Among his other talents, he was a behaviorist. He sensed what he "won" was not all he expected. Newhart's face, even via Skype, carried more than just his steely gray eyes, hairless jaw, and thick, pewter-colored hair.

"What's the rest of it?" Jefferson knew his friend and former college roommate well enough to know there was more to come.

"You've got to make some changes in your lifestyle, my friend. The Montroses threatened to go public with what they call 'your decadent and lascivious behavior', which they claim makes you unfit as a parent. Not to mention what they allege is your abandonment of your wife and sons."

Jefferson's large hands gripped into fists, the muscles in his strong, square jaw twitched, his eyes went from dark brown to steely black, but otherwise he showed no signs of his growing anger.

"They wouldn't risk a public display. Tyler Montrose wants this situation kept quiet. He's got more to lose than I do. For me, it's a win-win situation. I get my boys back and I get the Montroses out of our lives for good."

"Jefferson," Newhart began, with a great deal of hesitation, deference, and concern, "I wouldn't call their bluff on this one, old friend. Although it's been five years, Felicia's death is still a fresh wound to them. The Montroses have some very powerful friends in high and other unsavory places. I believe they will stop at nothing to prove their position. Boston's blue-blood society tends to galvanize when it comes to old families and the 'them against us' mentality comes into play. Your life has been, shall we say, high profile, for quite a while. Remember, we used to live life in our youth to the fullest before I settled down with my Laurie."

He did remember, all too well. "What is that supposed to mean, Craig?"

"Dare I mention Geneva of Geneva Cosmetics, the Contessa de la Gardo Ramose—*and* her daughter, Semina Surret Boviar, Madam—"

"Enough," Jefferson said, his powerful hands still clinched into fists. "What does this lifestyle change entail?"

"Because your boys are still minors, the court expects you to develop a stable home environment for them. In other words, a full-time father. The court understands your career involves frequent foreign travel, but you've got one year to demonstrate to the court your career goals and aspirations will not have an adverse effect on your sons or interfere with the parent-child relationship you need to establish. Moreover, you've got to win back your boys' love and trust. That will weigh heavily on the court's decision concerning permanent custody. Your sons have been with the Montroses for the past five years since Felicia's death. They were adamant about wanting to stay with their grandparents rather than to live with you. The court is very respectful of your position, and the judge is being very lenient in this matter because these are your biological sons. The judge is concerned your estrangement from your sons has not provided them with an opportunity to develop a relationship with you. You're a psychologist, so you know the drill. To do that, you've got to put down some roots and stop living out of a suitcase."

"When do I get them back, Craig?"

Newhart leaned forward toward the video camera. "Jeff, have you heard a word I've said?"

He had heard every word, but it had been a very long time since anyone dictated the terms and conditions of his life to him, and he wasn't going to start now. The Montroses dragged him through the courts for years, but now he would have his sons back. Since September 11, 2001, his life had not been his own. He hadn't the time to lead diplomatic missions to Arab and African countries and, simultaneously, mount a court battle for custody of his sons. Now he was making the time, no matter what else was going on in the world. The final hurdle was crossed. He was getting custody of his sons. That's all that mattered.

"When, Craig?"

Newhart leaned back in his chair, his face demonstrating his concern. "You have one week to establish a residence. The boys will be delivered to you on Friday at Dulles Airport. They're coming back from a camping trip with their aunts, uncles, and cousins. Meet them at the Dulles International private jetport at 11:00 A.M."

"Is that everything that we have to discuss?"

"Well," Craig hesitated, knowing this would be a very touchy issue. "There is the matter of the transfer of Felicia's estate."

"Then there's nothing to discuss. I did not want her money when I was married to her and I certainly do not want it now."

"It's not a question of what you want, Jeff. You transferred the estate into a trust for your boys and gave control of the account to the Montroses. By law, the boys are entitled to it, and control has to rest with you as the custodial parent. If you'd like, I'll have my law firm's accounting department handle it."

"That's fine. I don't want to have anything to do with it."

"Jeff, you must be reasonable on this score. Felicia's estate is vast. Considering her place in the Montrose line of succession, your sons, once they reach the age of sixteen, inherit not only their equal share in Felicia's estate, but also a healthy controlling share of Montrose Global—one of the ten wealthiest corporate conglomerates in the world."

"I can provide what my sons need, Craig. Handle the rest of it."

"All right, Jeff, I'll take care of it. A full audit of the inheritance will take quite a bit of time—weeks, if not months, in any event. I'll have our CPAs contact Montrose Global and have the trust funds transferred."

When Jefferson closed his laptop, he was struck by the fact he didn't even know his boys liked camping. He didn't know *what* they liked or even what *they* were like. Jefferson III, his eldest, was only eight years old when he last saw him. Miles was six and Stephen was just two years old. Leaving them with their maternal grandparents seemed to be the best thing to do at the time, especially following the death of their mother.

The press and news media had such a field day with the circumstances surrounding the Montrose heiress' death it made Princess Di's death resemble a footnote in history. He could not protect his boys from the media intrusion the way the Montroses could at their compound in New England.

Little did he know then that the Montroses would blame him for their daughter's death and try to take his boys away from him. He wasn't stupid, but distraught over his wife's untimely death, he didn't make all of the right decisions. He should have known better. He may have been unschooled in the social mores of the rich and famous, but he was no novice when it came to the games people play. The Montroses never wanted Felicia to marry him—not a man from Nowhere, Georgia, even if he was Phi Beta Kappa. They were felicitous and tolerant enough, feigning acceptance of him as a scholar while he was a guest in their home, but they never expected or wanted him to marry their daughter.

When he and Felicia first met on campus at Harvard University, he never expected her flirtatious and nymphotic behavior would end up with her becoming pregnant. Then he had no choice but to do the honorable thing and marry her, even if he did not love her. No matter the circumstances, he wanted his unborn child and was prepared to make the best of a bad situation. Felicia made it clear; if he wanted the baby, he had to marry her or she would have an abortion. Simply put, he was trapped between the proverbial rock and a hard place.

He thought, in time, he would grow to care for her the way a man should care for his wife. He knew he would love his child regardless of its inauspicious beginning. He couldn't offer Felicia all the things her very wealthy family could, but, in order to be a father to his child, he had agreed to live in a twelve-room, four-thousand-square-foot cottage on the Montrose's estate until he finished his doctorate. It was his intention to move back to Georgia, with his wife and child, to teach, but Felicia and her family had other ideas of an acceptable career for him.

The Montrose's close ties in politics and old, New England money landed him a post in the Foreign Service. They would have done anything to keep him and Felicia apart, but they hadn't counted on him making a success of his career. Felicia relished the life of a diplomat's wife. It afforded her the opportunity to travel extensively in the company of the aristocracy into which she had been born. His career skyrocketed, aided by his appointment to prestigious United Nation's blue-ribbon panels, Mensa, the Heritage Foundation, the Brookings Institute, and advisory posts supported by presidential hopefuls. The political press often called upon him as an expert in foreign affairs, and his books were among those found on best-sellers' lists. Speaking engagements and lectures kept him in the public eye, domestically and abroad. His current post as Ambassador Emeritus and confidant to the President of the United States was just such an appointment.

Jefferson speed dialed his sister, Savannah.

"Hey, big brother," her joyful voice came through the speaker.

"Hey, yourself, kid." He was less than cheerful.

"Uh, okay, Jeff, what's wrong? Don't tell me it's nothing. I can hear it in your voice."

"You know me too well, Sam. Actually, it's good news. I'm getting my boys back on Friday."

"Great!" she squealed. "I know you've been trying for so long. You've been through quite a bit and spent a considerable amount of money to get to this point. I'm very happy for you."

"Thanks, I hope you mean that because I need your help."

"Anything, Jeff, you should know that. What can I do?"

"Your cabin up near Camp David, may I use it for the summer?"

"You don't have to ask. It's yours. If it weren't for you—"

"You earned it, Savannah."

"You are a hard man to say thank you to, Jefferson Alden Logan."

"Thanks are not needed between us, Savannah Alicia Logan. We're family. We're all the family we have."

"Dad and Mom would have been so proud of you, Mr. Ambassador."

"And of you, too, Dr. Logan."

They shared a few moments reflecting on the sad loss of their parents when Jefferson was in his last year of high school and Savannah was only twelve years old. Jefferson was no stranger to court battles. With no other close relative to give them moral support, he fought for custody of his sister and won, but in the back woods of Georgia, no one really cared about two children who had lost their parents. At least, not the way he had to wage an all-out war to wrestle his sons away from the rich and powerful Montroses.

"You're going to spend some quality time with them, I presume?"

"I've got to get to know them, Sam, and let them get to know me."

"That's not going to be easy for you or the boys, Jeff. The Montroses have done a pretty good job of brainwashing the boys into thinking you're some kind of three-headed animal."

"I know that. The boys don't want to come to live with me, but I've got some time to try to turn them around before the court looks at the custody issue again a year from now. Nothing, and no one, is going to separate me from them again."

"I believe you, Jeff, but remember you have to live, too. Perhaps settle down, find yourself a wife, and leave the Foreign Service. It's too dangerous these days; particularly the places where the President and Secretary of State routinely send you."

"I'll do what I have to do. A wife isn't a necessity."

Savannah laughed. "I guess not. Seems you're also able to get the honey without getting stung by the bees."

"I've been stung," he said, without joy in his voice.

Savannah noticed. "Come to dinner with me tonight, Jeff. Then you can tell me what's got you in such a blue mood. Maybe we could come up with some other things you, I, and my nephews can do over the summer."

"Can't tonight, Sam. I've got a reception at the Japanese Embassy at six, and then a trade delegation dinner at the Naval Observatory at eight. Why don't you come with me? I'll send a car for you."

"Uh, can't make the Japanese grip and grin, but I should be able to get clear to do the dinner. Have the car pick me up at home at seven-thirty."

"Will do. See you later, Sam, and thank you."

"I love you, too, big brother."

Jefferson clicked off the line and swiveled in his chair. He reflected on the struggles he had over his thirty-plus years. Most of his early childhood was happy with his parents and younger sister, but after his parents' untimely death in a plane crash, all of that changed. He and Savannah had to fend for themselves. Fortunately, his parents had insurance policies and a small, debt-free home. The airline also paid insurance claims and he sold their home for full price. The money helped put him through Howard University, Georgetown Law Center, and Harvard for his doctorate. Savannah attended a private boarding school in Asheville, North Carolina, college at Spelman in Atlanta, Georgia, and medical school at Georgetown University before the money well ran dry. He tried to hold the line with Savannah, but he wasn't her parent and she had grown up very independent of the values he learned from their parents. They had been very close all through their lives. They knew each other completely and shared everything.

Savannah never trusted Felicia and he often wondered whether it was racism, her sibling side showing, or her woman's intuition that caused her distrust of his deceased wife. Whatever it was, Savannah's instinct was right on target. Felicia was not a woman who could be trusted, as he later learned very painfully. His wife's scandalous behavior made the Hilton twins or the Kardashians seem like nuns in a monastery. Yet, for that matter, so did Savannah.

In his hurt and disappointment at Felicia's duplicity, he lashed out at all womankind, bedding too many to remember—except one. One he wanted, but never found. He shook off the intruding thoughts. Maybe she was only a figment of his imagination. Dwelling on the woman, he saw only once many years ago, still haunted him. He tried to find out who she was, but was not successful. Yet, something about her seemed familiar and was still very intriguing.

Jefferson buzzed for his Executive Assistant. When the man entered, he gave him a number of directives and assignments. "Oh, and contact the Protocol Officer for tonight's dinner and instruct him to add my sister's name to the guest registry."

"Yes, Sir, and will you be escorting anyone else to the reception tonight?"

"No, Yates, just Savannah."

"Very well, Sir. Your tuxedo is hanging in your office closet. Should I prepare something for your return?"

"No, thank you, Yates. I won't be having a late night supper or an overnight guest tonight. You may have the evening free, if you so desire."

"Very good, Sir." Yates slightly bowed out of the room.

CHAPTER 3

hat time should I pick you up?" Bill asked.

"I'm not in town. I'll meet you at the usual location at 18:30," Dakota answered.

"You should spend the night in town at my safe house rather than try to drive up into the mountains in the dark."

Dakota didn't respond. She knew what underlay Bill's suggestion and she wasn't going for it.

"I suppose, by your silence, your answer is no?"

"See you later, Bill," Dakota said before she disconnected the satphone call.

She was not ready for this or anything else, she mused, as she strolled out of her kitchen to the deck overlooking the lake. She wrapped one arm around her waist and sipped her black coffee. It was cold and bitter to the taste. Nothing was as it should be. She couldn't even make a decent cup of coffee. If she couldn't read a cookbook's directions, she would starve to death. However, energy bars and high protein drinks constituted her usual fare. This was no kind of life, but what there was of it was slipping through her fingers. Her body was not performing. She was losing her edge. *What would I do if I have to leave the...* She shook off the troublesome thought, as she tossed the remaining coffee over the railing on to the grass below. She checked her watch. She had time for a swim before she had to leave. The mountain lake could be cold this time of the year. The spring had not released its grip for summer's approach. The mountain lake residents usually did not come in any significant numbers until summer had made its appearance in all of its warmth, splendor, and lushness. She often hazarded chances to swim alone before their arrival.

Dakota slipped out of her warm-up suit, socks, and running shoes, and positioned herself at the edge of her dock. She executed a perfect dive into the water, but did not immediately feel the bone-chilling cold. The deeper she swam the colder the water. The mountain lake, to her way of thinking, was a boiling cauldron compared to lakes in the high country of the Northwest where she grew up, learned to swim, and only two seasons existed: winter and the hard freeze. Living in an orphanage on the edge of the Indian Reservation had its advantages though. The Native American population knew how to exist in the cold and desolate terrain. She was an outcast in the tightly knit community because of her mixed African American and Native American heritages. The children in the orphanage did learn survival skills. Swimming in icy waters was one she learned well. Being isolated and living alone was another. Those skills and experiences proved to be a perfect basis for the US Navy SEAL and Israeli Mossad training where she excelled.

Dakota pushed off the bottom of the murky lake and swam upward, as her lungs began to burn. She felt no pain in her legs, as she moved smoothly through the water. A good sign, she thought. She still had a chance to get her edge back before it was too late. What else did she have?

Later that afternoon, Dakota entered the high-fashion house early and went immediately to a private dressing room. Bill entered moments later, carrying a shimmering, long, black, evening gown. She slipped out of her warm-ups and reached for the hooks for her bra.

"Here, let me do that," Bill said, standing behind her.
Dakota looked at him in the mirror and moved away. "I'm not an invalid. I can still take care of myself," she said to his reflection, as she unhooked her bra and it slipped from her shoulders.

Bill put a gentle hand on one of her arms and looked at her in the mirror. "No, you're not an invalid, Dakota," he said softly. "You're a very beautiful and desirable woman. Men like to do things for woman who they're attracted to. Undressing them is a particularly pleasurable experience." Bill continued to gaze at her. "Magnificent," he breathed out softly, just above a whisper.

She glimpsed him in the mirror. "Time?" she asked while removing her Native American pendant from her neck.

"On schedule," he answered, checking his multifaceted, custom Rolex watch.

Dakota held his stare until he backed out of the doorway and let the curtain fall before she sat on a settee. She never learned what to do with the frequent male overtures she received. Bill was among the most persistent, but she successfully dodged him for several years. Now he was turning up the heat and she wanted to douse the flames completely.

She rolled the black silky hose up her strong, shapely leg and noticed the surgical scars were only slightly visible. The plastic surgeons had done a very good job. Her finger traced the lengths of the scars and then she moved on. The garter holster held her weapon and slipped into place. She stood to open the curtain to face Bill. He handed a small, round patch to her, which she positioned on her right, bare shoulder, pressed it, and ripped off the cover. A tiny, irregularly shaped disk, fashioned to look no larger than a beauty mole, remained on her skin. She took the gown from Bill and slipped into it. The floor-length frock easily slid over her shapely frame and clung to her curves like sealskin.

She checked her makeup and jostled her hair, shaking the long, black, thick, straight strands until they flowed over her shoulders like mercury. She moved swiftly, flipping her hair into a Victorian style.

Bill was still gazing at her in the mirror, she noticed, but continued her preparation. The chopsticks looked like any other hair adornment. No one would determine their real purpose. She said nothing more, as she slipped into the diamond-studded, stiletto heels, while Bill slipped the stunning diamond ring on her finger and then a matching wrap around her shoulders. She moved toward the door, but Bill stopped her. Taking a small bottle of pricey perfume from his pocket, he dabbed a bit behind her ears, between her breasts, on her inner wrists and then leaned down, placing the scent between the slit in her gown along her inner thighs, without breaking his gaze.

Dakota looked away. He handed an evening purse to her and then opened the door, standing so close to her she had to brush against him to pass. In the underground garage, they climbed into the waiting limo that whisked them away.

CHAPTER 4

Nathan Flack shifted one hip onto the desk and waited. Shortly, Jefferson entered the office and Nathan quickly stood.

"You're early," Jefferson said, as he walked toward his desk, looking at the reports in his hands.

"Jeff, I just got the word. What's this about you taking a leave of absence?"

Jefferson smiled at his friend and confidant and stood behind his desk. "I've finally gotten custody of my sons. I'm taking time to get to know them again."

"I suppose that's a good thing, but for a year? I mean, you're in the middle of some very delicate trade negotiations. I could understand if you needed a week, or maybe two, but a year?"

Jefferson dropped the reports on his desk and looked at Nathan. "What's your father like?" He dug his hands into his pockets.

"My father?" Nathan's face was a mass of confusion.

"Yes, your father. What kind of person is he? His character? What does he like to do? What are his hobbies? Does he enjoy sports? What does he like to read? Who are his best buds? What are his favorite foods? What was he like as a kid? Has he traveled extensively? If so, where? What's his backstory? Does he have siblings?"

Nathan's face still showed confusion. He absently shrugged. "I don't know the answers to all of those questions. I guess he likes sports or reads. He's a high school principal. He's an honorable and principled man. I suppose he and my mother, who is a Boston Townsend, have a social life and I have aunts and uncles on both sides of my family, but...what do any of those questions have to do with you taking a leave of absence?"

"The answers to those kinds of questions are what my sons are going to learn about me and what I'm going to learn about them."

"Fax a message to them or something," he said, animatedly flailing his arms. "Call them on the phone or give them a copy of your bio, but, Jeff, you've got much more important things to do than to read nursery rhymes to your children, play catch or look at the boob tube, watching art imitate life. You're a very important diplomat, an artist, and master of the game in the global arena. You *make* the news; you don't sit around reviewing it. These upcoming negotiations are critical and sensitive, not to mention economically beneficial to the homeland."

"*Nothing* is more important to me than my sons, Nate. Not multibillion-dollar trade agreements. Not solidifying relations in the Middle East, or calming troubles in warring factions. Not the President's re-election bid. Nothing. That's what this big crunch is all about."

"Of course it is. It's a diplomat's quagmire, but it will have a far-reaching impact on the economy of this country and a few others in the world. Not to mention the fact the Middle East factions have agreed you are the only one who they could all agree on to open talks on behalf of this country. Your decision to take this little vacation could set the process back six months or maybe a year. Lives would be at risk. Anything could shift and change in that timeframe. You're the key to this entire plan, Jeff," Nathan implored. "We have to strike while the iron is hot. Forgive me for the cliché, but it's apropos *sine qua non*."

"No one is indispensable. The negotiations won't suffer, since you'll be spearheading the initial talks."

Pregnant silence ensued while Jefferson watched a myriad of realizations play over Nathan's face.

Nathan's frame pulled upright. *"Me?"* he asked in total shock and confusion. "I'm not the one to lead this team! Don't get me wrong, buddy, I'm a good second chair, but I don't have your intuition and savvy in international matters, particularly in the Middle East! I'm a research specialist. Ask me who has the Intel you need, I'm your man. Ask me who can be bought and for how much, I can tell you whether they're worth it. Ask me where the next military skirmish, insurgency or rebel uprising is going to break out, and I can give you a complete scenario, but to sit across the table from the likes of Al-Assad or Mubarak or Hussein, eyeball-to-eyeball, and hammer out an agreement the way you have done? That takes a cool head and intestinal fortitude. That's why they call you Ambassador and me Mister."

"*Summa cum laude*, Georgetown Law Center. State Department attaché to Japan, Spain, and France. Chairman of the delegation to the—"

"Window dressing," Nathan said, holding up one hand to stop the litany he knew would follow. "They needed a token Black and I was in the right place at the wrong time."

"Well, you've done it again. Let's just say you're one brother without rhythm. Your timing may be off as far as you're concerned, but for my purposes, you're the right person at the right time."

Nathan shook his head in disagreement. "Man, you have my respect, but this is not the right move. This project takes a level of dedication I don't have and doubt I can garner."

"Nate, you've been on my team for four years, and I trust your judgement. It's time for you to move up. You have my confidence and my support. More importantly, the President, the Cabinet, the Secretary of State, and the Joint Chiefs have approved your selection. I just left a meeting with the President shortly before I called you to meet with me."

Nathan started to protest again, but Jefferson held up a hand, silencing him. "There's no use in arguing the point. We don't have much time. Tonight, after the reception and dinner, we'll start the briefing sessions. By the end of the week, you'll be picking and leading your own team." He checked the clock on the wall simultaneous with the knock on the door. Yates entered and Jefferson looked up.

"Your car is here, Sir."

"Thank you, Yates. Have you arranged to have Savannah picked up?"

"Yes, Sir. She'll join you at the Naval Observatory."

Nathan perked up considerably and looked from Yates to Jefferson. A grin sliced his handsome face. "Savannah is joining us tonight?"

"Later." Jefferson grinned. "She's busy before that, but I thought you might like to see her."

"With all due respect, Mr. Ambassador, I'd like to see *a lot* of her," he said, beaming.

"In the biblical sense, I presume."

Nathan just smiled diplomatically, and Jefferson grinned and shook his head.

CHAPTER 5

A military-uniformed honor guardsman opened the car door of the limo and Bill stepped out, followed by Dakota. They made an impressive-looking couple, as they ascended the steps to the brightly lit front entrance of the Naval Observatory. Bill was resplendent in his couture black tuxedo. His looks and height won him an appearance on the TV show *Blue Bloods* as a young Tom Selleck and as the deceased son of Tom Selleck's role. Black hair combed straight back from his forehead in a Gatsby Era style complemented his patrician nose and deep-sea blue eyes. His lithe body appeared to have been sculpted by one of the grand masters of the art form on a very good day.

Bill and Dakota slipped past other guests who waited in the receiving line to greet the visiting dignitaries and the President. Once inside the cavernous building, they moved to the bar and ordered drinks while they furtively scanned the room.

"How many?" Dakota asked.

"Seventeen hundred. All of the usual suspects," he said. "The Congress, the Diplomatic Corps, and a host of captains of industry. Anyone I need to corner?"

"Yes, we need to work with a few."

"Male or female?"

Dakota glanced at him with a fixed smile. "Does it matter?"

Bill grinned. "Not necessarily." He tilted his head to one side. "You're even more beautiful and alluring when you smile. I wish you felt it inside."

Dakota continued unobtrusively scanning the growing crowd. She spotted contacts she would have to cultivate for her new assignment. Casually taking Bill's arm, she smiled broadly. "Curtain going up, stage left," she said lowly.

Bill's arm bent at the elbow and together they moved toward a cluster of people.

Jefferson greeted his sister, Savannah, as she arrived at the massive Naval Observatory anteroom. They gave each other a kiss on the cheek and a hug. Then her attention went to Nathan Flack at Jefferson's side.

"Mr. Flack," she acknowledged and smiled with guile, offering her hand.

"Dr. Logan." He smiled, lifting her hand to his lips and turning her palm up for his kiss. "Always a pleasure to see you."

"It hasn't been that long, Mr. Flack."

"A lifetime to me, Dr. Logan," he said smoothly with the telltale signs of longing in the lower timbre of his voice and devilish play of his eyes over her body.

Jefferson looked away, amused by his sister's staged politeness and Nathan's role in the games they often played in public. He sensed their private meetings were in complete contrast to their public personae. Perusing the room, he meandered through the crowd. He was approached every step of the way, as he, Savannah, and Nathan advanced through the opulent rotunda.

A while later, over the shoulder of the Mexican diplomat, Jefferson's eyes caught the sight of someone he almost believed didn't exist—the figment of his imagination. He watched her move from one cluster of people to another for more than twenty minutes, on the arm of a tall man, while he simultaneously carried on conversations with congressmen or senators, governors, presidential hopefuls, corporate executives, entertainment or sports icons, and military leaders, such as Admiral Clarence Gordon, head of the Navy's west coast operation and the Pacific Rim. Jefferson was, at one time, intrigued with the Admiral's beautiful XO, Lieutenant Stacy Greene. He had every intention of following up on that connection until now. His heart rate quickened and his breathing lowered. *There you are.* The woman who had flitted in and out of his consciousness for far too long. Her tall, svelte body was a masterpiece in motion. The black, shimmering gown, simple, but elegant, cascaded effortlessly over her subtle hourglass shape. Jefferson finally whispered his directives to Nathan, whose eyes scanned the room and rested on the object of the Ambassador's attention. Nathan acknowledged his instructions, excused himself, and moved away toward his appointed mission.

When he felt the slight pressure from Dakota's hand entwined on his arm, Bill whispered, "Problem?" in her ear, as if telling her a lover's secret.

"Could be," she said quietly and smiled affectionately, as if she approved of her lover's thoughts. She had seen him before. Ambassador Jefferson Logan was breathtakingly handsome—drop-dead, masculine gorgeous—a youthful looking Luther Vandross clone, only more sensual. Tall, six-foot-five, and striking in the tailor-made Adolfo tuxedo he wore. His close-cut hair—thick, jet-black, wavy with a hint of gray at the temples. Sparkling white teeth and bedroom eyes. A voice cut through her thoughts.

"Nathan Flack," he said, extending his hand to Bill Chandler, but extending his sweeping glance to include Dakota.

"William Chandler, Mr. Flack." Bill extended his hand for the traditional handshake.

"Ambassador Jefferson Logan sends his regards and asks whether you and your charming companion would join him at his table for dinner?"

"My regrets to the Ambassador, but my fiancée and I have already accepted an invitation to dine with the Malaysian Commissioner of Commerce at his table."

"Your fiancée?" Nathan asked with surprise, looking at Dakota. "You're a very lucky man, Mr. Chandler." Again, looking at Bill. "Uh, perhaps you don't remember me. We were at Georgetown Law together. I believe you were in the class that followed mine. You were in the honors program, as I recall, with Vivian Alexander, David Carter, Melissa Charles, and Alan Lightfoot."

"Yes, a few years behind you. You have a good memory, too. You were specializing in international law and were on the foreign affairs debating team, as I recall," Bill returned.

"Your specialty was international contracts, wasn't it?" Nathan asked.

"Yes, but I'm in sports and entertainment law now."

"You are associated with a very impressive law firm and still enjoying a very successful acting and modeling career. I've seen you on a number of national and international political talk shows. Your companion? Are you also a model and actress, Ms.—"

Bill interceded. "Uh, no, my fiancée is vice president of a computer networking, hardware, and software company." Bill lifted Dakota's hand to his lips and kissed it lightly.

"Oh, perhaps I know the company," Nathan said, probing for more information.

Dakota had purposefully chatted with others while Bill carried the conversation with Flack, but she could feel the eyes of the Ambassador on her from across the crowded room. She had felt his gaze for some time and their eyes had met briefly on more than a few occasions during the evening.

An attractive man, she thought—tall, lean, and muscular. Dignified, befitting his position. She had seen him before, but avoided contact. Nonetheless, she was familiar with his dossier—a very well respected international affairs legal scholar, academician, and a ladies' man. Perhaps that was why his gaze was disturbing. He enjoyed quite a reputation among those known to run in the upper echelons of society. The jet-set culture. A group who knew no territorial boundaries, played hard, and lived fast. Certainly not the life she had led, but she had been the observer. It was her job. She turned back to Bill.

"Darling," she cooed, "if you'll forgive me, I'm going to powder my nose before dinner."

She handed her glass of champagne to Bill, nodded to Nathan and the other guests as she started to depart. Bill captured her around the waist, lowered his head, and kissed her gently on the lips.

"Hurry back, honey," he crooned.

Dakota gave him a clinched-teeth smile. "Count the seconds, darling," she nearly growled.

Jefferson's eyes followed Dakota, as her statuesque figure glided out of the Rotunda. He also witnessed the kiss from her escort. She was the epitome of elegance and grace, he noted. Beautiful beyond description or belief. Tall, slightly muscular, slim, and leggy. Exotic in appearance, with a golden reddish tone to her supple-looking skin. A number of heads turned, surreptitiously observing her as she passed. She could have been on the cover of any internationally well-known, fashion magazine or perhaps a movie star, he decided. Shortly, Nathan returned to give the expected report to Jefferson. As Jefferson digested the information, his eyes scanned the room for the Chief of Protocol. Nathan was dispatched for another mission. Jefferson saw Dakota reenter the anteroom and move to rejoin Bill Chandler.

Jefferson thought himself to be a moral man. He prided himself on being one who would not breach the sanctity of another man's marriage. The woman who had haunted his dreams for several years was another matter altogether, and not a figment of his imagination at all. She was flesh and blood and not yet a married woman. There was still time to negotiate, despite the ring on her left hand. It was his intention to take full advantage of that opportunity.

"Who are you scouting, Jeff?" Savannah asked, as she craned her neck to follow his gaze.

"The lady in black," he whispered to her.

Savannah squinted slightly. "I know her, I believe. She looks familiar."

Jefferson's head snapped in his sister's direction. "A patient, perhaps?"

"No, I believe—"

"Dr. Logan," a male voice drew their attention.

"Yes," they both answered in unison, as they turned.

"Mr. Hawkins," Savannah said and smiled seductively. "It's a pleasure to see you again." She turned to her brother. "Ambassador Jefferson

Logan, this is Mr. Jacob Hawkins, President of BlackHawk International. Jacob, my brother, and his deputy, Mr. Nathan Flack."

Jacob shook Jefferson's hand and nodded at Nathan.

"Mr. Ambassador, it's a pleasure to meet you."

"Thank you, Sir," Jefferson graciously acknowledged. "I've met your father, Ambassador Jake Hawkins, Sr. I'm surprised he's not in attendance tonight."

"My father is still on vacation, I believe. He and his wife are in the Caymans."

As they conversed, Jefferson noted the nearly imperceptible shift in Hawkins' demeanor. The tension in Nathan was less obvious and he watched the interplay of the two men around his sister. Her aloofness couldn't be more obvious. The messages the threesome's eyes sent each other were, however, unmistakable. A rivalry was afoot and Savannah was the epicenter of their attention.

Jefferson's concentration was momentarily averted, as his eyes caught the nod from the Chief of Protocol, as he passed by them.

The dinner bell sounded and the august group went in to be seated, following the President, the First Lady, and their entourage of leaders from the Arab, Asian, and African countries.

"There's been a change," Bill whispered, as he and Dakota entered the posh enclave, waiting to take their seats.

"I suspected as much," Dakota said, returning his whispered comment. "I notified Delta of the potential problem. Is someone covering—"

"Taken care of. Harris will move to your spot with the Malaysians and Webster will move to mine, but what—"

"I'll explain later," she whispered, as she noticed Savannah waiting with her brother beside their table.

"Dakota Sinclair, isn't it?" Savannah asked, as they took their seats at the table for ten.

"Yes," she answered. "Savannah Logan. We were at Spelman together, I believe."

"You were a few classes ahead of me. You were a senior my freshman year, but I remember you were a triathlete. Swimming and diving?"

"Track and field," Dakota answered, keenly aware of Jefferson's close scrutiny. "I'd like to introduce my fiancée, William Chandler, Esquire."

"Of course, I've seen your photo on the cover of many fashion magazines. You're known on the continent as the supermodel Chandler," said Savannah. "You're with the law firm Alexander, Carter, Chandler, Charles, Lightfoot, and Towson, I believe."

"You're correct. Although Vivian Alexander Montgomery is no longer in the law firm," said Bill. "However, you probably already know that since Vivian was also at Spelman while my fiancé."

"Yes, I'm aware."

Her voice was like velvet to his ears: low, husky, and seductive. Up close, her skin looked unadulterated, fresh, and satiny smooth. Light, rosy-brown sugar with deep onyx-like mesmerizing eyes. A perfect oval face, with unusually high cheekbones, made her look very exotic. Native American and African American, he decided. Not too many generations removed either. The silky, thick-looking texture of her hair piled on her head in a Victorian style with wisps dangling around her face gave her an innocent appearance, but he seriously doubted it was in her character. His eyes dropped to her full sculptured mouth, as she lifted a soupspoon to her lips. As her hand moved down again, his eyes followed her long neck to the clavicle and then down to her breasts—full, prominent, and luscious.

His tight groin told him she would be delicious to taste. His mouth went dry, although he sipped his water. His eyes rose more slowly and surprisingly briefly met hers. Something there, he noticed. Something deep and mysterious. A sadness that outwardly did not show. An alertness that did. The eyes, fringed with long, black, sable-like lashes, closed deceptively after they quickly swept the table of diners. Alert to her constant scans, he wondered why.

Every nerve ending was alive and aware of the sensual perusal of Jefferson Logan's eyes. He participated in lively dinner conversation, but his eyes never stopped scrutinizing her. She felt somehow bare under his flickering contemplation. Something deep in Dakota's core responded to his gaze, as she attempted to divert her attention. Her left hand went slowly to Bill's thigh and, on cue, he turned his handsome countenance toward her, bent, kissed her softly on the shoulder, and then moved to kiss her behind her ear.

"What are you doing to the man?" he whispered against her ear.

She smiled her best semblance of a loving response to Bill, briefly covering her mouth with her napkin. "After the next course is served, let's make some excuse and move on," she whispered.

"Mr. Chandler," Jefferson said, interrupting what appeared to be Bill's overly amorous attention to Dakota. "I understand you have your own line of men's apparel."

"I do, yes. I developed a taste for comfortable men's wear and, with some up-and-coming young designers, incorporated it into a business. The label is called Risqué."

"Do you envision growing and expanding your business into the foreign markets the way you have with *Stallion*?"

Bill smiled. "I'm surprised, Mr. Ambassador, that you're familiar with my production and entertainment company."

"I'm sure nothing much surprises you, Mr. Chandler," Jefferson said.

"There are those who have...surprised me, but to answer your question, I export to a few international markets, but I have no desire to grow Risqué and compete with the Oleg Cassini's or Bill Blass' or Carlos Ortega's of the world. *Stallion* found its own market naturally. Foreign markets are more accepting of the beauty of the human form than those markets stateside."

"Perhaps we should talk further about that and our U.S. economic plan for exporting American fashion to the Middle East in a more deliberate manner. We're fighting a trade deficit and need to export more American goods and services abroad to level the playing field," Jefferson said.

"Mr. Flack has already made me aware of your interest in having more American industries vie for position in Third World and other foreign markets. I agree that manufacturing and jobs would increase, domestically, but I seriously doubt the trade deficit will be balanced on the back of *Stallion,* or even Risqué, for that matter."

"Ms. Sinclair, do you export your computer hardware and software?"

"Certainly, to those countries that do not have trade embargoes pending or in place," she answered smoothly. "However, I'm only a sales and marketing representative. The market locations are dictated by the company's upper management team."

She sensed Jefferson directed his question to draw her out into a fuller conversation, but she also sensed he already knew the answers to the questions he posed. His penetrating gaze washed over her and her attention focused more fully in his direction. Clean shaven with a mustache that barely moved. A seriousness in his strong, square jawline and chin. Thick eyebrows and lashes accentuated the masculine contour of his face. Yes, yes, he did resemble the singer Luther Vandross. His broad shoulders barely moved as he talked. No revealing body language, that was enlightening, she noted. He kept himself in check, forcing anyone to deal with his words instead of his evasive thoughts and motion. The consummate ambassador: unreadable, unpredictable, unfeigned.

Under the table, Bill's hand on her knee brought her back to herself. Never had a man's gaze so enlivened and enthralled her. It also confused and even frightened her. He was not a man who could be dismissed like so many others who thought she was of easy virtue. She took calming breaths silently and slowly, her chest rising and falling in a non-pronounced fashion. *What is wrong with me?*

Fortunately for her, Savannah picked up the conversation, mentioning former classmates of theirs from Spelman, like Vivian Alexander, JaiHonnah Hawkins, Constantina Justice, Kristen Bryant, and Cheryl Lawrence and what they were now doing. Dakota didn't clearly remember many of the people Savannah mentioned, but then, unlike Savannah, Dakota was a loner in college. Listening to Savannah's chatter permitted Dakota a mental break to ponder other, more important matters, like the contacts that were her primary reason for being at this trade delegation dinner. Slowly, she slipped back into her necessary façade.

Jefferson was fighting the battle of his life. Dakota's presence across the table from him was a mistake, he now knew. He didn't make many missteps, but this was a lollapalooza. She had him in an emotional prism. He could visualize himself holding her in his arms and capturing her sexy mouth in his. Stroking her body and molding it to his, joining with her lithe body and bringing them to a place where only consummate lovers were allowed. The vision was as jarring and palpable, as it was problematic for himself at this turning point in his life. For his sons' sake and his own, he had to find a way to pull back from his growing fascination with the mysterious beauty, Dakota Sinclair.

As the next course was served, Bill's affectionate kisses on Dakota's neck and shoulder, and whispers in her ear caused Jefferson's fist to tighten involuntarily. It wasn't seeing two lovers participating in a shared moment of intimacy or even watching another man being so attentive to a woman of color. Rather, the emotions were specific and basic, primal and territorial. He had taken possession of her in his thoughts and this man was in his territory.

However, the vision of her giving herself up to Bill Chandler, imposing as he was, did not quite wash with Jefferson, though. Something was askew, he sensed. Her smile did not sparkle like a lover's smile. She had no excitement in her demeanor, although he detected it in Bill, but, of course, William Chandler was a very successful actor and model accustomed to practiced poses. He was also an attorney with a sterling reputation so he was capable of extreme discipline in his outward appearance. Those thoughts gave Jefferson hope that his intuition and assessment of the relationship between the beautiful, alluring, and sensuous, the incomparable Dakota Sinclair and the very debonair William Chandler was not solid…at least not yet.

Dakota felt the eyes of Jacob Hawkins on her as well as the Ambassador's, but Jacob's stare across the dinner table gave her a sense of familiarity. He was the brother of another former classmate, JaiHonnah

Hawkins. Perhaps they had seen each other on Spelman's campus, but she believed she would have remembered him if they had met.

Yet, something about him made her feel uncomfortable. Not like Jefferson's gaze, though. That, she sensed, was a signal of nothing more than just lust. Rather, Jacob Hawkins seemed to be searching his memory as if he knew her or that she reminded him of someone. She felt it the moment he entered the room. She dismissed the feeling. Perhaps the fact he was obviously of mixed heritage, just as she, sparked a feeling of connection. He, too, was of African American and Native American descents.. From what she read about him in the society pages and financial reports, he was the eldest son of a wealthy Texas industrialist who was the Ambassador to an array of African countries. His father, Jake Hawkins, owned BlackHawk Holding, a Fortune 500 company. He had turned over the operation of the company to his son-in-law, J. Roderick Baylor, a former basketball superstar and self-made multibillionaire in his own right. Baylor married JaiHonnah Reise Hawkins, Jake Hawkins' only daughter, an architect and engineer by trade, and also an underclassman at Spelman when both she and Savannah were there. Dakota believed she never met Jacob until this day, but she and JaiHonnah had been friendly toward each other for that one year they were in school together. From what Dakota remembered about JaiHonnah, she and Jacob were as different as night and day.

There was another brother though, Adam Hawkins, who JaiHonnah loved fiercely and talked about incessantly. Adam also headed companies in the BlackHawk conglomerate, but spent time designing, engineering, and racing Formula One cars in international sports events and competitions. Whatever it was she sensed about Jacob Hawkins had not been there when she knew JaiHonnah.

Now was not the time to dwell on it though, she reminded herself. She would have new background data run on everyone at the table just to be thorough. Nor was it time to focus on the disquieting thoughts she was having about the all-consuming presence of Ambassador Jefferson Alden Logan.

The seven-course meal ended and the lights lowered. The President stood and began the round of speeches and toasts. Jefferson studied Dakota's face in profile and noted her eyes, even in the darkened room, seemed to search constantly. *A huntress*, he thought. Still, he could not discern her purpose. What was she searching for or for whom? Her gaze rarely landed on any particular person, except Jacob Hawkins. He made a mental note to study that development further.

Bill continued, he noticed, his ardent attention to her in the darkened room, leaning toward her, whispering close to her ear. Although the charade still annoyed Jefferson to see Bill's arm possessively around Dakota's shoulders, he was more in control of his emotions. Bill and Dakota's relationship was a puzzle he was determined to solve. *Connect the dots*, he thought.

The audience's none-too-quiet or subtle gasp, as the President announced Jefferson would be taking a leave of absence to teach and write a book, clearly had a profound impact, but he had expected that. Hushed and somewhat frantic murmurs greeted the news and then the spotlight shifted to him. He stood when the applause forced him to his feet and bowed his head slightly toward the President and the audience. When the President announced Nathan Flack would become the newest Special Envoy, Jefferson gestured for Nathan to stand beside him. Jefferson applauded Nathan with the rest of the audience and then both men sat as the spotlight shifted back to the President.

Jefferson noted the traditionally-covered heads of the Middle East statesmen were in constant motion with their aides as they sat on the dais. The Sultan of Oman made direct eye contact, telegraphing his displeasure with the news. The King of Qatar, representing easily the richest people on earth, sat in fixed stare. President Ali Abdullah Saleh, of the Republic of Yemen, rapped his fingers on the table. The Monarch of Bahrain, where Jefferson spent a few quiet weeks with La Countess, looked away, perhaps in anger. They would all send emissaries to him the following day, he knew, but they would soon learn nothing would deter him. Just as he would not be dissuaded from his attention to Dakota Sinclair. The potentates would cool their rancor, he was sure, with Nathan Flack at the helm, but his fire and, yes, desire for the mysterious Dakota Sinclair would not be assuaged.

"What was that all about?" Bill quietly asked, as they waited for their limo to pull to the front of the Observatory.

"What was what about?" Dakota asked, not looking at him.

With his arm tucked around her waist, he pulled her more securely to his side to whisper in her ear. "You know what I'm talking about, Dakota. You and the Ambassador. The man was fixed on you like a heat-seeking missile all evening."

"Perhaps it was you who he was obsessing over."

"I seriously doubt that."

"It's not beyond the realm of possibility," she said, moving toward the limo, as the driver got out and opened the door for them. "According to his dossier, the man has an insatiable sexual appetite. Perhaps his tastes and preferences run in more than one direction. In any event, his interest is of no consequence. We've accomplished what we set out to do. CompuCorrect will have a firm foothold in the Middle Eastern countries once the Alliance of Arab, Asian, and African States' Agreement is inked."

"That assumes the players will continue to want to negotiate with Logan out of the picture. Something tells me that, although Nathan Flack is capable, more than a few countries will not take very lightly Logan's decision to withdraw at this time. There will be repercussions and fallout from the bomb the President dropped tonight."

"I sense Jefferson Logan will never be completely out of the picture. The timing of Logan's withdrawal may have been inopportune, but, of course, that's no longer my management area. My successor can carry CompuCorrect into that market," she said testily.

Bill turned his head to look at Dakota. "Is this an emotion I detect?" he asked with some surprise.

Emotion. She had none to speak of, she thought. She could not recall any emotion strong enough to register with her—that is until tonight.

Something had gripped her and dug in deep. Something she could not taste, touch, or feel, but it was as real as her heartbeat and as distant as the next galaxy. It was as if she had stepped into another reality. Something was drawing her to Jefferson Logan. Something she never felt before in her entire life.

Her thoughts went to him and his regal, all-engulfing presence. A proud African prince came to mind. Tall, strong, and virile—disturbingly so. She actually thought of him in another context. As if telepathically, he was sending signals and feelings to her. Something in his eyes was kinetic and disturbing. An emotion that could not be confused or covered.

She sensed it before in England when their paths briefly crossed at another social/political event with the Prime Minister, the Queen, and the President, but then her focus had not been altered as it had been tonight.

As a child, she had dreams or visions the old Algonquian told her were things from the past or things to come in the future. She never understood how he knew of such things.

"Dakota, what about Savannah Logan?"

"I remember her. As you heard during dinner, we were both at Spelman College at the same time with your friend, Vivian Alexander. I was a senior. They were freshmen, but we were not communicative."

"You're never communicative, Dakota. Most of the time I don't instinctively know what you're thinking and that's dangerous for me. Since we're not going to be working the same market, don't you think it's time to get to know each other better?"

Dakota turned only her head toward Bill. "That takes an emotion that might be confused with human nature. As you have already determined, I'm devoid of passion, sensation, or sentiment," she said with icy coolness. "You know me well enough for what we have to do."

Bill retreated. "For now, perhaps," he said lowly.

Jefferson had observed the curvature of Dakota's spine when she walked toward Bill who had held her wrap. The sway of her hips was from walking, not enticing, but that heart-shaped butt of hers sent a signal he could not ignore. Yet, something seemed off about her gait. He couldn't quite figure out what it was.

She was braless and, from where he stood, there was no question her panties, if she was indeed wearing any, would not cover a fly's butt. She was every bit a woman with gazelle-like movement, swift of foot. A runner, in deed, he had thought, as he watched her move. He wanted desperately to undress her and take the chopsticks from her hair. He would run his fingers through that silky mass... His thoughts were interrupted with a hand on his arm.

"Steady, big brother," Savannah said at his side. "You're eyeing her like she's dinner and you're starving. I happen to know there were, at least, ten women here tonight who you've sampled, but you haven't looked at another woman since you spotted Dakota Sinclair."

"What's her story, Sam?" he asked, as they waited for his limo to arrive.

Savannah shrugged. "Beats me. I haven't seen her since my first year in college. To be honest, we weren't close. She was a loner, as I recall. Wasn't a leader or a follower. Good student. Excellent triathlete. Didn't date. Frankly, I'm mystified about this engagement thing. She never seemed to show any interest in any of the guys around Atlanta, but then, she was ahead of me. She was a senior, while I was a freshman. Perhaps she had something going on back home."

"Where is home for her?" he asked, as he watched Dakota climb into a limo with Bill and be whisked away.

"Montana, Wyoming, Nevada, the Dakotas, perhaps, hence the name. I don't really know. I was only around her for about eight months. As I've said, she wasn't one of the crew I hung out with. I do recall JaiHonnah, Jacob Hawkins' sister, seemed to be friendly with Dakota. Tate Kennedy, the astrophysicist and space engineer, I believe, had feelings for her. They were both tri-athletes, but beyond that, their relationship didn't go anywhere. He was too young for her. Why are you so interested?"

Jefferson gave her a non-descriptive glance. Then he looked over his shoulder at Nathan and Jacob Hawkins waiting in the line behind them and changed the subject.

"What's the game plan, Sam?"

"Uh, the KIS method. Keeping it simple. You drop me off at home. I'll figure out the rest from there."

"You're playing a dangerous game. Nathan is a good man and he has some very sincere feelings for you. Jacob Hawkins, on the other hand, is the dangerous type and a little too close to Roderick Baylor for your comfort, I should think."

Savannah looked away. "As for Roderick Baylor, he's in the past, Jeff. He's married now to Jacob's sister, JaiHonnah. I can accept that. If you're implying that my interest in Jacob has anything to do with Roderick and JaiHonnah, you're wrong. There was a time when I thought Roderick was in my future. Clearly he had other ideas about his future, and me, well, I wasn't in it.

"You could have warned me you were going to recommend to the President that Nathan take your place."

Jefferson slipped his arm around her waist and kissed Savannah on her temple. He knew Roderick Baylor meant a great deal more to her years ago, and she was disappointed when they ended the intimacy in their relationship. They were still friendly toward each other, and Roderick's wife, JaiHonnah still one of Savannah's sorority sisters and patients.

He hoped Nathan could and would fill the void for her on a romantic level, but Nathan wasn't the action-packed, devil-may-care, mystery man Jacob Hawkins was on the international scene. For all her worldliness, Savannah lay somewhere between the two extremes of the men who flanked her literally and figuratively on the right and left. His concern was she might be caught in the middle of two aggressive and dynamic personalities. If she needed his counsel, however, he'd be there for her, just as she was there for him with Felicia. Still, what was he going to do about the incomparable Dakota Sinclair?

CHAPTER 6

Later that same night, Dakota's 300ZX smoothly climbed the hills the way she still wanted to do. She cornered a curve in the road like a dream and the engine roared like a lion, then purred like a kitten on the straightaway. Dakota downshifted, as she reached the crest of another hill and noticed distant headlights in her rearview mirror. Someone had been tailing her and keeping a discretely distant pace. She remembered a truck pull-off on the downhill side of the mountain. As she rounded a bend on the darkened roadway, she turned off her lights and took the road in the moonlight. She knew this stretch of road so well she could do it in her sleep. Passing the familiar sign post, she pulled onto the truck ramp, snapping her car into a one-hundred-eighty-degree turn and waited for the other car to approach. It didn't take long before the familiar BMW whizzed by. She pulled out of her hiding place, flipped on her high beams, and hugged the bumper of the car ahead of her. As it pulled onto the dirt road in front of her cabin and skidded to a stop, Bill leaped from the car.

"Damn it, Dakota! What do you think you're doing? You were driving like a maniac in these mountains! This isn't a ride at Disney World! You could have killed yourself!"

Dakota peeled herself out of her ZX and slowly flexed her neck from side to side. Then she met Bill's gaze in the moonlight.

"You're getting sloppy," was all she said, as she started past him.

Bill deflated. "All right," he huffed. "I'm pissed off because you...well, you know."

Dakota didn't look back. She did know. She had spurned Bill's attempts to get close to her. She appreciated his desire to be her friend, but nothing more. Even that was an anomaly for her. She didn't make friends and didn't have any to speak of.

She crossed the first security sensor and clear, white light suddenly bathed the cabin. The house lights snapped on in the interior, as she approached. Bill followed. Dakota stopped at her front door, pressing a series of numbers on the electronic lock. The door popped open and she turned to face Bill, putting up her arm to block his entry.

"Well, aren't you going to invite me in?" he asked.

Dakota continued silently studying him.

"Look, it's too late for me to try to go back down through these mountains tonight," Bill argued.

She looked around him at his car and he followed her gaze. He knew what she was thinking, but sleeping in his car was not his idea of something to do.

"I'll be gone in the morning. Scouts honor," he said, raising two, not three, fingers.

Nevertheless, Dakota relented and walked into her cabin. Bill followed and closed the door behind him. She hung her car remote on a hook, opened a panel on the wall, and reset the alarm. The exterior and interior lights flicked off and the house was suddenly pitch-black.

"Hey, I can't see," Bill said, finding himself suddenly in the dark.

"In fifteen seconds, your eyes will become accustomed to the dark. Incoming at two o'clock," she said simultaneous with a blanket and pillow landing on the sofa next to where Bill stood.

He pinned her voice to be coming from the loft above. How she could move so silently and swiftly without disturbing the air around her was still a mystery to him. Shortly, his eyes did become accustomed to the dark and he saw, but could not hear her moving in silhouette above. As silently as ants crossing the dessert, she slid into bed. Bill disrobed in the dark silence and stretched out on the sofa.

"Dakota, smooth move," he said to the darkness.

She didn't answer him, but he didn't expect she would. Dakota was a woman of few words. She didn't waste time on idle conversation. Twice that day, he had seen her uncharacteristically display feelings or emotions, which was more than he had seen in the eight years he had known her.

He cupped his hands behind his head and focused on the loft above him. He'd give anything to be up there with her at that very moment. His eyes finally drifted shut on that thought.

CHAPTER 7

When Jefferson and Nathan reached Jefferson's residence on Embassy Row, their work began. Jefferson was anxious to clear his workload and schedule, and begin the process of untangling his complicated life. He predicted meetings from early morning to well after midnight would fill his next few days, affirming and reaffirming his decision to step down as the international trade negotiation leader.

Nathan would be included in each session with the foreign dignitaries, and then, after each session, he would brief Nathan on his thoughts of what needed to be done. Threats of various nations to pull out of the delicate accord would not daunt him. He was adamant in his decision. Now five-forty in the morning, he finished his session with Nathan, who just left. He quietly sat with fingers steepled, reflecting on the tasks behind him and the ones to come. Yates knocked and simultaneously entered his office.

"Mr. Ambassador, here is the report you requested." Yates placed the red-jacketed material before him, awaiting further instructions.

Jefferson opened the file and pulled the two sheets of paper from the jacket. He read them both in ten seconds and looked up at Yates.

"Is this all?" he asked with furrowed brow.

"Yes, Sir."

Jefferson closed the file and handed it back to Yates.

"Will that be all, Sir?" Yates asked quietly.

"Yes. Get some rest, Yates."

"I will, Sir, when you do." Yates nodded and left the room.

Jefferson returned to his reflective pose. If he was to believe the file he just read, Dakota Sinclair didn't exist. At least not in the same sense others did. She had no credit cards. Never purchased anything. Never saw a doctor or a dentist. Her driver's license listed her office address and her passport information did not reveal much more. Not even her college transcript was included. The company she worked for was based in California, with offices in San Francisco and Santa Barbara. The only telephone number listed for her was an international satellite skyline with an unlimited range and unlisted number. She could be anywhere at this moment, he noted. Around the corner or around the world. He had a lead, though, and he would follow it up. He reached for the intercom on his desk.

"Yates, clear my calendar for dinner. This is what I want you to do."

***

Bill lifted his head at the sound of the vibrating phone in the pocket of his shirt that lay on the table next to the sofa.

"Chandler," he answered.

"Mr. Chandler, please hold for Ambassador Logan," Yates said on the other end.

Bill glimpsed his watch and waited. It was seven in the morning and the cabin was silent. He thought the noise from the phone or his voice might have caused Dakota to stir, but he heard nothing, only silence. Sitting up on the sofa, Bill cleared the sleep from his eyes.

"Mr. Chandler," Jefferson said. "My apologies for calling so early in the morning, but I hoped you and your fiancée would dine with me this evening at my residence."

"Mr. Ambassador, this is very short notice, but what did you want to discuss?"

"I'd like to continue our discussions concerning your joining the trade delegation to the Middle East. Perhaps Ms. Sinclair could be encouraged to join you on the delegation."

Bill stood and walked up the steps to the loft. The bed was made as if no one had slept there, and Dakota was nowhere to be seen in the cabin.

It still mesmerized and infuriated him how she could move so swiftly and silently, usually without detection.

"Uh, Mr. Ambassador, Dakota is still asleep and I don't want to wake her," he lied. "We did get to sleep rather late last night. May I respond to your invitation later in the morning when we've had an opportunity to check our schedules?"

"Certainly, should we say before noon today?"

"That should be ample time. Good day, Mr. Ambassador."

Bill didn't have to guess why the Ambassador extended the invitation. He knew exactly why. Jefferson Logan surreptitiously watched Dakota the evening before, and Bill had watched him as he usually did to cover Dakota's back.

A word with the Chief of Protocol confirmed Nathan Flack arranged for the change in the dinner seating plans. That, too, came as no big surprise to him, but it interfered with his and Dakota's carefully laid plans to garner more insight into their primary market areas.

At least it interfered with his plan, but not with Dakota's, to any great extent, he discerned. She cornered her quarry and completed her mission in the ladies room like the consummate professional she was.

In the many years he had known her, nothing rattled her or interfered with her goals and objectives. Nothing and no one. Jefferson Logan was treading on dangerous ground, if he thought Dakota's attention could be diverted. Many men tried and all failed miserably. Even him, he had to admit. Jefferson Logan would soon learn the futility of his interest. "Well, the bigger they are, the harder they fall," Bill mouthed the cliché to the empty cabin.

A niggling thought rose. Dakota had been elusive because she was always mobile, but now she was grounded. This was going to be a new experience for her and he could not be around to monitor this situation or cover her back. That was a chilling thought.

Bill descended the stairs from the loft and looked around the expansive, empty cabin. It was a place of peace and serenity, but held no warmth or love. If Dakota walked out of that place today, she could carry all of her belongings in a tote bag. None of her essence was anywhere in the rough-hewn cabin. Only the bare necessities. No pictures. No plants. Not even a book or a CD. The cabin was a reflection of the owner—aloof, distant, and detached—a mystery.

Bill walked through the open-concept kitchen and looked through the glass wall toward the lake. There, in the rising, early morning mist, he spotted her. She was clad in black warm-ups, moving to the cadence in her head, as she meditated through her Tai Chi routine. Graceful as a swan, her body moved in perfect rhythm, barely moving the mist that surrounded her.

Bill silently walked to her and joined her in the willowy, contemplative, and deliberate maneuvers. Mind and body became one in deep reverence with a strong current of awareness. When they finished and she turned and observed him with the obsidian stare for which she was well known in the ranks, he knew he had overstayed his time. He nodded and removed himself from her presence, as she continued her yoga exercise routine.

Later, when Dakota reentered her cabin, she pulled a specially designed container of frappe from the otherwise empty refrigerator. She pulled a paper cup from a holder and filled it with the thick, fruity liquid. Then she glanced at Bill sprawled silently on the sofa.

"What is it?" she asked, not looking at him, as she replaced the jar in the refrigerator.

"Logan called. He wants us to join him for dinner."

Dakota didn't immediately answer. She tossed her empty paper cup into a small incinerator.

"The usual excuse will do," she said, as she went to the alarm panel and waited.

Bill knew he was being dismissed. It happened too many times before. He rose from the sofa and walked to the door. His hand on the knob, he did not turn to look at her.

"Dakota…" he said, feeling the emptiness and futility of his thought. He changed his mind about telling her how much he cared for her. "I'll take care of it."

Bill closed the door behind him and Dakota waited until she heard the roar of his car's engine before she reset the alarm. She ascended the steps to the loft, disrobed, and entered the shower. The pain in her leg was not as bad as it was the day before. Maybe she could get back to where she wanted to be in her body and in her mind. She blanked her mind of all other external thoughts and refocused only on the tasks ahead of her.

***

Savannah rolled to her side and immediately saw the long, black, curly, and silky tresses of Jacob's hair on the pillows next to her. Vaguely, she recalled the evening before. As soon as Jefferson's limo pulled away from her townhome on Foxhill Road in Georgetown on the Potomac Canal, another one replaced it.

She knew Nathan and Jefferson would immediately go into discussions over the President's announcements. She and Nathan argued because he did not tell her he would be stepping into her brother's shoes. She knew what that would mean for their relationship and she was furious. Nathan would have no time to be with her during the night or anytime in the near future. She wasn't a nun and didn't want to live a monastic life.

She had just opened her front door when Jacob exited his limo and stood on the narrow sidewalk, stoically looking up at her. It was difficult to disguise their desire. It came in cascading torrents, as his eyes raked over her. Wordlessly, like a big cat stalking its prey, he climbed the black, curved, wrought-iron steps to her, his eyes burning into hers. His well-groomed, blatant masculinity and his jaw set resolutely, spoke to something wild within her. She was consumed with lust by his provocative scrutiny of her. Without pretense or preparation, he backed her into her home, removed her wrap, and began her complete seduction.

When the telephone rang later that night, she noted the number. It was Nathan, she knew, but she heeded Jacob's breathless instruction in her ear, as he stroked in and out of her, to let the telephone ring. Her body and mind separated. One relishing the more urgent fornication and the other paralyzed by disquieting thoughts. His touch was electric and full of possession. His mouth on her back sent sensations to her core. From behind, he relieved her of her gown pooled at her waist and then he inflamed her breasts. Near nudity, he lifted her chin until his mouth covered hers over her shoulder, while with his free hand he played her core like a concert guitarist. He bent her over a sofa and took her where she stood, teasing and tormenting the wildness within her until her senses left her, but that savageness within her turned to dread now in the cold morning light. She turned away from him and the pain her body endured through ecstasy now ached from being ravished.

The telephone rang and she reached for it, but Jacob stayed her hand before she could answer it. He took the receiver from her.

"Yes," he answered and then grinned derisively. "No, she won't come to the phone. She's not finished making love with me." He hung up and grinned at her. "Are you?" He asked more as a statement than a question.

Savannah knitted her brow. "Who was that?"

"Nathan Flack." He grinned unemotionally, as he lowered his mouth to her tender breast.

Savannah winced as much from the pain of his biting touch against her chaffed breasts as from the vision of the pain that would be in Nathan's eyes and in his heart. She started to rise, but Jacob held her back. He covered her body with his, clamped her hands together above her head, and thrust himself inside her, urging her with obscenities against her ear. He was a master of seduction and, again, her body and mind battled the contradiction. Her body won another battle, her mind struggling to win the war.

***

Jefferson disconnected the call and sat back in his executive chair, steepling his fingers in deep thought. Bill Chandler would join him for dinner, but Dakota Sinclair was "unavailable." Something to do with a previous engagement out of town that could not be rescheduled. Chandler was glib about it, saying his fiancée was a workaholic, but Jefferson sensed the real reason for her inability or unwillingness to join them for dinner. She had gleaned his ceaseless concentration on her the night before. Generally, he was not revealing unless it suited his purposes in critical or high-level negotiations, and certainly not in his private affairs, but he believed Dakota had a sixth sense that alerted her to his interest. Round One in these intimate negotiations went to Dakota Sinclair, but the deal was not yet inked. She could not run from him forever.

The knock at the door distracted Jefferson. "Yes," he said, sitting forward at his desk.

Nathan entered with his iPad under his arm and his briefcase in hand. "Good morning, Mr. Ambassador."

Jefferson glimpsed him and knew immediately from his tone and demeanor something was askew. He had a premonition of the problem.

"Nathan, we've known each other a very long time, so I'm going to take certain liberties with you that, under ordinary circumstances, would be outside of the bounds of our professional relationship." When Nathan did not respond, but nodded, Jefferson forged ahead. "You are about to embark upon a mission that will require you to be excruciatingly careful, in full possession of your faculties, digest and sort through a constellation of ideas, and remain meticulous in your deliberations. To accomplish this mission successfully, it will require that you put aside your private life for a more auspicious occasion. I have confidence your expectations of yourself, and mine for you, will not lead to any uncertainties in your professional tasks. However, your private life could be distracting if you do not resolve to distance yourself from that which may become perplexing—namely one ferociously independent Savannah Alisha Logan."

"In other words, don't screw up because I'm feeling torn to shreds over Savannah."

"You're an enormously articulate man, my friend, and, as usual, right on point."

"She's pissed because I've been appointed to take on this task. Not to belabor the point *ad nauseam*, your sister is driving me crazy."

"Family trait. My mother, rest her soul, did that to my father until the day they died. While they were alive, he survived, as will you."

Nathan placed his iPad and briefcase on Jefferson's conference table, stuffed his hands in his pockets, and began slowly pacing the room. "Has Savannah said something to you?" He turned toward Jefferson, searching his mentor and friend's face. "About me, I mean?"

"Savannah generally keeps her own counsel. However, I would strongly suggest you make the time to resolve whatever is between you and my sister before you leave on this mission. You will be involved in very delicate, often secret, and usually dangerous deliberations for six months or more. You will not have time to deal with your insecurities about your relationship with Savannah."

Nathan, his hands still in his pockets, approached Jefferson's desk. "Is that how you've handled the pressures, Jeff? Put all manner of personal and private emotion and physical pleasure out of your mind for the sake of the mission?"

Jefferson looked into Nathan's eyes and said, with deliberate emphasis, "Nothing and no one is more important. You must be prepared to sacrifice everything you hold dear and risk everything, including your life. Hundreds, sometimes thousands of lives depend on your skill and abilities."

Nathan understood. He, indeed, witnessed Jefferson's single-mindedness when the mission required it. Jefferson risked it all, and lost his wife and his sons in the process. Nathan wondered whether he had the courage to put his life on the line as Jefferson had done time and time again for his country. A question he fervently hoped would never have to be answered.

***

Later that evening, Jefferson looked up from his newspaper when Yates escorted Bill Chandler into the library of his home.

"William Chandler, Esquire, Sir."

"Thank you, Yates." He stood and extended his hand to Bill. "Good of you to come, Mr. Chandler."

"Thank you for inviting me, Mr. Ambassador. You have a very impressive residence," Bill said, as he looked around at the well-appointed library, decorated in forest green with stark white trim. Its books shelved to the high ceiling above, deep rich mahogany Louis XV furniture, hardwood floors, Persian rugs, and expensive artwork. "Is that a Russet?" he asked, walking toward the impressive figurine on a Grecian pedestal and then studying it closely. It was crafted by a young, cutting edge artesian who was gaining notoriety. He was also a fellow operative.

"You know art?" Jefferson asked.

"Some," Bill answered blithely, with a slight shrug. He put his hands into his pockets and continued his slow perusal of the library and its treasures.

"May I offer you a drink?" Jefferson asked.

"Stoli, neat," Bill said, shifting his eyes to Yates. What an odd man, Yates, he thought. Outwardly, he seemed the consummate butler or manservant, but Bill sensed there was far more to the man below the surface.

Yates nodded slightly toward Bill and then turned toward Jefferson. "And you, Sir? Your usual?"

"Yes, Yates. Thank you," Jefferson said, still observing Bill.

Yates left the library and Bill continued looking closely at some articles of fine art more than others. He knew Jefferson's eyes were on him, as he regarded the many plaques and awards that graced one entire wall.

"It is unfortunate your fiancée was unable to join us this evening," Jefferson said conversationally to Bill's back.

"That fact was clearly obvious when I returned your call this morning. Frankly, Mr. Ambassador, and," lifting a brow in question, "of course, you expect frankness from me..."

"Certainly," Jefferson answered amicably.

"Frankly, I'm pleased she was not available to join us."

"Oh? Why is that?"

Bill turned, hands still in the pockets of his elegant designer suit that bore his label, and struck an arrogant and authoritative pose while leaning against the large Grecian-styled fireplace. "My fiancée is a very provocative woman. You and I might have spent the entire evening thinly veiling our desires for her and eye-wrestling to the death."

Jefferson grinned disarmingly. "Would we now? Unlike most of the artwork you've been admiring, I do not regard women, even a woman who is as beautiful and charming as Ms. Sinclair, as a curiosity to be gawked at."

Bill smiled enigmatically, a strong current of awareness beginning to course through him. "Yet, your curiosity has been piqued, has it not? Or, that's at least what I observed."

It had, but fortunately, Yates returned at that moment, carrying a tray with the men's drinks and held it up to Bill and then to Jefferson. The men retrieved their drinks and observed each other.

"To women," Jefferson said in a toast.

"To Dakota," Bill answered, tapping his glass against Jefferson's.

Both men drank, regarding each other over the rims of their glasses. Then Jefferson motioned Bill to the high, wingback chair next to where he had been sitting. Bill took the seat and Jefferson sat across from him. Placing his drink on the table that separated them, Jefferson steepled his fingers.

"Have you and Ms. Sinclair known each other for very long?" Jefferson asked.

"Quite a while now."

"Where and how did you two meet?"

"Several years ago in Visp."

"The French Alps? You ski?"

"Yes, as does she." What he didn't say was they were both on a dangerous mission at the time. He was a veritable rookie sent to cover Dakota's back. He was a high-fashion model at the time, a great cover identity that fit in with the jet-set crowd he ran with. The first sight of her on cross-country skis was indelible. She was pure poetry in motion. She crossed the mountain range from Spain with vital information. As instructed by her superiors, he took her to a safe house where she was able to code the information and uplink it to a satellite as it passed overhead. From that time forward, they worked many missions together. She became his team leader and he, and other members of her squad, held her in awe.

"That's interesting. I understood, from my sister, that Ms. Sinclair was a triathlete, but I thought she mentioned running."

Bill leaned forward. "I've never been the diplomatic type, Mr. Ambassador, and I'm clearly no match for you in that department, so shall we dispense with the pretense and go straight to the heart of the matter, and likely the reason for this dinner meeting?"

Jefferson nodded briefly and Bill continued.

"Dakota Sinclair is exactly as you've witnessed and, no doubt, investigated. She is a very private person. What is important for you to know about her is that she is my fiancée. Any man would be incensed and, perhaps, even intimidated if a man of your stature were as inquisitive about a woman he intends to marry."

"But, of course, you're not."

"You're right. I'm not. I'm very secure in my relationship with Dakota. She and I are very much in love and she has agreed to be my wife."

Jefferson lifted his drink to his lips. He drank slowly and deliberately, replaced the glass on the table and laced his fingers.

"If I believed that, Mr. Chandler, you wouldn't be here tonight trying to convince me there is something between you and Ms. Sinclair. Of course, we both know there isn't."

Bill sat back in his chair and leisurely sipped from his drink. "Oh and why is that?"

Jefferson's disarming smile resurfaced. "Because, Mr. Chandler, you're gay."

Bill regarded Jefferson closely, took another sip of his drink, and placed the glass on the table between them before he responded. "Actually, the politically correct reference is bisexual. There is a difference."

"Only to someone who is homosexual. Ms. Sinclair, I believe, is not. Therefore, Mr. Chandler, let us 'dispense with the pretense', as you so aptly put it. Who is Dakota Sinclair?"

"A woman who enjoys the pleasure of my company. Subtlety never was one of my strong points either. I don't wear my homosexuality as a badge of courage or my heterosexuality as a badge of honor. I am a sexual being, however. I feel gratification from both sexes equally. I don't have a preference. Ms. Sinclair is fully aware of my proclivities and she remains my faithful companion...and lover," he said, as he leaned back in the comfortable chair. "You are, of course, a person of considerable influence and, no doubt, you have the means and opportunity to pursue this matter. My question, however, is to what end? What is your motivation and what do you hope to gain?"

Jefferson was not about to open that door to Bill Chandler. His motives were purely personal and not open to discussion. In his desire to gain more insight into Dakota Sinclair, he had slightly lifted the diplomatic veil. That would not happen again. He took the tactful way out.

"As I have said publicly, Mr. Chandler, I'm interested in having you *and* Ms. Sinclair join the trade delegation. In making that decision, I must assess not only the companies represented, but also the people involved. Ms. Sinclair represents CompuCorrect International, a company that enjoys an unblemished, impeccable, and respected reputation in this country and abroad."

"It does, yes, but it is my understanding her company is looking at other markets. Markets that don't include Asia where, I believe, your trade delegation is planning to focus its attention. Given that fact, coupled with the fact that you have abdicated your position with the trade delegation, I doubt my fiancée would be interested in joining Nathan Flack's delegation—if, in fact, that's what has spurred your interest in her or the company she represents."

"Are you suggesting there is some hidden agenda or ulterior motive in my interest?"

"Let me just say, Mr. Ambassador, discretion is the better part of valor."

Jefferson let that remark pass unchallenged. It was not Dakota's corporate relationship he was interested in, it was Dakota, and Bill Chandler knew it.

"Dinner is served, Mr. Ambassador," Yates said, interrupting the discussion.

Yates' timely announcement relieved Jefferson of the need to discuss Dakota further, while Bill was prepared and alert. He smiled to himself. Before the evening was over, he'd get the information he wanted. He and Bill went into dinner.

CHAPTER 8

Hi, Sam. Looks like you have a full house tonight," Dr. Sandra Lewis, another OB/GYN specialist, said, as she joined Savannah Logan at the nurse's station.

"Four in labor. I'm going to be here all night it seems," Savannah said, as she continued reviewing medical charts.

"Chuck Montgomery's wife, Vivian, is one of your patients, I see."

"Yes, it's their second baby since they were married three years ago, and Chuck is acting like it's their first. Doctors make the worst expectant fathers," she mused.

"Vivian seems to be handling it like a champ."

"She's a judge. She's accustomed to theatrics—even from her husband."

"Speaking of fine specimen, how is that devastatingly handsome brother of yours?"

Savannah glimpsed Sandy. "Jefferson is fine, Sandy."

"Seeing anyone?"

"I wouldn't know, although he did show an interest in one of my former classmates last night," she said more as a recollection than as an answer to her friend's question.

"Spelman, huh?" Sandy surmised.

Savannah smiled. "Yes, Sandy, Spelman."

Sandy sighed. "I knew I should have gone to school there instead of Stanford. All of you Spelman women find the most interesting and fascinating men. Vivian and Chuck, you and Nathan, and JaiHonnah and Roderick—" She broke off her thought when Savannah looked up. "Oh, Sam, I'm sorry. I forget sometimes that you and Roderick...well, you know what I mean, don't you?"

"Yes, Sandy, I know. Don't worry about it. I'm over Roderick."

"Yeah, especially since you've got that phine, phine, super phine Nathan Flack. Now that's what I call a man!" she said with enthusiasm. "When are you going to put that man out of his misery and marry him?"

Savannah thought a moment. "Sandy, do you have some time to do an exam for me?"

Sandy looked at her quizzically. "What? Do you need help with your patients? I thought you had this all under control, as usual."

"Uh, I do, Sandy, but…"

Sandy's eyes brightened and she smiled broadly. "You mean—"

"No, nothing like that. I'm not pregnant, but…"

Sandy's eyes narrowed as she looked at Savannah. Then she looked around to assure they were alone. "What is it, Sam?" she asked with concern.

Savannah suddenly felt embarrassed. Her body still felt ravished from her experience with Jacob Hawkins. It was the first time they slept together and her body told her it would be the last. She regretted having been with him, especially after Nathan called. She was angry with Nathan for agreeing to take her brother's place as the head of the US trade delegation, but a cooler head now prevailed.

Nathan was so very patient with her, allowing her to be independent and not demanding she make any commitments she was not ready for. Still, his patience would not last forever, she knew, especially if he felt he wasn't the only man she was intimate with. He had plenty of options just as her brother had, but in recent times both men limited themselves, while she had not.

"Well, hello, Nathan," Sandy said and smiled broadly.

Savannah snapped out of her revelry and looked up over her shoulder. Nathan was standing behind her.

"Hello, Sandy," Nathan said, looking at Savannah. "Could we talk, Savannah?"

"Well," Sandy said, grinning. "That's my cue to check up on my patients."

"Sorry to interrupt," Nathan said apologetically.

"Uh, you don't have to go," Savannah said to Sandy and then turned to Nathan. "I'm swamped, Nate. Couldn't we—"

"No, Savannah, we can't," he said without a smile anywhere in the vicinity of his face.

Savannah sensed the tension in Nathan's stoic demeanor, as did Sandy.

"Look, you two. The doctors' lounge is empty. Why don't you go in there? I'll cover for you, Sam."

Savannah started to protest, but Nathan touched her arm and she rose from her seat.

"Uh, thanks, this won't take long," she said, as she permitted Nathan to guide her to the doctors' lounge.

Savannah walked as confidently as her body would permit, each step an effort to mask the discomfort. Once inside the lounge, Savannah walked directly to the Keurig. Anything to delay the confrontation she knew would come. She avoided Nathan's telephone calls all day. Now, at nearly midnight, he was there for an explanation and she had none to offer. What could she say? Her life was in turmoil. It wasn't that Nathan wasn't important to her because he was. She cared about him, but her disappointment over a failed romance with Roderick Baylor made her question her appeal as a woman. She wasn't fooling herself. After Roderick rejected her and married JaiHonnah, she needed the gratification and ego boost that multiple suitors afforded her, and she needed time to build her confidence again. Regrettably, judging from Nathan's uncharacteristically forceful demeanor, her time with him just ran out.

Savannah's unsteady hand poured cream into a coffee cup, as Nathan looked on. He noticed her labored movements and guessed the reason for it, but he would not let the jealousy and anger that seethed within him boil to the top and overflow. He kept himself in check, practicing the control he learned from years of watching Jefferson in stress-filled conferences. He prayed he would be as seemingly dispassionate as Jefferson could be, but Savannah was trying his patience to the nth degree.

"How are you, Nathan?" Savannah nervously asked.

"You already know how I am, Savannah." Nathan's deep-throated, melodic voice seized her.

For a moment, the passion in his declaration stunned her. She could not turn around to look at him, but with his next words, he left her no room to maneuver.

"Look at me, Savannah," he directed.

Savannah turned slowly, not raising her eyes to his. She could see his strong, tall frame hard as steel before her.

"I said, look at me," Nathan said again, his voice not rising.

Savannah lifted her eyes to meet his. She exhaled slowly and nervously worried her bottom lip. He was magnificent...and he was angry.

"What is it, Nathan? Why are you here so late?"

"Stop asking me questions you already have the answer to."

Steadying her nerves, she brushed aside his statement with a dismissive flick of her hand to check her watch. "This is neither the time nor place for us to visit—"

"This is no social call and you know it. You know exactly why I'm here and I'm not leaving until you give me an explanation."

"I'm too busy to talk now. I've got four patients in various stages of labor. I need to monitor their progress and—"

"I'm supposed to be sympathetic, I presume? Well, not tonight, Doctor. I have obligations, too, but at the moment, nothing is more important than this conversation. Now either you tell me where I stand or I walk, and, make no mistake about this, if I walk out, I mean to walk out of your life for good."

That statement was delivered with the force of a sledgehammer and Savannah's brows knitted. "Don't give me ultimatums, Nathan. I don't respond to threats from you or anyone very well," she said angrily.

"That's no threat, Savannah. That's a promise," he said without a blink.

The tension in the lounge rose effortlessly and was so thick it could be cut with an ax. For Savannah, the thought of losing Nathan felt like a blade cutting through her body. She knew in an instant she had pushed him too far. Fortunately, Sandy interrupted their conversation.

"Uh, sorry for the intrusion, folks, but, Savannah, you're needed in Delivery Room 3."

"No problem, Sandy, Savannah and I are through," Nathan said with resolve, the double entendre purposefully delivered. "There's nothing to interrupt. I was just leaving." Nathan turned and looked at Sandy. "She's all yours."

Then he was gone. Savannah felt his swift departure deep in her core and flopped down on a sofa. It couldn't end like that! Not without asking him to continue to be patient, but he said what he came to say.

"Savannah, are you all right?" Sandy asked with concern, coming forward and placing a comforting hand on her shoulder. "What in the world is going on in here? I've never seen Nathan act like that."

Savannah shook her head. "Nothing, Sandy. Nathan must have had a bad day or something. He'll be fine soon. It's all of these long hours we've been working. We haven't had much time together. Now he's taken on more responsibility, which means we'll have even less time for each other."

"Girlfriend, Nathan looked like a man on a mission. If you want to go after him, I can cover for you in DR3 for a little while."

"No, that won't be necessary. Thanks anyway," Savannah said, knowing the real possibility existed that she was about to lose Nathan and she could not let that happen. She hurried out the lounge to go to her patient.

Nathan caught a cab at the hospital entrance and, within moments, he was walking into the Watergate Complex, which was within walking distance from his office at the State Department. He went directly to his condo without checking his mail or giving the desk clerk his customary greeting. Once inside his place, he stripped his tie from his neck and flung it across the room. *Why am I so angry?* Savannah had given him his answer. She was not going to commit to him. He had to move on. He had an awesome task ahead of him for the next year. He wanted her love and support, but he knew now it would not be forthcoming. His pride wouldn't let him back down from his position. It was over! Finished! He tore out of his clothes and went into the shower, turning the water on full force with a pulsating stream from three directions. He would wash her out of his system just as the hard force of water washed over him and down the drain.

CHAPTER 9

Dakota finished her early morning workout and limped into the house. Her leg was afire and the pain was excruciating. She tried to walk it off, but she knew from years of training and cross-country running that the problem was serious. Her doctors, the best in the business, told her she might never regain full strength in her legs. A year of recuperation would be necessary before they could determine whether there was hope. She never thought her body would not respond to her own rigorous training schedule, but it hadn't and the results were the pain and discomfort that now afflicted her.

She sat on the sofa and cupped her face in her hands. *No!* she thought. *This is not going to happen!* She closed her eyes and then her mind to the pain. Slowly, she breathed in and out, forcing her mind to disallow the gut-wrenching agony.

She took her thoughts to another place. A place where she was safe from harm. A cabin on the edge of the foothills of the Rocky Mountains. An old man who had taught her, but without touching her. The way of the Algonquians would save her. She was part Native American and part African American, but who was she? Who were her people? How had she come to live in the orphanage? Was she part Blackfeet or Cree or Ojibwa or Gros Ventre? Although she wore a piece of their jewelry usually hidden around her neck, under her clothes, and could speak the languages of the Northern Plains Native Americans, no one could give her answers. The old Algonquian, who made the piece of jewelry for her, had been the only one to talk to, but he could not answer her questions either. His advice and counsel, when she left the orphanage to go away to Spelman College, was to look ahead, not back. There was nothing to look back to. Two people had thirty-five seconds of pleasure and she had thirty-five years of pain. Who were those people and why had they abandoned her?

The pain in her heart was as great as the pain in her legs. She stopped her meditation when she heard a car pull up the gravel road. She rose and disarmed the security system. Then she walked to the front door and opened it. Bill stalked past her and into the cabin. His agitation palpable.

"I believe Logan is going to be a problem," he said without amenities.

"I thought you were going to handle it?" she said more as a statement than a question.

Bill turned and looked at her. "He's not an easy man to discourage, Dakota. I spent last night ducking and dodging him, but he picked me like a pro. When I left his house, I thought I had been successful, but, by the time I got home, I knew he let me go because he had gotten everything he wanted from me."

"Damn!" she said under her breath, her hands tightening into a fist.

"What can I say, Dakota? You have that kind of effect on men, but Logan, well, he's no ordinary man."

Dakota cocked an eyebrow in his direction.

Bill put up both hands. "The man is blatantly heterosexual, Dakota, and, besides, seducing him wasn't my mission. Still, he apparently bought the cover that I'm bisexual," he said, answering the question he knew was lurking behind her beautiful face. "Are you sure you haven't run into the man before? Maybe on some lost weekend?"

Dakota dismissed his comment with an annoyed flick of her hand and moved on. "You didn't come up here just to tell me about your evening with Logan. What else is on your agenda?"

"Actually, I did. Logan didn't buy the engagement business. We need to step up the cover. Maybe we should go through with the wedding and—" Dakota knitted her brow and Bill noticed. "Either that or move out of harm's way," Bill added.

"I'm restricted, remember? Officially, I'm still on medical leave."

"I remember," Bill said with a sly grin, "but your restriction—"

"Forget it," Dakota said, knowingly. "I'm not going from the frying pan into the fire. Not yet, at least."

"It's more like a raging inferno," Bill said smoothly. "You know how I feel. I want you, Dakota."

"You know it's not going to happen. Not now or ever, Bill."

"Well, at least, there is some good news."

"What is it?"

"He has a Russet in his collection."

Dakota's face lifted with curiosity. "I don't recall any covert action involving him in his dossier. Who planted a listening device in his home and how long has it been there?"

"I don't believe there was anything involving The Nursery. If so, Delta would have said something when I gave him a sitrep. Maybe he just bought it as a curiosity. He has an eclectic collection of art, but I'll dig deeper to see whether I missed something in his background."

"Activate the Song Bird. Learn things. Let me know if you find something."

"Copy that."

CHAPTER 10

Savannah heard no word from Nathan in over two days. Usually, when they did not spend the night together, he would call every morning before he got up and every night before he went to bed. It was well after three in the morning when she left the hospital. She started driving toward her town house and then changed her mind. Instead, she headed for the Watergate Complex. Just as she was about to pull up to the lobby door, she saw Nathan come out of the front and instruct the valet to hail a cab for his companion, her friend, Dr. Sandy Lewis. Savannah didn't know what emotion to feel first—anger or hurt.

As Nathan opened the door of the taxi for Sandy, she gave him a big hug and kiss on the cheek. The rage began to build effortlessly within Savannah. *How dare Sandy move in on Nathan!* Savannah fumed silently in her car. *And him! What does Nathan think he's doing?* All of the recriminations came raging to the forefront. *Sandy and Nathan!* Her *Nathan!* Just because they had a little disagreement didn't give either of them license to carry on an affair behind her back! She and Nathan had an understanding after all! They had been together for over a year. Perhaps "together" wasn't the right term, but they were lovers. He couldn't have forgotten her already. Not in two damn days when they had just been together, she thought, but she tried to recall when last she slept with him. Finally, it came to her. It had been weeks! She was very busy, though, and so was he working with her brother in preparation for the trade mission. Then, too, Jacob Hawkins had been in town. Since Nathan was not around, she was spending a great deal of time getting to know Jacob. Nathan had to understand...or did he?

Nathan looked over the baseball schedule Sandy dropped off at his place. The State Department team, of which he was an organizing member, would be playing against the Georgetown Hospital team four times over the summer. He positioned himself in his bed and leaned his head back against a mound of pillows and the tufted leather headboard, wondering why he couldn't have fallen for someone like Sandy Lewis. She was bright, intelligent, attractive, easy going, and uncomplicated.

No, instead he had fallen for the opposite: Savannah Logan. And, fallen hard. Savannah. Sexy, aggressive, independent, every man's wet dream and more of a challenge than any woman he had ever known. He shook off the troublesome thoughts of Savannah. He had to forget about her. It was over and done. She made her choice. It was Jacob Hawkins, or whoever the hell the next victim of her desire happened to be, but it would not be him. Not anymore. He had taken the last smack in the face from her and he meant it. He tolerated too much. Never before had he permitted himself to be a doormat by any woman and he was tired of it now.

In the early days of their friendship, seeing Savannah out with other men wrenched his gut, but she always came back to him, as their relationship grew closer. She warmed parts of his life no other woman was able to touch. It was not just that she was a fantastic lover, nor was it her beauty, her position, or her prominence. Many women he knew had those traits. No, with Savannah, it was her essence. The stuff dreams of a future were made of. He could visualize her pregnant with his child or mothering the family they could have together...*together?* Hell, there was no *two* in together for them. It was Savannah Logan and Savannah was out of his life for good!

Nathan flipped off the bedside lamplight and tried to fall asleep. His eyes closed, but not his thoughts or his needs. His mind went directly to Savannah and his body reacted just as it usually did whenever he thought of her. He automatically reached for the telephone to call her and then hesitated. It was one thing to think he could dismiss her from his mind and body. It was quite a different thing to actually do it. He had to try harder, though. He could not continue to let his life be turned upside down by Dr. Savannah Alicia Logan. Not if he expected to remain in control of his sanity.

Savannah sat in her car for nearly an hour in front of the Watergate Complex. She was still visualizing Nathan holding Sandy in his arms and the kiss he and Sandy shared. The vision of Nathan and Sandy together was jarring, but she was getting nowhere just sitting and staring at the Complex. She had to have some answers.

Savannah inserted her electronic key in Nathan's door and walked in. The lights were out, but she knew her way to his bedroom blindfolded. She had done it many times before after Nathan gave her a key to his condo. The faint odor of Sandy's perfume still hung in the air. She went to Nathan's open bedroom door; the clock dial illuminated his body. He was lying on his back, one hand behind his head and one leg up and bent at the knee. She noticed the overnight shadow of coarse, facial hairs that never failed to tantalize her when they made love—and he was the consummate lover. His body was a masterpiece, well sculptured and masculine, she thought. Black hairs covered his cocoa-brown chest and were lost beneath the cover that rested below his navel. The imprint of his long, strong, and hard phallus tented the zillion-count sheets between his firm thighs. Suddenly, her body ached for him and his touch. She could stand it no longer.

While slipping out of her slacks and blouse, she continued to gaze at him. She noted the opposite side of his king-sized bed—her side of the bed—was undisturbed. If he and Sandy had been intimate, the sheets would have been on the floor. Maybe Nathan's relationship with Sandy hadn't progressed that far yet. If she had anything to do with it, Nathan wouldn't have a sexual relationship with any other woman.

Her eyes washed over him, as she slid out of her teddy and then between the sheets. She watched him sleeping for a moment and then lowered her mouth to his, licking softly at his lip. She stroked his chest, playing her nails against his hardening, raisin-like nipples. His breathing quickened and he moved his hand from behind his head to stroke her back. His other hand joined in the seduction along her thigh, cupping her butt and bringing her leg to rest across the firm trunk of his nude body. Savannah deepened her kiss, wallowing in the velvet recesses of his mouth. Her nipples hardened as she raked her nails across his rock-hard abdomen and found his member, thick and pulsating in her hand. She felt his body snap to attention. He moaned when she began to stroke him.

Nathan thought he was dreaming. Savannah was so often in his dreams. He very vividly recalled every inch of her luscious, silky-soft body. Her smooth skin, her scent, and her taste. His dreams often felt like reality, but this was no dream cupping him and stroking his phallus. When her mouth accompanied her hand, his life spun out of his control. She played him like a concert pianist, all fingers manipulating him, reshaping him too well and too easily. She knew how to love him. He recognized any effort to delay or distance himself from her was futile. Yet, he wasn't fooling himself. He wanted her. He wanted her desperately, completely, and permanently.

"You drive me crazy," he said through clinched teeth, his voice ragged. "All you have to do is touch me and you send me into orbit."

"It's called retribution for what you do to me," she whispered against his ear.

"Call it whatever you want, but I call it love," he said, as he rolled atop her, lathing the hollow of her neck.

Now it was Savannah's turn to gasp, as Nathan moved to capture her nipples in his mouth, calling forth her nature from her core. She stroked his thick, naturally wavy hair then threaded her fingers through it as his mouth slipped down her abdomen to her navel. His hot, wet tongue on her pubis sent waves of passion flooding over her and then he captured her core, the center of her being. No man made her body writhe with ecstasy like Nathan. Her toes curled involuntarily and her inner muscles constricted. He held her thighs immobile while he made sweet love to her. His expert ministration lasted a lifetime.

"Now, who's driving who crazy?" Savannah gasped. "I want you now, Nathan," she said urgently, as he caused her second orgasm to rage unchecked.

"It's been three weeks since I last touched you. I don't intend to end this in three minutes or three hours," he growled lowly against her core.

Savannah's back arched as Nathan worried her sweet spot and held her still during the exquisite agony. Her body writhed in ecstasy as he coaxed her nature from her core again and again. Then, with painstaking slowness, he licked and kissed his way up her trembling torso until he found her mouth waiting for him. He made quick work of protecting them both. Then, by degrees, he began to enter her smoothly, strongly arching his back with his downward stroke. Savannah's fingers urged him on, gripping his firm butt while simultaneously moving her posterior to a sensuous cadence in her head. His whispered, lust and love-filled words thrilled her and she responded to him in kind.

Nathan thought he would explode when Savannah tumbled him over and came up on top of him without breaking their union. If he did not know her profession to be in the medical field, he would have thought her a professional belly dancer the way she moved atop him. Her hips were mesmerizing, as she undulated them, tightening her inner muscles around him. He sucked in a ragged breath and felt his nature ready to brim over. His jaw locked, straining against the urge to release, but he held back, relishing the feel of her velvet softness.

Ultimately, it became too much for them both and they brought each other to a pinnacle not reached before in their intimate, yearlong relationship. Both were perspiring profusely from the experience and breathing hard.

"Woman, what you do to me!" Nathan choked out the words around the lump that had formed in his throat.

"It's only the beginning," she breathed into his ear.

Not long after, she began to rekindle his flame and they were again off on another journey of discovery.

CHAPTER 11

Jefferson parked his Land Cruiser at the curb in front of the private jetport at Dulles International Airport and walked up to the security checkpoint. The guard looked up and narrowed his eyes.

"All deliveries are made around back," he said, eying Jefferson closely, as if he had seen a wanted poster with Jefferson's face on it.

Usually, when Jefferson arrived at the airport destined for some foreign land, security and aides surrounded him, but today no entourage accompanied him. He was alone and dressed casually in well-worn jeans, an old T-shirt, and his favorite old designer jacket. He was accustomed to the manner in which some people regarded Blacks that seemed to be out of their element. Under ordinary circumstances, Jefferson might have taken offense and had the man chastised or even fired, as he had done with others who took liberties because of his race, but today was the day his sons were coming to live with him and that was paramount in his mind. Besides, fighting discrimination had always been his forte. He, however, did it on a global basis more often than on the domestic front. Facing the man, he made eye contact.

"Jefferson Logan," he said clearly and distinctly.

"Logan? You mean Ambassador Logan?" the guard asked, disbelieving the sight before him. "Is your boss in the car or something?"

Jefferson looked away a moment and then turned back to the man with a leveling gaze.

"No, the President is in Arizona. *I'm* Jefferson Logan."

The man's eyebrows furrowed. "You? Uh, do you have identification?"

Jefferson reached into his pocket, retrieved his State Department credentials, and held them up to the guard's face.

The guard flushed red, gulping audibly.

"Uh, uh, I'm sorry, Mr. Ambassador," the man said sheepishly. "I was only doing my job."

"You're new here, aren't you?" Jefferson asked, putting his credentials back in his pocket.

"Uh, yes, Sir. I've only been on the job a week, Sir," the guard said nervously.

Jefferson grinned disarmingly. "Well," he peered at the nametag on the guard's shirt, "Mr. Pritchard, keep up the good work."

"Uh, yes, Sir. Uh, thank you. You may go in. Your party will be arriving shortly. Help yourself to the buffet."

Jefferson nodded to the guard and entered the jetport lounge. Disregarding the lavish buffet laid out for his and the Montroses' arrival, he focused on the big, private jet being guided into its docking port just outside the huge hanger bay doors. He wasn't sure what to expect from his sons, but seeing the largest of the Montroses' corporate jets, he knew what was coming from their patriarch. Although he had spoken with his boys on the telephone, he had not seen them in some time. The battles that raged between him and Tyler McKenzie Montrose started the moment Felicia introduced him as her husband and it had never waned. Tyler turned white as a sheet and Clara Smith Montrose, his mother-in-law, fainted. All manners of ugly reprisals and recriminations ensued because of his and Felicia's impromptu marriage.

Felicia was a rebellious person throughout her life. She had done things to her parents simply to rile them, as he later learned. Her parents spoiled her rotten, never requiring her to be responsible for her own actions. Instead, they placated her often-horrendous behavior, covered up misdeeds, and succumbed to her every whim.

After their marriage, when Jefferson would not let Felicia have her way, she behaved much like a petulant child. His attempt to deal with Felicia as an adult failed. She treated him like less than a man and their sons as toys and bargaining chips. When she tired of both him and the boys, she was off on one junket or the other with her jet-set, blue-blood crowd.

Although their marriage started on the wrong foot, they never had a chance to develop a real relationship. He had been away too often and too long on one diplomatic mission or another for most of their married life. Sex was all she wanted from him, but that resulted in the birth of three sons he both loved and cherished.

Later in their marriage, Felicia's frequent, open, and highly publicized affairs were the proverbial straws that broke the camel's back. Felicia was arrested for drunk and disorderly conduct, hobnobbing with her equally irresponsible crowd, while he was in Washington, DC. He gave her an ultimatum: Either she was going to come to Washington with him and raise their sons, or he would file for divorce and for custody of their boys. The Montroses feared little, given their great wealth and influence, but the threat of the negative media attention and publicity that an ugly divorce would engender did strike fear in their hearts. Felicia swore it would be ugly if he ever tried to leave her. She did, however, move to Washington with him. That turned out to be a mistake as well.

While he was on a special, six-week assignment in London, Felicia was caught in an FBI drug raid, along with two congressmen, various sundry lobbyists, a few sports figures, and other entertainers. He could have tolerated being the laughing stock and the butt of many cruel jokes and cartoon caricatures in the press and news media if at any time he felt there was love between him and Felicia, but he soon learned there was no love to be had.

All of these factors affected his relationship with his sons over the years. Now he was prepared to put the past behind him and move on with his boys as his primary focus. Only the Montroses stood in the way of that goal. They had battled him for the love and affection of his sons and for their custody. No matter what lay ahead for him and his children, Jefferson intended they would face it together as a family and without the influence of the Montroses.

The jet docked and Jefferson was not at all surprised to see the patriarch himself, Tyler McKenzie Montrose, coming down the steps, accompanied by his battery of lawyers. Jefferson anticipated such a move, but he was not going to be intimidated. He waited for Tyler to enter the lounge and stood with his head up, back straight, legs apart, and arms akimbo.

Tyler McKenzie Montrose, III, a short, stocky man with beady, green eyes, a thick pelt of wavy silver hair, had a reputation for being as cunning as a poisonous snake and not nearly as even tempered. Despite his sixty years, he still had a commanding presence. He inherited his wealth from his forefathers, but he also parlayed that wealth into an empire in his own right. He headed three multinational corporate conglomerates and ruled over them and his family with an iron fist. Tyler's own four sons, who were younger than Felicia, never lived up to Tyler's expectations, but Felicia, his only daughter and firstborn, had been his prize. Except for her marriage to Jefferson, she could do no wrong in Tyler's eyes. As a result, Tyler's sons long since gave up trying to please their father and simply took advantage of the leisurely, and often, decadent lifestyles their heritage and inherited wealth afforded them. Jefferson believed Tyler saw in his and Felicia's sons, Jefferson Junior, Miles, and Stephen, an opportunity to reshape the Montrose future, but his sons were Logans, not Montroses, and Jefferson had plans for his sons that did not include them becoming Tyler's clones. Their grandparents would have a place in their lives, Jefferson conceded, out of respect for Felicia's memory, but he was their father, not Tyler.

"I'm here to offer you whatever you want to withdraw your claim to the boys," Tyler said without the customary salutations.

"Bring my sons to me, Mac. They're not for sale and I resent the implication that any amount of inducement would dissuade me from raising my boys."

"You're not fit to be a father to them!"

Jefferson held his temper and turned to Tyler's attorneys. "Instruct your client to relinquish custody of my sons or I'll assure the courts will find him in contempt as a civil matter and the Attorney General will file kidnapping charges against him in a criminal action this very day."

"How dare you!" Tyler blared.

"How dare *you*!" Jefferson shot back. "I want my boys and I won't wait another damn minute!"

Tyler's puffed-up frame was met by Jefferson's determination. The attorneys huddled and then one whispered to Tyler, who actually slapped the attorney's face. He brushed off another one.

"They don't want you, Jefferson!"

"I want them! *Now!*" Jefferson said firmly.

As if on cue, Jefferson saw his sons being guided down the steps of the aircraft. They looked like tin soldiers to him, as they marched toward the lounge.

"You'll pay for this!" Tyler stormed. "This and much, much more!"

Jefferson turned away and looked at the sad faces of his sons.

"I already have," he said, modulating his voice.

Jefferson moved toward the boys, but Tyler stepped between them.

"I've told you how stubborn and unfeeling Jefferson Logan can be," Tyler said, bending to talk to his grandsons. "He has refused my offer to let you permanently stay with me and your grandmother, where you belong. However, it will only be for a little while and then you'll be back with us for good," Tyler said. "Your place is with those who love you, boys. Now remember that. If you need anything at all, you call me."

Jefferson held his temper, but if Tyler went on for one more second, he might have forgotten Tyler was an old man.

"This way," Jefferson said, guiding his sons away.

An entourage of porters followed, carrying luggage they loaded into and tied on top of Jefferson's new, extended Land Cruiser.

The ride from the airport out of the populated areas was quiet, as Jefferson drove through the twisting road toward his sister's mountain retreat. Jefferson fought to hold on to his temper. What was upper most in his mind was his boys and not Tyler McKenzie Montrose, but he knew he had a lot of fence mending to do with his sons. Years of fighting for custody of them and, finally, he won. Now the hard part would begin— winning his boys' respect, trust, and most importantly, their love.

The three boys sat in the back seat of the SUV nearly motionless for more than an hour. Jefferson consciously chose not to force himself on any of them. There were not the customary hugs or kisses or any other show of emotion or affection Jefferson would have wanted his reunion with his sons to be. Time would cure that, he silently speculated and then affirmed in his mind. Time to show his sons he cared about them, loved them, and wanted them to be with him. He was willing to risk everything—including his career—to be with them.

"Where did you go on your trip?" Jefferson finally asked, breaking the uneasy silence that had prevailed for nearly two hours.

Both Miles and Stephen looked toward their older brother. Jefferson Junior's silence was thick.

"Canada," he answered curtly without further commentary.

"That must have been exciting," Jefferson Senior answered. "Would you tell me about it?"

Jefferson Junior remained quiet, clearly not interested in carrying on a discussion. Miles nervously shifted in his seat and started to speak, but Jefferson Junior cut his eyes at his younger brother and Miles stilled.

"Father required that we prepare an exposé on the journey. It will be published in Father's *Wilderness Weekly*. You may purchase a copy and read the—"

"Tyler Montrose is your grandfather. Not your father. When you speak of him to me, you may refer to him in that term. Have we an understanding, Jefferson?" the Senior said more harshly than he intended, but he wanted an understanding from the beginning. He was their father, not Tyler Montrose. Jefferson glimpsed the three boys in his rear view mirror, but their stone-like faces gave him no solace. Silence again reigned inside the car. Then Jefferson Junior spoke.

"We will accede to your will. However, you will address me as J. Montrose Logan."

The battle lines were drawn, Jefferson Senior thought silently, but his diplomatic demeanor kicked in.

"On that score, there is room for negotiation," he said more to himself than as a response to his son.

Clearly, it was going to be a very long, hot summer.

Jefferson pulled into the gravel-filled, circular driveway in front of a four-thousand-square-foot, ultra-modern, post-and-beam constructed cabin. He got out of his SUV and opened the rear door. Then he untied the luggage from the roof and began placing the bags on the ground. When he looked up from placing the last piece of luggage on the ground, he noticed the boys had not moved from their seats.

"I could use a hand with this luggage and these groceries," he said, opening the other door to the back seat.

Again, Miles and Stephen looked toward Jefferson Junior for direction. Jefferson looked straight ahead.

"Have the servants assist you," he said coldly.

"There are no servants here. It's just us," Jefferson said, leaning an arm on the top of the door and the other on his hip.

Jefferson Junior turned only his head and glared at his father. "You expect *us* to carry luggage? We're not porters or butlers, Mr. Logan!" Jefferson Junior indignantly spat.

"It's your luggage, son," Jefferson Senior said calmly with a smile. "You insisted on bringing it, you can carry it."

Jefferson Junior raged. "I will not!"

"Suit yourself," Jefferson Senior said, with a laconic shrug. "Miles, Stephen, it's your decision as to whether your luggage gets into the house. We can make this a group effort, if you'd like, or not." Jefferson carried three full bags of groceries into the house on each of four trips.

Miles and Stephen sat stone-faced, looking straight ahead. On the fifth trip, Jefferson Senior lifted his own luggage and proceeded into the house, leaving his sons to make their own decisions. Every step away from the car for Jefferson Senior was labored, but he had to establish the ground rules. He could not let their arrogance continue unchecked. He prayed his strategy would work, but his level of confidence was less sure than when he dealt with hostile, international leaders. In his diplomatic milieu, he knew his strengths and his opponents' weaknesses. Here, he was out of his element.

He had good role models in his parents, but their untimely deaths left him to raise himself and become a parent to his sister all too soon.

He did the best he could under the circumstances, but his sons were another thing all together. With Savannah, they were in the same boat. They shared the loss of their parents together. With his sons, he all but abandoned them after Felicia's death and the guilt of that fact tore at him. It made him do foolish things, like have affairs with women he did not or could not love. Women who he should never have been with, but for what they could offer him in terms of information. He was not proud of how he used women, but he had no excuse to offer. That was his life—or was it? Had his career been a convenient way of running from the memory of his loveless marriage? He shook off the pain and opened the door of the cabin, never looking back to see what his sons' reactions had been. *Everything in its time,* he recalled his father cautioned. Jefferson remembered.

The cabin was a mixture of rustic and modern, open-concept, post-and-beam construction, and very elegant, befitting his sister's exquisite taste. African art adorned the high, cream-colored walls in the open common areas. The loft balcony and upper three bedrooms traversed the width of the cabin and highly polished, solid, hardwood floors gleamed and glistened in the late afternoon light. Jefferson opened the draperies to the panoramic view of the lake. He paused, folding his arms across his chest. He always felt at peace here. He could hear the birds and the sound of nature all around him in the dense forest. The comfort found here was much like his early, carefree childhood in the small Georgia town where he and Savannah were born.

Opening one of the French doors, Jefferson stepped out on to the expansive epee wood deck and walked to the railing. Bracing his hands on the railing, he closed his eyes and listened. Just like it had been in his rural Georgia hometown, the tension was beginning to drain away from his shoulders and neck as he rolled them from side to side.

Father, Mother, he prayed silently, *guide me. No task has been as great as the one that I now face.* The image that came to him surprised him. Dakota Sinclair. Her face was as vivid as the setting sun glimmering through the dense trees and on the lake. Her movement across his mind had been frequent, irritatingly so. He could not shake her from his conscious thoughts, but why should she invade his thoughts now? And, in this place? He had not gained greater insight into who she was. None of his contacts turned up anything more about her than he already knew. She existed, but she was still a mystery, an enigma, almost an illusion.

He talked with Kenneth Alexander, currently Lieutenant Governor of California. Kenneth was the owner of CompuCorrect International, although he took no active part in the operation of the company now during his public service. Kenneth was well respected and admired. He had a family who was also held in high esteem. Kenneth's wife, JeNelle, was a congresswoman. His sister, Vivian, a sitting judge on the federal district bench, and Savannah's former classmate. Kenneth was a man who had proven he could be trusted, but Kenneth offered no additional information about Dakota Sinclair. She was a vice president assigned to the international division of the company.

She was not well known in social circles; she worked alone, and produced quantity and quality export and import agreements for the company. There ended what Kenneth would tell him about her, but why? There had to be more. There had to be something. Even more perplexing was why Dakota's image captured him so completely. His thoughts were deep and focused. He opened his eyes and looked across the lake. He could barely see the other cabins that surrounded the waterfront.

"Mr. Logan." A small voice penetrated Jefferson's thoughts, tugging at his consciousness.

He looked down to his left side at the small up-turned face that stared back up at him.

"You may call me Father or Dad, if you like, Stephen," he said and smiled tentatively.

The boy looked down at his shoes. "May I use the bathroom, Mr. Logan?" the boy asked.

Jefferson inhaled. "Certainly, son," he said, reaching to guide his son back into the house.

Stephen sidestepped his touch on his shoulder and never looked up. Jefferson opened the door and Stephen entered.

"There's a bathroom in your room or you may use the one over there," Jefferson said, pointing toward a hallway.

"Thank you, Mr. Logan," the youngster politely said, as he scurried away.

Jefferson silently registered his deep disappointment, as he watched his son move away from him. He wanted to call to him, to hold him in his arms, and tell him how much he loved him, wanted him, and needed him. Yet, he realized that it was far too soon.

Turning his attention away from Stephen's retreating back, he chanced to look through the front windows at Jefferson Junior and Miles still outside standing by the SUV. He could see the fury in Jefferson Junior's demeanor, as the boy paced back and forth. Jefferson exhaled and shook his head. Jefferson Junior certainly had leadership ability, he thought. The younger two boys followed his lead without question. He had to be patient though. If he could win Jefferson Junior's trust then Miles and Stephen would follow his lead. In the alternative, if he could win over the two younger boys, Jefferson Junior might come around. The dangerous strategy might backfire if he failed with them all. A year was too short a time to win their love and respect, he thought, but he had changed the position of nations in far less time than that.

***

Dakota paced her cabin like a trapped animal. The walls were closing in on her. She was beyond cabin fever and stir crazy. She needed to expend her energy. Slipping on her hooded jogging outfit, she left the cabin. She stretched and limbered her muscles, cleared her mind and measured her breathing. Then she was off. She ran at a cadence in her mind. Each step geared to stretch her endurance, blind herself to her pain, and put her mind in a trance. She remained acutely aware of her surroundings, though. These days, more cars were on the winding backcountry roads that led to the mountain retreats. That meant more people. People asked too many questions. Questions she didn't want to answer. Crowds bothered her.

She felt closed in by them and unable to be completely free the way she was in the wide-open spaces of the Dakotas as a child.

"Hey, baby!" someone shouted at her, as she ran along a roadside. "You fine mammajamma!"

Dakota ignored the voice and kept up her pace.

"Hey! You hear me talkin' to you!" the voice continued, annoyed, while honking his horn.

Dakota continued to run, not looking at the sleek, white, convertible sports car filled with young men.

"Let's go, Todd!" another voice said. "Forget her! We got women waitin' up at the crib. That old broad ain't worth it!"

"No bitch is gonna diss me!" the voice shouted back.

The car swerved out of the lane and onto the gravel behind her, but Dakota didn't change her pace along the roadside. Then the car pulled out and ahead of her and stopped. The driver got out, swilling a bottle of beer and tossed it away, as Dakota approached.

"Man, you're wacked!" someone in the back seat yelled, as the other four young men climbed out of the car.

Dakota sized up the situation. They were young, drunk, and stupid, but they were lying in wait on either side of the car that blocked her path. She had no way around the situation and, therefore, no choice. Touching the patch on her shoulder, for a while, she ran in place counting out the distance and the time in her head. When the time ticked off, she picked up her pace and approached the car and young men. When she reached the car, her left foot scaled the rear bumper, the right foot the trunk, the left foot the top of the front seat, the right foot the top of the windshield and the left foot the hood. The now astonished and angry young men yelled their expletives as she continued her run. They jumped into the car and began to speed after her.

Before they reached her, angry alternating red and blue lights approached from both directions, the unmarked SUVs screeching to a halt around the sports car. A black, Apache, attack helicopter hovered overhead with armed marksmen standing on its skids with weapons drawn and trained on the young men.

"*Holy...*" she heard one of the young men exclaim, as she continued to jog along the roadway. "*What the...*"

***

More than an hour had passed and the boys were still milling around in front of the cabin. Jefferson completed preparations for dinner, cooking a hearty meal and setting the table. He looked through the front windows and saw a hooded figure jogging up the gravel roadway at a steady pace. The movement of the person was somehow familiar, but his thoughts were on his sons. His patience was waning as he watched them still standing by the open car. The boys noticed the jogger, too, and watched as the person approached and ran past them. Moments later, a van pulled up. Several men got out and approached his sons. Jefferson immediately rushed out of the cabin as the men reached for the luggage and the boys moved toward the van. He recognized one of Montrose's attorneys. He was the same one Tyler had slapped.

"Mr. Ambassador," the attorney said with reluctance. "I have a Restraining Order..."

Jefferson narrowed his eyes at the attorney and stalked past him to his sons.

"Go inside!" Jefferson ordered quietly through clenched teeth, glaring at Jefferson Junior.

The boys' fear was evident when they cringed, but Jefferson Senior did not modulate his firm tone. He knew that intimidation was not the way to gain the respect of his sons, but seeing that van pull up to take his sons away called up fears he never experienced before.

"Now!" Jefferson Senior said when the boys seemed reluctant to move.

With that last instruction, the boys scurried away to the cabin. When his sons were out of earshot, Jefferson turned his attention to the attorney. He glared at the younger man who tried to offer up the folded document that was clenched in his fist.

"Uh, I'm sorry, Mr. Ambassador, but—" the words caught in his throat and his protruding Adam's apple bobbed spasmodically. "I, um, I knew this was a bad idea," the man said, as he backpedaled away from Jefferson. "Leave the bags," the attorney ordered his helpers. "I'm going to look for a new line of work," the man said, getting into the van.

The other men complied and were soon on their way. Jefferson turned in time to see the three surprised faces scrambling away from one of the cabin windows. He stood next to the abandoned luggage, his arms akimbo, and waited. He didn't have to wait very long before the boys slowly came out of the cabin and walked toward their father. Wordlessly, each boy grabbed a bag, pulling it toward the cabin. Jefferson picked up two bags and followed them into the house. After several more trips, all of the luggage was inside. The boys stood in silence with heads bowed. Jefferson Senior towered over them.

"Wash your hands and let's eat. You can unpack later," he said to the tops of their heads.

Dejectedly, the threesome moved away toward the first floor bathroom.

"Jefferson," he called to his eldest. The boy stopped and turned to face his father. "Nice move," Jefferson Senior said. "You and I will have a game of chess after dinner. Loser washes the dishes."

The boy looked up and blinked in stunned disbelief, shifted from foot to foot, and then headed for the bathroom following his younger brothers.

When the boys were out of sight, Jefferson grinned. It *was* a nice move, he mused, but his hands were still shaking. Those men could have easily been enemies instead of Tyler's flunkies. The danger to his sons was obvious and enormous, particularly when several heads of foreign nations were livid over his decision to withdraw from leadership of the trade delegation. Some of those nations were known to have instigated or suborned terrorist attacks and kidnappings in the past. His fear was part of the reason he initially believed his sons would have been safer with Felicia's family at their New England compound. The Montrose Mansion was built to resemble Downton Abbey; more castle than a home and the compound was better guarded than The White House.

Many atrocities were perpetrated against American citizens, domestically and abroad, in some country's desperate attempt to turn world opinion against America or to focus the world's attention on some internal issue. He, himself, had been at the forefront of negotiations to free American captives and many citizens from other countries from terrorists. Some radical terrorists had even targeted him for capture or elimination. Yes, the threat to him and his loved ones was real and immediate.

He had purposely chosen Savannah's cabin because it was secluded and had no telephone, but he had forgotten about the car phone or the ability of his car's GPS system that was trackable. His sons obviously used it or a cell phone to call their grandfather. It amazed Jefferson that his sons, probably Jefferson Junior, had memorized the route they took to reach the cabin. At least, enough to give directions. That made Jefferson both proud and sad. Proud because his sons were bright and resourceful. Sad because they used their skills to find a way to get away from him. He wanted no intrusion on his time with his sons. However, he also did not want his sons to feel like prisoners, but he'd have to remember to lock the phone in the glove compartment. He sensed that, although he had his way on this occasion, there was more to come. He would have to be more alert to both his sons' behavior and the external real and present dangers.

CHAPTER 12

I love you, Sam," Nathan crooned against her lips in the throes of passion. He arched his back with each downward stroke. "I need you and I want to marry you before I have to leave." He drew in a ragged breath.

"Oh, Nate," Savannah shuttered, as she gripped his moisture-slick back and dug her fingers into the hard muscles of his flesh. She arched her hips and cried out his name in ecstasy, over and over again.

Savannah was dizzy with passion as Nathan intensified his cadence, sending her spinning over another edge. She closed her eyes as the sensations rippled through her body. Her need for him was great. Greater than she dared to admit, but she could not commit to him. Not yet, at least. Now she needed to be with him. To feel the love flowing over her when they were together. Again, her back arched involuntarily, giving in to him and giving up to him the unbridled passion within her. The power of his physique and his deft movements were sending her over the edge. At that moment, she would have promised him anything—everything— including the promise to marry him.

Nathan was lost in his love for Savannah. Her silky skin tantalizing him and torturing him. He tasted all of her and basked in the flame she ignited in him. Her hot, wet kisses drew groans from deep in his core and unintelligible sounds from his throat. His body nearly burst when he felt her release the honey nectar flowing around his phallus sunk deep within her. He never had enough of her. Bracing against his release, he felt her body shudder beneath him.

"Savannah!" he rasped in advance of his pending release.

The telephone rang, freezing them in midair.

Savannah recovered her senses and tried to reach for the telephone.

"Baby, please. Not now," Nathan groaned, his body still filled with unleashed tension.

"I've got to answer the telephone, Nathan. It might be important. I'm on emergency call at the hospital," she said, sighing.

Nathan exhaled deeply, painfully separated himself from her, and rolled on to his back in absolute, total, and painful frustration. He was still trembling with desire while sweat continued to stream down his face and over his body. He choked back his disappointment and wiped his face with the palms of his hands.

"Nate, I'm sorry," Savannah said, as the telephone continued to ring.

Nathan didn't answer, but she knew he was battling the pain of his failed release.

"Dr. Logan," she answered.

"Hello, lover," a low voice said on the other end of the telephone.

Savannah shot a quick look over her shoulder at Nathan. His ridged body still unspent.

"This is not a good time," she whispered lowly.

"It's a very good time for me." Jacob laughed derisively. "Send him home. I'm waiting for you."

"No!" she spat out more loudly than she intended. "I'm busy!" she said more quietly.

Savannah felt Nathan move next to her and knew he was listening.

"I'm not coming," she said, as she hung up the telephone.

An uneasy moment hung in the air.

"That wasn't the hospital, was it, Savannah?" Nathan asked, as he rolled to his side, facing her.

"Nathan, I—"

"Never mind!" Nathan flung at her, as he rolled off the bed in one fluid motion, snatched his clothes from the chaise lounge in the corner of her bedroom, and began to dress. "I've had it, Sam! I can't love you any more than I do this very moment, but you can't or won't make up your mind whether you want him or me! Well, I'll make it easy for you!

I leave for Asia in a few days. If we're not married before I go, I won't be coming back to you! You can do whatever the hell you want!"

The fury and pain in Nathan's eyes were palpable. He stormed from the bedroom, slamming the door so hard the windows rattled. Savannah leapt from the bed, grabbing a robe as she sped toward the door. Snatching it open she pleaded, "Nathan, please!" to his back, as she fumbled to put on her robe at the top of the balcony.

Nathan stopped on the wide, circular staircase and turned toward her.

"Please what?" Nathan shouted. "Please be patient, Nathan?" he mocked. "Please understand, Nathan? Please give me time, Nathan? Well, Savannah, I've been patient! I've tried to understand and I've given you time! Too much time, it seems! If you can't love me now, if you can't commit to me now, then I'm through begging for your love! I don't just want to sleep with you, Savannah! You're not the flavor of the month! Some damn one-night stand! Unlike you, I'm not afraid to make a commitment. I'm not ashamed to say out loud that you're the woman who has my heart, my soul, and my body in the palms of your hands! I'm in love with you, but I won't be a fool for you!"

"Nathan, please, I do love you. I just can't marry you, yet. I have this need...to—"

Nathan turned away from her. "To be free!" he said scornfully, finishing her thought. "Well, Savannah," he growled, while trying unsuccessfully to stuff his shirt in his slacks, "whatever makes you happy! I love you too much to tie you down." Nathan continued down the steps and out the door.

"*Nathan*!" Savannah screamed, as she clung to the balcony railing and slid to the floor. Tears blurred her vision and burned her eyes. "I love you," she whimpered, as the heart-wrenching tears continued to flow. "I love you."

Moments later, the doorbell rang. Savannah's head snapped up. Maybe Nathan had come back, she thought. He should have used the key she gave him, but that didn't matter now. Savannah gathered herself and fled down the steps on quick bare feet. She reached the door, wiping the tears from her eyes.

"Nate—" she started, as she flung open the door. She froze in her tracks. "Jacob."

Nathan's fury was subsiding, but not his resolve as he drove through the dark, quiet streets toward his condo. That was the last straw. Jacob Hawkins had the uncanny ability to interfere every time he was with Savannah. He had warned Jacob to stay away from her, but the man was not to be dissuaded. Savannah had not discouraged Jacob Hawkins either. Nathan knew the battle he was fighting and Savannah was worth it, but not if they weren't in it together. Not if Savannah couldn't tell Hawkins to get lost. Nathan's ego couldn't take any more. He loved Savannah with every fiber of his being, but she didn't love him back. Not the way he needed. The thought tore at him as he gripped the steering wheel while speeding through the streets. Suddenly, a car pulled away from the curb, but it was too late.

"*Oh my, God!*" Nathan yelled just before everything went black.

CHAPTER 13

Heard you had some problems," Bill said, as he watched Dakota move toward her refrigerator. "Sorry I wasn't here—"

"You're not my babysitter. I'm a big girl. I handled it."

"So I heard. I've warned you about running alone."

Dakota shook her head and pursed her lips in brief frustration. There had been five men. If there had been two or even three she could have handled the situation without involving her team members, but defending herself against five men in her weakened condition was asking for trouble.

"Why are you here?" she asked, cutting to the chase.

Bill huffed in frustration. "Always the loner. Never let anyone inside—"

"Same question," Dakota said, turning toward Bill and eyeing him directly.

"Logan. He's like no one I've ever encountered before. He's on the hunt. A heat-seeking missile. He's turned on a lot of heat and he won't let up. I'm joining Nathan Flack's trade delegation. I drew the textile industry while you, Mrs. Dakota Sinclair Chandler," Bill said, laying a newspaper down on the counter before her, "are soon going on a very high-visibility goodwill tour to African countries with the Vice President's wife."

A very vivid expletive slipped from her lips.

***

Jefferson put down his cup of coffee, as he looked closely at a shadowy picture on his iPad. He clicked on the article and read it carefully.

Erron to Africa

The wife of Vice President Richard Erron will make a goodwill tour of African nations and bring medical supplies, books, and other gifts furnished by American industrialists to countries in desperate need.... Among the representative corporate interests will be Mrs. Dakota Sinclair-Chandler, Vice President of the prestigious CompuCorrect International conglomerate and the bride of wealthy attorney and entertainment magnet, William Anthony Chandler. The newlyweds were reported to have been married secretly this week and to have honeymooned briefly on a private island in Bimini.... While his wife introduces new computer technology to the African school and library systems, Mr. Chandler will take time from his many lucrative interests to join a high-level State Department trade delegation to developing Third World countries for talks.... The stunningly beautiful Mrs. Dakota Sinclair-Chandler, pictured above, is quoted as having said she is none too happy her new husband is going abroad so soon after their nuptials and blissful retreat. Mr. Chandler echoed his new bride's sentiments and added they still plan to start a family this year. Also on the tour will be...."

Jefferson put down the iPad and steepled his fingers before him. *Married? Is it possible I was wrong?* Had he misread the situation? If not, what was the rush? Pregnancy? Not likely in this day and age of contraceptives. Why a secret marriage? Lifting the iPad again, he noted with frustration Dakota's face was somewhat obscured by Bill's hand, apparently in an attempt to block the photographer's shot. Jefferson understood why someone wouldn't want his or her privacy invaded by the press and news media. Still, why would Bill care? A part of Bill Chandler's career had been as a model and actor being photographed for high-fashion designers and chic magazines. Looking closer, Jefferson noted Bill appeared to be keeping Dakota from being photographed. Why? The thoughts swirled around in his head, but the pieces never fit. Jefferson pulled his cell phone from his pocket and pressed one number.

"Good morning, Mr. Ambassador," the voice said on the other end.

"Good morning, Yates. I have a task for you."

"Yes, Sir. I read this morning's newspaper. I've begun the research, Sir."

"Good. I'll be looking forward to the report."

"Yes, Mr. Ambassador. I will forward it to you as soon as it is assembled."

"Thank you, Yates."

"You're welcome, Mr. Ambassador. Have a good day."

Jefferson hung up. He was not at all surprised Yates began an investigation without instructions. The man was a master and knew him very well. He lifted the coffee mug to his lips and slowly sipped the strong, black liquid. Soon a plan began to hatch in his mind. The cell rang and Jefferson looked at the number display.

"Good morning, Sam," he answered.

"Jeff, I need your help," Savannah said with some urgency.

Jefferson sat forward in his seat. He was expecting this call.

"Sam, Nathan is fine. He wasn't seriously injured. It was just a fender bender."

"*Injured?* Jeff, what are you talking about? Nathan was in an accident? When? Why didn't you tell me? Where is he?"

"Calm down, Sam. Yes, Nathan was involved in a minor accident two nights ago. He asked me, for obvious reasons, not to divulge the information or details. He's preparing for his trade mission. He has gone into seclusion with members of the delegation to hammer out the United States' platform before they leave for the talks with the foreign countries. He cannot be reached."

"You can reach him," she implored urgently. "I know you can. I want to—no, I *must* talk with him!"

"Not now. He has to stay focused. I'm sorry, honey. I've already told you more than I should. If the press and news media get a hold of this information, they'll make a field day out of it. These are very delicate negotiations, so I cannot tell you more."

"That's not all you know, is it?" Savannah snapped.

"That's as much as you need to know. He's fine."

"You don't understand. Two nights ago, we had a disagreement, an argument really. Nate left angry. I'm probably the reason for his accident."

"Perhaps, when he returns, you'll have an opportunity to—"

Dial tone.

Jefferson never denied Savannah anything she wanted or thought she needed, but now was different. More, much more, was at stake than her pique at him or the state of her relationship with Nathan. If anything went wrong with the mission, Jefferson would blame himself. That was how he approached every decision he made in his life. It was his decision to leave the delegation and put Nathan in charge. If anything did go wrong... Jefferson stopped in mid-thought when he heard movement in the cabin. One of his sons was awake. Another day of the tug of war between him and his boys would begin. The past two days were unproductive. Barely a word passed between them. Today would be different. He was determined the silence would be broken and he planned carefully how that would happen.

***

Savannah sat on the side of her bed, still fuming from her brother's refusal to put her in touch with Nathan. She sprawled across the bed feeling totally helpless. She reached for the T-shirt she found after Nathan left that fateful night and pulled it to her. It still carried his heady, masculine scent. Visions of them together danced in her head. The rhythm of her heart picked up a beat. The tips of her breasts hardened. Ripples of raw electricity shot through her and she curled into a ball. Nathan couldn't have meant the things he said to her, she reasoned. It was *not* over between them. "Nathan," slipped from her lips as if a prayer. She hugged the shirt tightly to her body and squeezed, the vision of total bliss..."Nathan," she said again and again.

***

Nathan removed his rimless eyeglasses and pinched the bridge of his nose between his eyes. Besides his fatigue, something was tugging at his senses and, in his opinion, rendering his participation in the discussions useless. He briefly touched the sutures on his temple and then palmed his face in one hand. Dragging his hand downward, he looked at his face in the mirror, willing his thoughts to stay still.

Only a few days passed since he was with Savannah, but it felt like a millennium. Then twelve hours in the Emergency Room with Gail Conway, the driver of the other vehicle. Now twenty-two straight hours of discussions with the trade delegation industrialists. Sleep was what he needed, but his body was still charged. The adrenaline was still coursing through him like wildfire. He was operating on another level beyond sex and sleep deprivation.

"Mr. Flack," Dr. Peterson Rockwell interrupted, "here is the medication I ordered. You should really take them now—"

Nathan held up one hand. "Thanks, anyway, Doctor, but, as a representative of the pharmaceutical industry, you know those pills will make me drowsy. I can't afford that now. We're close to a negotiated platform. We have to keep going until we reach closure on these issues. If we cannot come to agreement between us, we cannot expect to convince the warring factions and neutral countries that commerce with the United States is preferable to the continuation of hostilities and even terrorism."

"You've persuaded everyone around the table to take your position on every major point so far. You've gained the respect of them all. For a first meeting, I would describe this as a total success."

"If I've had a modicum of success, it's as a result of two factors: First, the reputation of Ambassador Logan, whose message to the legation was clearly fashioned to dispel any doubt that I have his total and complete confidence and support. Secondly, to the unexpected support of Bill Chandler who pressed as hard as I have for unity on each major issue. Those two factors have gotten us to where we are now. The tougher issues are yet to come."

"You're referring to the U.S. military presence in certain countries with whom we will need to negotiate."

"Yes, the military have our industrialists very edgy and with good reason. The Intelligence communities, the CIA, Interpol, MI5, the Knesset, tell us there are factions who do not want these meetings to succeed and may take aggressive action to interrupt or scuttle the talks. Taking these discussions to the heart of the problem areas, rather than to The Hague or other safer havens, is geared to show our trust and goodwill, but our oil and natural gas industrialists aren't convinced we will be able to ward off terrorists' attacks without a heavy military presence."

"Our military interests want a role in determining where to put more military bases."

"We're working at cross purposes, if we allow an increase in the military's role, rather than seeking ways to reduce our armed forces presence. Now is not the time for failure. The Ambassador knows that and so do I. I'll sleep when we take off later today. For now, I have to remain alert and in control, and that means no drugs."

Peterson put the medication into the pocket of Nathan's suit jacket, which was hanging on a rack near the hand towels in the men's room. "You'll need this later," he said, patting the pocket.

"A few hours of sleep will be all I'll need," Nathan said, retrieving the medication and returning it to Dr. Peterson. "Prescription or not, they're still drugs."

"And you don't do drugs," another voice said.

Nathan and Peterson turned in surprise toward Bill Chandler standing in the doorway. Nathan nodded toward Peterson who silently bowed out of the men's room.

"No, I don't do drugs," Nathan said, as he washed his hands and shook off the excess water. He reached for a hand towel as he regarded Bill in the mirror that spanned the alcove area.

Bill cupped his hands under the running faucet and drenched his face. "You're a very cautious man, Flack, despite the fact your family owns one of the top pharmaceutical companies in the United States."

"You're well informed, Chandler. Yes, my mother, Priscilla Townsend Flack, is a descendant of the Townsend family. She's a physician, as are my grandparents. You wouldn't have taken drugs offered to you either, I'll bet."

"Certainly not from a representative of the pharmaceutical industry who is in competition with your family and who sees having close personal ties to the man who can open foreign markets for drugs as an ace in the hole."

Nathan only snorted.

"You're good in there, Flack," Bill commented, as he doused his face again.

"So are you, Chandler, but I question why I've received so much support from you."

Bill's cool and easy smile sliced his handsome face, as he wiped the excess water away. Nathan handed a towel to him.

"Because you deserve it. You've stuck to the point and stood your ground. Solid ground, with purpose and foresight. You haven't changed since your days in law school."

"Nor have you," Nathan added. "By the way, congratulations on your marriage."

"Thanks. Dakota is a fascinating woman and I'm a very lucky man," he answered smoothly.

"Where were you married?" Nathan asked.

"In DC," Bill said nonchalantly, but cryptically, tossing the paper towel into the trash and rolling down his sleeves.

"Oh? When?" Nathan continued to probe.

Bill briefly regarded Nathan in the mirror and then raked at his thick, black, wavy hair as if the question held no consequence. "The day after my dinner with Ambassador Logan, as a matter of fact. It occurred to both Dakota, and to me, there was really no reason to delay, particularly in light of this *trade mission*." He punctuated the goal with healthy skepticism.

Nathan eyed him carefully, but was not distracted by Bill's insightfulness. He forged ahead carefully. "A small ceremony?" Nathan asked blithely.

"Small and private. We left immediately on our honeymoon. I highly recommend that approach should you and the lovely Savannah Logan decide to tie the knot when this is over."

The mention of Savannah's name almost caused a visible reaction, but Nathan maintained his composure. "It's difficult to imagine that you'd leave your new bride so quickly after your wedding for a mission that could take weeks and probably months to complete."

Bill smiled wryly. "Dakota and I aren't kids experiencing the first blush of newfound romance. We can distinguish lust from love. Ours is a deeper commitment," he said assuredly, but he needed to divert Nathan's pointed questions. He delivered the intelligence that he planned. "What about you and the good doctor? I thought you two would have issued an announcement by now."

Nathan nearly faltered. He wanted nothing more than to hear that Savannah wanted to be his wife, but his ultimatum to her two days earlier failed and he still bore the scars deep in his heart of that fateful night. He was not about to resurrect them now.

"Savannah Logan is a wonderful woman for whom I will always feel lasting friendship." He tried to pass by the hurt and deliver his statement confidently.

"Oh, I see," Bill said, knowingly.

"Gentlemen," a voice came from the doorway, and both men turned toward one of the aides to the delegation. "We have a signal from the State Department's Asia Desk. There is some concern about our departure for the Middle East, it seems. The Secretary has ordered a stand down while the CIA runs a full investigation on the situation."

"For how long?" Nathan asked, his brow furrowed.

"Unknown at this point, Sir."

Bill slipped into his expensive silk-blend suit jacket and straightened his Hermès tie. He checked his watch. Right on cue, he thought to himself.

"Well, if we tie up the remaining issues, I'll just have enough time to have breakfast with my bride," he said, winking at Nathan. "You look as if you could use some sack time, too, Nathan."

Nathan checked his watch. He could use some sleep, there was no debate about that. "Let's take eight hours and let everyone get some rest. We'll tackle our outstanding matters better with clear heads."

"Eight hours it is," Bill said smoothly, as he slipped through the door.

***

"So far, that's what we've accomplished. We only have a few, relatively minor, remaining issues to resolve, Mr. Ambassador," Nathan said, as he finished briefing Jefferson over the telephone.

"Nate, this is your show, not mine. You need not report to me on the outcome of your meetings."

Nathan slowly blew out a breath. "It's a habit, Jeff. One that's hard to break."

"You sound exhausted."

"I am, I suppose. We took an eight-hour break and then went back into a lock-down session. I'm beyond feeling it now. I'm still operating on that last gallon of coffee."

"Get some rest. You know from experience these CIA Intel operations generally take a little time. From what you've told me, you've done a fine job. Rest well."

"Uh, Jeff, before you go, let me mention that Chandler has been an unexpected asset to the discussions with the other industrialists. However, I'm not sure I'm reading his motives correctly."

"He's a tough read, but I'm sure there's more to Bill Chandler than what meets the eye. He reminds me of the character, the Scarlet Pimpernel."

"And his, uh, wife?"

"Wife? Not likely."

"Seems solid to me, Jeff."

"Yeah, like Mata Hari," Jefferson said quietly.

"What was that? I didn't quite hear you."

"Rest your mind, Nate, and, by the way, Savannah is trying to reach you."

"I know. I had several messages waiting. I should tell you, Jeff, it's not going to work out between us. In fact, it's over."

"I understand, my friend. No need to explain to me. Savannah is the one you need to tell."

"I will, but later, after I've rested."

Nathan put down the telephone and rested his head back against his soft leather, high-back executive chair. He loosened his tie, unbuttoned his shirt at the collar, and chanced to close his eyes for a brief moment.

The telephone rang and Nathan cursed, as he pressed the intercom button on his console. "Sadie, I said, no calls," he spat out.

"I know, Mr. Flack, but there's a Ms. Conway at the Security Desk in the lobby asking to speak with you."

"Conway? Who is she, Sadie?"

"I'm not sure, but she said you two met by accident."

"Accident?" Nate said, trying to remember. Then it dawned on him. "Oh, Gail Conway." *I must be more tired than I realized*, he thought.

"Yes, Sir. Should I have her admitted?"

"What does she want, Sadie?"

"She said it was personal. Do you want a dossier run on her first?"

Nathan exhaled slowly. He was fatigued, but thought, considering the circumstances surrounding the accident, there was no harm in seeing her for a few minutes. "No. Have Security bring her to the office. I'll give her ten minutes."

"Yes, Sir," Sadie acknowledged and then hung up.

With his fingertips, Nathan rubbed his aching temples. He felt as if his head was splitting in two, and a million thoughts were running through his mind, most of them involving Savannah. He didn't want another scene with her, nor did he want to put himself in harm's way. She was too much of a temptress. He had to stick to his decision. They were over and done. If he didn't cut off their relationship, he'd forever be her slave. No, he thought, he needed to end it. He wouldn't let her persuade him to hold on to the illusion they would ever marry. At thirty-six, he wanted some stability in his life. Someone who could accept the love he had to offer and return love in equal measure. Someone... Nathan's thoughts were eclipsed when Sadie knocked at his door and then entered. A woman who he almost didn't recognize followed her.

"Ambassador Flack, Ms. Gail Conway," Sadie pleasantly announced, stepping aside to let the stunningly attractive young woman enter.

Nathan hastily buttoned his shirt at the collar, straightened his tie, and rolled down his shirtsleeves, fastening his French cuffs at his wrists.

He reached for his jacket on the back of his chair, slipped into it, and extended his hand.

"Ms. Conway, I apologize for keeping you waiting. Please come in," he said. "May I offer you something? Coffee or tea, perhaps?"

"No, thank you, Mr. Ambassador." Her velvet tones and soft smiling countenance lifted his spirits. Her hand was small, soft, and warm in his. Her light-brown eyes encased in long, lush lashes were the most striking feature on her lovely face.

"May I get more coffee for you, Sir?" Sadie asked.

"Uh, yes, Mrs. Hilton. I'd appreciate that," he said, smiling at his stately Executive Assistant.

Then Nathan turned his attention to Gail Conway. "Have a seat, Ms. Conway," he said, showing her to the leather sofas on the far side of his spacious office.

"I'm sure you're wondering why I've come, Mr. Ambassador," she said, walking slowly toward the large floor to ceiling window overlooking the skyline of Washington, DC. She kept her back to him and he noticed her tall, statuesque body shrouded in a perfectly fitted, peach-colored business suit, the long slit in the back of the skirt revealing very shapely, aerobicized legs.

"I presume your visit has something to do with our accidental meeting," he said smoothly. "Have you recovered from the experience?"

Gail turned and looked at him. Something within him jolted, wanting to sooth her troubled brow.

"Yes," she said quietly. "I'm here about the accident. I, uh, I wanted to pay for the damages to your car. I mean, it was completely my fault, but I don't want to report it to my insurance company. I mean, I do have car insurance, but, well, the truth of the matter is I shouldn't have been there in the first place," she began to ramble, clouds building in her eyes.

Nathan sensed she might cry at any moment. He went to her and guided her to a seat.

"Ms. Conway," he began soothingly, "it's really not as bad as that. My insurance company will repair my car. You need not concern yourself with making—"

"If he finds out, he'll know I followed him," she said abruptly.

"He? Who are you speaking of, Ms. Conway?" he asked, his brows bunching.

Gail lowered her head and looked at her hands in her lap. "My fiancé."

"You were following your fiancé?"

She pressed her lips tightly together and looked away. "Yes, I'm ashamed of what I did, but I had to know the truth."

"Ms. Conway, obviously this is very stressful for you. As far as my car is concerned, I'm sure my mechanic can repair the damage at a reasonable rate. If you'd like to contact the garage, you can set up any arrangement that is comfortable for you."

Gail looked up at him, a smile edging around her mouth.

"Thank you, Mr. Ambassador," she said. "I'd like to show you my appreciation for your kindness that night and today. May I take you and your wife to dinner?"

"I'm not married," he said, smiling, "and the name is Nate. You don't have to stand on formality here. It's not necessary for you to make amends for the accident by taking me out to dinner. I was as much to blame for what happened as you were. I was driving too fast and not paying close attention to what I was doing."

"Oh, but I insist. I've inconvenienced you and you've been very kind to me. I understand you stayed at the hospital until I was released and then arranged for a car service to take me home."

"It was the least I could do—"

"Please, Mr. Ambassador..." Her long sable lashes swept down and then up. Her countenance sweet and innocent. "I mean, Nate, I feel I owe you so much."

Her youth and beauty momentarily entranced Nathan. "Perhaps another time. I may be leaving town at any moment."

"Well," she said, fishing in her purse, "my offer still stands. Here is my business card. Please call me when you're available."

Nathan took the card just as Sadie entered, bringing a fresh pot of coffee.

"Sir, you have an important call on your private line and several other messages," Sadie said, setting the tray on the coffee table.

Nathan stood and went to his desk. He was expecting a call from the White House, where the Secretary of State and the National Security Council were meeting with the President. He expected new instructions would be forthcoming, but when he looked at the telephone number displayed on the console screen, he didn't pick up the line.

"Take another message, Mrs. Hilton," he said to her.

"Yes, Sir," she answered, eyeing him carefully.

"Ms. Conway, are you sure you wouldn't like to have coffee?" Nathan asked, pouring a cup for himself.

"Well," she hesitated while looking at her watch, "perhaps just one cup," she agreed, smiling shyly.

***

"I'm sorry, Savannah, but he won't take your call," Sadie answered.

"I must talk with him. He's being unreasonable."

"I won't get in the middle of this, but you know as well as I do Nathan Flack is one of the most reasonable men alive. Now, I understand you want to talk with him, but he's really got his hands full. He hasn't really slept in days and he's pushing himself to the limit. Give him time, chile," she said warmly.

"Sadie, I can't lose him," she said desperately.

"I know, Savannah."

Savannah hung up the telephone and palmed her face in her hands.

"Headache?" Dr. Chuck Montgomery asked, as he entered the doctors' lounge and brewed a cup of coffee for himself.

"Man ache," Savannah answered, raking her fingers through her long, bronze, flowing hair.

"Uh, do I want to know this?" Chuck asked, skeptically.

"Men!" she fussed. "Why do they have to be so—so—so *male?*"

"This is a trick question, right?" Chuck chortled, sitting down across from her on another sofa and stretching out his long legs on the coffee table before him.

"It's Nathan. He's being a bear," she fussed.

"Oh," Chuck said nonchalantly, as he sipped his coffee. "In other words, he's not responding to the whip."

"'The *whip?*' What do you mean, '*The Whip?*'" she asked indignantly.

"You know exactly what I mean, Sam. You and Nathan. The man bends over backward to please you and you whip him like he stole something."

"Humph!" she fussed. "Nathan has everyone fooled. He's—"

"Hi, y'all," Sandy said cheerfully with a big smile, as she entered the lounge.

"Hey, kid," Chuck said.

"Hi, Sandy," Savannah said drolly. "What are you doing here so early?"

"Late, you mean. I delivered twins about an hour ago. Say, Sam, how's Nathan? He didn't look too well the other night."

"What, when you visited him at his place?" Savannah asked facetiously.

"His place?" Sandy asked, confusion evident on her face. "No, I mean when he was brought in through the Emergency Room. Apparently, he and this lady had been in an accident. Nathan had a mild concussion, but... Hold up. What's this about me being at his place?"

"I saw you there, Sandy. It was three in the morning and—"

"Oh, the night I dropped off the baseball schedule and roster. He asked me...hey, wait a minute. You don't think that I...damn it, Sam, what's *wrong* with you? Yes, I find Nathan attractive, but I would never go after him. We're only friends."

"Never mind that. What's this about Nathan and a lady?"

"I thought you knew. Nathan was involved in an accident with this woman. He got banged up a little, passed out cold, according to the emergency crew. Head injury from his airbag. A few contusions and abrasions. Will Tompkins was the attending physician until the State Department suits arrived. The man has clout. The woman wasn't badly hurt, but Nathan insisted she be checked out thoroughly by his doctors."

"Why does everyone know about this but me, and who was this 'woman'?"

"Beats me, but don't look at me with those green-eyed monster ideas of yours. I'd never make a play for Nathan—that is, unless you willingly step aside," Sandy teased. "Ms. Woman, on the other hand, well, I don't think I could say the same about her."

***

Nathan was laughing when he walked Gail to the door of his outer office. A security guard was waiting.

"Then I'll see you at eight?" Gail asked, with a broad smile on her face.

"Sure, Gail, I'd love to have dinner with you."

"Until then," she smiled, as she walked through the door.

Nathan closed the door and turned to see Sadie standing arms akimbo, glaring at him.

"Nice lady," he said, sheepishly digging his hands in his pockets and walking toward his office while whistling.

"Uh-huh," Sadie hummed knowingly. "Don't give me that 'nice lady' business, Nathan Jerome Flack. I know what you're up to."

"Right now I'm not up to much. I'm going to a hotel and get some rest." He smiled at her.

"You're up to no good, young man. And that 'nice lady' doesn't hold a candle to—"

"You know where to find me, if you need me," he said, breezing by her.

Sadie shook her head and huffed. "Don't believe bull horns will hook, do you?" she grumbled, but Nathan went into his office and closed the door. Sadie knew the lay of the land though. She worked for the State Department a lot of years. She picked up the telephone and put some people to work.

CHAPTER 14

Dakota walked out of the doctor's office and headed to the elevator. She had not made the progress she wanted and expected. Although the bones knitted, the MRI she just underwent indicated the pain she was experiencing was possibly emanating from a pinched nerve. The doctors were recommending surgery. According to them, the recuperation time would not be long. She impatiently paced in front of the elevator, waiting for its arrival.

"Dakota," a voice came to her when the elevator doors opened.

Wordlessly, she strode into the box. When the doors opened again on the first floor, she quickly walked out. Bill Chandler matched her pace, stopping her with a hand to her arm.

"Look, I told you, I don't need a babysitter," she said stoically.

"What did the doctors say?" He released his hold on her arm.

"Nothing I wanted to hear." She continued her pace.

Bill caught up with her. "Look, how about we go somewhere and talk, maybe have a cup of coffee? Greenfield Brothers isn't far from here."

"Talk? Talk about what? They've said it all. Either I take the therapy for one year, or I have the surgery, which will lay me up for a month. Either way, I'm out of the loop."

"Dakota," he said soothingly, reaching for her.

She moved out of his reach. "What are you doing here anyway? I thought you were supposed to be on a flight—"

"A delay. Look, let's just take a walk. Put our heads together. Maybe we can come up with something—"

"I'm outta here," she said, turning toward her car. A severe pain shot through her body and she winced, nearly stumbling.

Bill noticed, grabbed her, and held her in his arms.

"It's going to be all right, Dakota. I promise, it's going to be all right," he said soothingly, kissing her on her forehead.

Dakota didn't pull away. Affection was something she didn't understand or know how to handle, but at that moment, with her life crumbling around her, she felt alone and in need of human contact. She hated that need. It reminded her too much of her childhood where there was no one to comfort her. No one to hold her when she was alone and lonely and afraid. Especially when she cried. She was an outcast. A half-breed, the bullies and others called her. No mother. No father. Not even a relative she could look to, only an old man who lived on the edge of the reservation—the grounds caretaker for the orphanage where she grew up. He taught her how to hunt and fish, to survive in the wilderness, but not like a parent or even a friend. He was just Joe Eaglefeather. A loner like her. A man with no relations. In all the years she was around him, he never said a kind word to her or showed her any affection or sympathy. Just the way to close yourself off from the world and survive.

Two, well-dressed, Black men, carrying briefcases, walked by Dakota and Bill, eyeing them with condemnation showing in their faces.

"Now ain't that just the *shit?*" one man said to the other, looking directly at the warm embrace between Dakota and Bill.

"Yeah, and sistahs always bitching when we crossover! They need to check their own attitudes."

Dakota was keenly aware of them. So was Bill, whose smile eased into a triumphant grin.

Later, after a quick lunch and coffee at Greenfield Brothers near Capitol Hill, Dakota and Bill silently walked along the waterfront at Haynes Point, as airplanes landed and took off from Washington's Reagan National Airport.

"Where are your rings?" Bill asked.

Dakota dug into her pocket, retrieved the rings, and put them on her finger.

"You're not supposed to be without them," he reminded her. "This thing with Logan is heating up. You have to be careful."

"I *know*," she said, agitation and frustration reflected in her tone.

Bill grabbed the back of his neck with one hand and stretched. Dakota noticed.

"How are the talks going with Flack taking the lead?"

"Better than I expected. He's no fool and certainly no pushover. He's a shrewd negotiator. Logan made the right choice picking him. He's got Logan's systematic and objective approach, but with more risk than Logan usually allows himself." He stretched his body again before he continued. "By the way, Flack grilled me on our marriage. I'm not sure whether Logan sent him on that mission or whether he was doing the reconnaissance for his own edification."

"What's your game plan?"

"None, at the moment. The pattern is full," he said, again grabbing the back of his neck.

Dakota looked up into the fatigue on his handsome face. "Let's go. You're tired," she said, turning to walk away.

"Dakota," he called to her retreating back. She stopped, turned to look at him. "Those men—the ones back at the doctor's office…"

"What about them?" she asked absently.

"Is that why we haven't moved beyond a professional friendship? Because I'm white?"

Dakota looked away in frustration then eased her tension. She sauntered toward him until they were nearly chest-to-chest. Then she raised her head slowly to look up into his handsome face, with beautiful, startling blue eyes.

"No, it's because you're too tall," she said seductively.

An easy grin sliced his concerned face. "One day, Dakota," he snorted. "One of these days."

CHAPTER 15

Jefferson watched the reaction of his boys, as he put the puppy down on the floor in front of them. Only Stephen knelt to greet the new addition.

"It's a mutt!" Jefferson Junior scowled with disdain. "Grandfather only lets us have animals with pedigrees. Our dogs win Best of Show every year. That *thing*," he sneered, "should be destroyed."

"No!" Stephen squealed protectively, holding the fat, frisky puppy close to his chest. "Don't you hurt him, Jay!"

"Silence!" Jefferson Junior raged.

"No! If you hurt him, I'll tell—" Stephen paused, glimpsing Miles and then his father. "Just don't you do it," he said more calmly, but tightly to Jefferson Junior.

Miles bent and put a hand on Stephen's shoulder. "He won't, Stevie. I promise. It will be okay," Miles said soothingly. Then he looked up at Jefferson Junior. "Won't it?" he said, eyeing his elder brother.

Jefferson Junior snorted derisively and walked away. Miles turned back to Stephen and smiled reassuringly.

Jefferson was watching the interplay between his boys. They were holding something back. Something they didn't want him to know. He was trying to forge a relationship with them, but he didn't want to press. Not yet, at least. He wanted them to come to him on their own accord without fear of reprisal. He wanted them to see him as someone they could depend on and share their confidences with, someone they could trust, but that time in their relationship had not yet come. Then he spoke. "What should we name him?" he asked Miles and Stephen.

"Hercules," Stephen piped up easily, smiling at the frisky pup that eagerly licked his face as he still held him in his arms.

"Do you agree to that name, Miles?" Jefferson asked.

Miles nodded. "Yes, that's okay."

"Hercules it is then," Jefferson said.

Stephen's big, brownish-green eyes looked up at him. "Thank you, Mr. Ambass...Mr. Logan...Father," he said, getting to his feet.

"You're welcome, son." Jefferson nodded to his two boys, his attention captured by the warmth in his son's eyes.

Miles guided the seven-year-old out of the door, as Jefferson watched.

It took nearly a week, but finally one of his sons called him father. It wasn't much, but it made Jefferson's heart sing. It was the right choice, he thought to himself. He had driven to the dog pound in the small town, not far from the cabin, and purchased the puppy. Now they had something to start with. Something to focus on. He tried other approaches. Taking walks together. Downloading movies to watch. Playing catch or board games. Going fishing and swimming. Things that parents typically did with their children. Things his father did with him as a boy, but nothing seemed to spark a conversation between the four of them. They simply did as he requested, wordlessly. They still barely talked to him though, although they talked quietly among themselves out of his earshot, sharing their secrets with one another. This was a strategic opening, though, in their silent negotiations. There was a glimmer of hope, too.

Stephen "Stevie," Jefferson smiled to himself, had defied Jefferson Junior and Miles had come to Stevie's support. Miles, the middle child, was the mediator, the one willing to negotiate, he thought to himself. Jefferson Junior's hold on his eleven-year-old brother was slightly easing. Time and patience would win out, he thought. He had both in abundance and determination as well. He watched Stevie and Miles playing and laughing with Hercules in the yard. The sight warmed him, but he looked toward the closed bedroom door where he knew Jefferson Junior sat, probably brooding over his brothers' defection. He wondered what it would take to get Jefferson Junior on his side. What would it take to make them a family?

CHAPTER 16

S o, when I found out he was seeing other women, I just couldn't take it any longer," Gail Conway said, her eyes near tears.

Nathan reached across the dinner table and rested his hand on hers. She looked up at him and smiled sweetly.

"Well that's the whole sordid story," she said. "Three boyfriends and all of them dumped me for other women. I guess a girl from Minnesota doesn't know how to handle herself in the big city; certainly not a city as sophisticated as Washington, DC."

"Sounds like the men you've known simply didn't realize what they had," he said, reassuringly.

"I guess the old fashioned values of commitment, love, and respect are just that—old fashioned. All I've ever wanted was to love someone and have him love me back. He didn't have to be rich or handsome, just honest and forthright. Someone who wanted to be a team player, but so far all I've found are the playas." She laughed at her own joke.

Nathan exhaled slowly, a hurt-filled smile on his face. Gail put her free hand on his.

"You've been hurt, too, I see," she said, with comforting strokes. "It's hard to imagine any woman would walk out on you, dump you for another man. You seem to have all the qualities any woman would find appealing. You're handsome, intelligent, virile, sensitive..."

Nathan looked up into Gail's soft, doe-like eyes. Although very beautiful, she looked nothing like Savannah. He eased his hand back from hers.

The band began to play. "Enough about romantic misadventures," he said, smiling. "Would you like to dance?"

"I'd love to," she said, smiling brightly.

*****

Savannah walked out of the hospital toward her car and pulled up short. Her assigned parking space was empty. Perplexed, she looked around the doctors' parking lot. Her car wasn't where she had parked it. She frowned, trying to remember whether she had forgotten and left her car unlocked. She checked her purse and found her keys. Confusion crossed her face.

"It wasn't stolen," the low timber voice whispered in her ear.

"Jacob," she muttered. "I told you over the telephone I didn't want to see you."

He pulled her back against the hardness of his chest. "Now make me believe it," he whispered, nibbling at her ear.

She turned her head away from him. "I told you I love another man. Why can't you accept that fact?"

"I love many women, but, like you, I'm no fool. I live to love. You, I enjoy loving. Just like you, I enjoy loving freely with no shackles to bind me to any one person. You are a very exciting woman, Savannah. You have a wildness in you. An untamed spirit."

Savannah felt the desire beginning to rise in her. She tried to pull away from him, but he held her fast. "Let me go, Jacob." She breathed the words.

"Anything you want." He rakishly grinned, releasing her, but not moving away. "Anything," he whispered. "Anywhere in the world."

Savannah turned to face him. "Where is my car?" she asked, moving away from him.

Jacob's roguish and raw masculinity poured through the polished *façade* of his finely tailored attire. His expensive, heady musk teased her senses. His jet-black hair pulled back away from his face and tied in a ponytail at the nape of his neck. His black band-collar shirt, white dinner jacket, and white bow tie pulled loose around his strong neck, accentuating his reddish-brown skin, tanned from his recent business trip to Jamaica. His coal-black eyes raked over her and she felt her nipples harden, unbidden against her silk tank-top.

"My car?" she asked again.

"In the garage of your townhouse," he said smoothly. "My car is over here," he said, touching her elbow.

"How dare you—" she started, but he closed off her words with a searing kiss, driving his tongue into her mouth.

Jacob held her with one massive hand behind her head, her body involuntarily slamming into his. She pushed with one hand against his chest, but could not budge him. He only deepened his ravaging kiss, her struggles giving him more tenacity. She stopped struggling, as he pulled her to his waiting limousine.

The limousine moved sleekly through the streets before Savannah noticed they were not headed toward her townhouse.

"Where are you taking me?" she asked, annoyed, yet secretly thrilled by his take-charge behavior. He reeked of wealth and sophistication. He had obviously been at some event that required he dress in the *haut courant* fashion forward attire of the day. He obviously had his pick of any woman, but he had taken liberties to be with her. That, too, thrilled her.

"You're going to finish what you started," he said, pulling her into his powerful embrace. Before she could utter a sound, Jacob had ripped her panties away and plunged himself into her.

He took her right there in the back of the limousine while the chauffeur drove slowly through the dark streets.

***

Nathan admired Gail's royal blue, silk, body dress, as he reached around her to open the door of the restaurant. She had a silky smooth movement that added to her bold femininity. Her thick, wiry hair twisted into a French roll gave him an unobstructed view of her long neck and the revealing curvature of her back. Once outside the restaurant, they stood waiting for the valet to return with his car.

"Does the evening have to end so soon?" Gail asked, looking up at him. "I haven't enjoyed an evening like this ever before."

Nathan was momentarily off center. He smiled at her. He had enjoyed himself, although thoughts of Savannah were ever present on his mind. He cleared his thoughts. "It's your evening, Gail. What would you like to do?"

"How about The Tap Room at the new waterfront in southwest DC? There's usually a great band there. Suddenly, I feel like dancing," she said, smiling brightly.

"We just did that," he said and smiled back at her, amused at her crisp, clear, wide-eyed smile.

"No, I mean *really* dancing. You know, blue-lights-in-the-basement kind of dancing."

Her smile was infectious, he thought. "Oh, you mean the sweat-popping-off-your-nose kind of dancing," he said, teasingly touching her nose. "I haven't been keeping up with the latest dances, but sure. Why not? Sounds like fun."

Gail pushed up on the tips of her toes and softly kissed his cheek, just as his rental car arrived. He opened the door of the convertible and helped her step in. As they pulled into the stream of traffic, a traffic light caught them. They chatted, smiling at each other. Gail's eyes were glistening. She was very charming, animated, and vulnerable, he thought. He was in need of her rapt attention, remembering how he had angrily left Savannah with his needs painfully unfulfilled. He would not take advantage of the situation with Gail, though. He was still deeply in love with Savannah; that thought nagged at his conscious.

Gail shivered slightly and Nathan noticed.

"Cold?" he asked. "I could put the top up on the car."

She slid closer to him and placed her head on his shoulder.

"No, not really. I love this convertible," she cooed. "Just exhilarated being with you, Nathan Flack. You're restoring my trust in men."

Nathan put his arm around her. "You're far too trusting, Gail."

Savannah blinked repeatedly, as she peered through the darkened windows of the limousine. That was Nathan in the car next to the limo, but she wondered whom the woman was snuggling up under his arm. The traffic light changed and she watched intently as the limo turned the corner and Nathan's car continued across the intersection. Confusion and then anger seized her. *How can he do this to me?* she fumed silently. He had refused to take her calls and now she knew the reason why. He was seeing someone else!

She was so infuriated she didn't notice Jacob's sinister grin. He loved it when a plan came together.

The limo pulled to a locked gate that slowly swung open. The car went under a portico and the driver opened the door. Savannah didn't question Jacob's decision to bring her to his father's impressive and stately mansion in the heart of Embassy Row in northwest Washington, DC. Her brother's home was only a few blocks away. As they walked to the door, a butler opened it and bowed slightly. Savannah walked in, still seething with anger at Nathan in the arms of another woman. Jacob guided her into one of the salons. She paced the small, intimate room like a caged animal, ignoring Jacob, and deep in thought.

For a few moments, Jacob stood watching Savannah while he pulled his white bow tie free and loosened more buttons on his monogrammed shirt. Then he moved to the bar and poured two brandies. Approaching Savannah, he held one out to her.

She looked at the offered snifter, took it, and, in one gulp, downed the brandy. Placing her empty glass on a table, she then took Jacob's empty glass from his hand and placed it beside hers. Reaching up, she firmly grabbed his shirt at the collar and ripped, as she tore open his shirt, the buttons flying as she trapped his arms by his sides. With a wild energy exploding in her eyes, she dropped his pants and briefs. While she disrobed him, Jacob grinned his delight in her aggressive manner. All caution gone, Jacob's nearly nude body stood before her, proud and unabashedly masculine. She pushed against his chest until he fell back onto one of the intricately embroidered sofas, his arms still trapped by his sides, and then slowly she began a seduction as she disrobed. Their eyes locked together when she mounted him. Her finger clawed his long, silky hair from its Native American leather tie. When she yanked his hair to bring his mouth to hers, Jacob didn't even wince. His eyes glowed with an energy that matched hers. She tormented him and then took him in a frenzied attack. *To hell with Nathan!* she vowed silently. *No man will possess me! No man!*

CHAPTER 17

Dakota strolled through the woods, deep in her own thoughts. It was more than a week ago since she last ran, but the walk through the hilly terrain kept her muscles toned and limbered. The deep, dark woods were alive with animals she noticed only slightly in her conscious thoughts. On she went, moving without real purpose, deeper and deeper into the woods. Suddenly, she stopped, lifted her head, and turned it slightly toward a sound uncommon in the woods. She silently moved toward the sound. Parting the leaves of the low hanging bushes, she watched a little boy who sat on a log, whimpering. She turned her head in each direction, listening. She heard no other sounds. Then she looked back at the boy. She started to back away. Surely, she couldn't just leave this child there with no one else in the immediate vicinity. She sighed in silent frustration.

"How long have you been lost?" she quietly asked so as not to frighten the child.

The boy's greenish-brown, doe-like eyes looked up at her. "I'm not lost. Hercules is," he answered, wiping his tearstained face with the back of his hand and rising to his feet.

"Hercules?" she asked, moving into the clearing where the boy now stood. She squatted to his height.

"Yes, ma'am, my dog. He ran into the woods and I can't find him."

"Oh," Dakota said. "Well, your dog will find its way home. You should be running along. Your parents will be looking for you."

The boy dropped his head. "I don't have any parents," he muttered quietly, looking at the ground.

Something in his tone grabbed at Dakota's heart. This child was hurting badly and not just from the loss of his dog. She knew that kind of despair. She had lived it.

"Come with me," she said, extending her hand toward him.

The boy looked up at her. "Where are we going?"

"To find your dog."

***

Jefferson was nearly frantic. It had been more than three hours and no results. He had searched the woods with Miles and Jefferson Junior for more than an hour before he called for help. The local sheriff had called in trackers with bloodhounds.

How could I have let this happen? His boy was missing and so was the dog. The fear he had been kidnapped edged his thoughts, but he had to remain positive and strong for his other two sons. Jefferson Junior's anger was apparent, but so was Miles' concern and fear.

"It's my fault, Father," Miles said, owning up to his father's prior warnings not to venture too far away from the cabin. "I should not have let him go after Hercules."

Jefferson lowered himself to Miles' height. He put his hands on the boy's stiffened body, pressing gently. "We'll find him, Miles. I promise you that. When we do, he's going to be all right. I should have been with you instead of in the house making lunch, so, if anyone is to blame, it's me and not you."

He pulled Miles into his embrace and Miles reciprocated by putting his arms around Jefferson's shoulders and burying his face in his neck. Jefferson's heart nearly burst with joy and sadness. It had to be all right, he told himself. Stevie just had to be all right!

"Mr. Ambassador, we're about ready to start, Sir," the Sheriff said. "We'll comb the area thoroughly. He couldn't have gotten too far. Little kids are always losing their way in these woods. We've never failed to find them. We'll let you know when we find your boy."

"Thank you, but my sons and I are coming with you."

"Sir, this could—"

"That's my son out there, Sheriff. You will not leave me and his brothers behind," Jefferson said firmly, leaving no opportunity for further objection.

"Yes, Sir," the Sheriff acquiesced, clearly taken aback by Jefferson's vehemence.

"Over here!" someone shouted.

Everyone turned toward the excited voice. There, coming through the crowd, was a tracker carrying Stephen who held Hercules in his arms. Jefferson moved swiftly toward them and gathered Stephen into his arms, kissing his face and hugging him tightly. After some of the fear and tension drained from Jefferson, he finally trusted his voice not to falter.

"Stevie, are you all right?" he asked, still holding the boy closely, his voice strained.

"Hercules was lost, Daddy, and an angel lady and I found him," Stephen said, easily awed by all the confusion around him.

Tears were fighting their way to Jefferson's eyes when he heard Stephen call him "Daddy." He buried his face in Stephen's chest, as Hercules licked both of their faces. Miles was standing next to him and Jefferson gathered the boy to his side, rubbing his back while his shoulders shook from release of his pent-up fears. Then he spotted the tear that dropped from Jefferson Junior's angry face. His eldest son knuckled away his tears and stalked toward the cabin.

Later that night, Jefferson tucked Stevie in under the covers. Hercules took up his position beside him on the bed.

"Son, you mentioned a woman helped you find Hercules," he said quietly. "Who was she? I'd like to thank her for finding you...your dog."

Stevie yawned sleepily. "I don't know her name, but she is a very pretty angel," he said, putting his arm around Hercules. "She runs a lot."

"Oh?" Jefferson said and smiled. "Was she young?" he asked. "What did she look like?"

"No, she was older, like you. Maybe fifty or something."

Jefferson stroked Stevie's small head and chuckled. "I see, but I'm not quite fifty, yet, son. I'm forty."

"That's old, isn't it, Daddy?"

Jefferson chuckled. "That depends on your perspective, Stevie."

"Was my mommy old?"

The question caught Jefferson by surprise, but he recovered quickly. "No, Stevie, your mother wasn't old. She was young, only thirty-four when she…when she left us."

"Oh," he said absently, "are you going to leave us again?"

Another lump caught in Jefferson's throat. "No, Stevie, not for a very, very long time, I hope."

Stevie turned away from Jefferson. "That means you'll go away though, doesn't it?"

Jefferson inhaled deeply. He understood the depth of his son's question. Separation anxiety. "I'm very healthy," he said, as he began stroking the boy's head again. He couldn't stop touching his son, reassuring himself again and again that the boy was there in the bed safe from harm. "Everyone goes away, eventually, but, if I can, I'll stay around until your grandchildren have grandchildren," he said. "Now, what story should we read tonight?"

Stevie grabbed one of the new books they recently bought and settled in hugging Hercules to hear *Bella and the Muddy Puddle* by Catherine Lowery. Ironically, it was about a little girl who gets lost in the woods.

Stevie was fast falling asleep. Jefferson bent and kissed him gently and patted Hercules, whose eyes had also closed. He stood, placing the book on the shelf, and watched his son sleeping for a few more moments, turned out the light, and closed the bedroom door. Next, he went to the bedroom where Miles was sitting up in his bed reading.

"Lights out soon, son," he said to Miles.

"Is Stevie all right?" Miles asked.

"Yes, he's asleep."

Miles went back to reading his book. Jefferson entered the room and sat on the side of the bed.

"What do you like to read?" Jefferson asked.

"Mystery stories," Miles answered absently, not looking up at his father.

"Who is your favorite author?"

"Gina Rawlins and Kiavi Littlefeather."

"Oh, yes, I know Ms. Rawlins."

"I know. She told me."

"You've met her?" Jefferson was surprised.

"Yes, Grandmother invited her to do a private reading at Montrose Manor last spring."

"I see." Jefferson recalled the brief interlude he and Gina shared.

"Do you sleep with all the women you meet?" Miles asked. "Grandfather said you do. He said that you probably have bastards all over the world, and, just like most Black men, you don't want any of them."

His sons certainly didn't take it easy on him, he thought, but his anger was focused on the racism that Tyler Montrose inflicted on his son.

"No, son, I don't sleep with every woman I meet, and most Black men do want and take care of their children. I have been with other women, but I have only the three of you. No other children."

Miles seemed skeptical, but accepting of his father's word. He didn't press any further and Jefferson looked at him questioningly.

"Any more questions?" he asked.

"Not at the moment," Miles said absently, as he diverted his attention back to his book.

"Good night, son," Jefferson said, as he leaned to kiss Miles' forehead.

Miles turned away. "Is that why mother died? Because of your other women."

Jefferson stopped in midair and reseated himself. He looked at Miles directly.

"I was faithful to your mother, Miles. I never slept with another woman while she was alive. I was away when your mother was in the automobile accident, but I feel responsible—"

"You need to get some rest, handsome," Savannah interrupted from the doorway. "It's been a pretty adventurous day." She crossed the room and kissed her nephew all over his face, making him giggle. "God, you get better looking every time I see you," she said, smiling at Miles. "You're going to break a lot of young ladies' hearts with that smile of yours, too."

Miles blushed, as he hugged Savannah. "Good night, Aunt Savannah," he said and smiled, and then looked at Jefferson. "Good night...Father," he said, metering his tone.

"Good night, son," Jefferson said, rising and smiling at his boy.

Outside Miles' closed door, Savannah glared at her brother. Jefferson didn't have to ask what clouded her eyes. He turned toward Jefferson Junior's door and found it locked. He placed his hand against the door.

"Good night, Jefferson," he said to the closed door.

Only silence greeted him. Savannah stormed away. He followed her slowly, his hands dug deep into his pockets. He closed the door to the hallway and watched Savannah pacing the floor. With irritation obvious in her demeanor, he knew what to expect.

"When are you going to stop blaming yourself for what that irrational woman did to herself?" Savannah's angry words flung at him. "If I hadn't stopped you in there, you would have taken all of the blame! Tell them the truth, Jeff! She was bipolar and refused to take her meds! She was controlling! She was a sick woman! You didn't make her that way! You did everything in your power to help her! It was Tyler Montrose who stood in your way! He and Clara turned a deaf ear to your warnings! Have you forgotten how often you pleaded with them to stop interfering in your marriage and let you get her the help she so desperately needed? But, *noooo*, they wouldn't hear of it! Not even from a psychologist with your impeccable credentials. No daughter of the rich and powerful Montrose family was going to see a shrink or be committed to a mental institution! She was *'just high spirited,'* according to them! High spirited? The woman needed a keeper!"

"Enough, Savannah!" Jefferson raged.

"*Enough?* Enough is what I said to you on countless occasions when she publicly displayed herself nude riding on the hood of some fancy sports car in the middle of Georgetown and embarrassed you! Enough is what you should have had when you caught her sleeping in your bed with other men! *Ménage à trois* being her favorite position!"

"Sam!" he said, pulling her into his embrace and rocking her. "Stop it! You're getting yourself all worked up. It's over, done, and forgotten. Now what's the real reason for these hysterics?" he gently asked.

Savannah buried her face in her brother's chest and sobbed. "You're a good man, Jeff. You tried so hard to be a good husband. I know what Felicia put you through. Every day it was something new you had to bail her out of. No man could have held up under that kind of pressure, especially since her family thinks you were to blame for her death."

"I was to blame, Sam," he said, quietly rocking her in his arms. "I didn't try hard enough to help her. I didn't recognize the symptoms of her illness before it was nearly too late."

Savannah looked up into his eyes. "You did everything you could, Jeff. She didn't want to be helped. In addition to her illness, she was a spoiled, little rich girl. Making you bend and twist to her every whim obsessed her. When she couldn't succeed with that, she threatened to harm the boys...."

Jefferson put a finger to her lips.

"It's over, Sam. Felicia can't hurt them now. Please, let's not dredge up the past." He kissed her forehead. "Besides, to you, I can do no wrong. It's in the Sister Book: Thy shall always put thy brother up on a pedestal whether he deserves it or not." He smiled at her and held her face, wiping her tears with his thumbs. "Now, what else has you so upset?" he calmly asked, holding her shoulders and looking into her eyes with a quizzical smile on his face.

Savannah couldn't help the slight smile her brother wrought from her. Then they both heard a sound from the closed door to the hallway. Jefferson went to the door and opened it. The hallway was empty. He listened and knew one of his boys must have been listening, but he couldn't tell which one. He walked to each door, but only heard silence. Maybe he had been wrong. Then he heard Hercules scratching at the door. He opened Stephen's door and Hercules sat in a puddle on the floor. Jefferson shook his head at the frisky puppy that wagged his tiny tail and grinned his doggy grin.

"You should have done that when you took your romp in the woods," he gently scolded the pooch.

Later, after giving Hercules a quick bath while Savannah cleaned the mess the pup had made, Jefferson showered, wrapped himself in a terry cloth robe, and returned to the great room. The night in the mountains held an uncharacteristic chill in the air. Savannah sat on the floor before a small fire in the fireplace, hugging her legs to her chest.

He poured two glasses of brandy, handed one to her, and then sat on the sofa near her. She would talk when she was ready, he knew. For now, he would not press her. For a long time, they sat quietly together, watching the flames devour the fragrant logs and sipping the flavorful brandy.

Savannah curled up at her brother's feet and laid her head on his knee. Jefferson soothingly stroked her loose, untamed hair.

"You know, I remember seeing Mom and Dad sitting quietly together in front of the fireplace at the old house," he began. "He'd have his arm around her and she'd snuggle close to him."

"They were very much in love, weren't they, Jeff?" Savannah asked quietly.

"Yes, I believe they were. They used to hold hands all the time and kiss when they thought we weren't looking." He mused at the pleasant thoughts.

"I remember they used to make you take me for a walk after church on Sundays, so they could be alone together." She smiled, looking up at him. "They couldn't wait to be together."

"They were together, every night and every day." He smiled at the memory. "They did everything together, whether it was working or playing."

"They loved each other, and us, so much." Savannah sighed. "I remember they loved teaching at our school, too."

"They were together for twenty years, Sam. They knew and understood what love was. It was the invisible threads that held us all together."

"I never heard them fuss or fight. Did they have arguments?"

"If they did, they never let it interfere with their relationship. Mom knew how to handle Dad. It didn't take much with him. She'd just look at him and he'd melt."

"Daddy was no weakling," Savannah said, pinching Jefferson's leg.

"Ouch," he said, laughing. "No, he was a strong and principled man and she idolized him. He adored her. He just liked the way she sweet-talked him into her way of thinking—mostly things to do with you, I might add. You were his heart, his little girl. He wouldn't let you out of his sight, but Mom didn't want him to smother you or over-protect you. She used to say, *'If you love someone, set them free. Let them soar to the heights of their imagination'* and boy did you have imagination," he teased.

Savannah rolled her eyes and pursed her lips. "Humph! Daddy was one thing; you were another! You watched me like a hawk and you know it. That's why Mama wasn't worried about me. She knew wherever I was, you wouldn't be far away, and you weren't. Every boy I met, you met."

"You were all too often time enough for me, too, Sam."

"Not anymore, I suppose," she said, looking up into his eyes. "Why didn't you warn me that I was losing Nathan?"

"Have you lost him? Or, is it that you haven't found yourself yet?"

"Have you?"

"Neither of us has recovered completely from our parents' death, Sam. We want in our lives what they had in theirs—unconditional love."

"Everything changes over time."

"It does, honey, but that doesn't necessarily mean it's a negative change."

"It has been for me. Every time I've been happy, something came along to change it."

"Mom and Dad didn't want to leave us. They had no control over what happened to them. They were coming home from a teachers' conference when the plane crashed."

"Intellectually, I know that, but Roderick—" she cut off her thought.

"Roderick found the love he needed in JaiHonnah Hawkins. That wasn't to say he didn't care about you. He just cared about her more."

"What about Nathan? He professed to love me and want me. Now he's deserted me, just like—" She sobbed.

Jefferson bent and held her.

"No," she said, getting to her feet. "You can't kiss the hurt and make it go away anymore. I'm not a little girl! I'm an adult! I'm going to take what I want from men! I won't be hurt again!"

Savannah walked away and up the steps to her bedroom. Jefferson cupped his hands over his face. He wanted to hold her and dispel her fears of rejection, abandonment, and loss, but she was right. She was an adult now. She was capable of making her own decisions and very vulnerable to making her own mistakes. Everyone had a right to make mistakes, he thought to himself. He had made more than a few, he recalled. One that could have lost him his child today, he chastised himself.

Jefferson sprung from his seat, grabbed the back of his neck, and slowly paced the floor. Then he went to his sons' rooms to check on them again. Jefferson Junior's door was still locked, but he opened it with a key that was concealed on a ledge above the door, and went in. The boy was asleep, balled tightly into the fetal position. The sheets tossed haphazardly about the bed. He noticed the mark on Jefferson Junior's leg before he covered his son lightly with a sheet and watched him sleeping for a few moments. He covered his face briefly with one hand, bracing against the painful vision of how that mark had gotten there.

He recalled coming home very late from studying one night. He had worked a full day and then went to the library on Harvard's campus to study. He expected Felicia would be waiting for him and angry. He wasn't disappointed. She was awake, but drunk. Jefferson Junior was a little over two years old at the time. He exchanged a few words with her and went in to his son's room to check on him, as he usually did. Felicia followed him into Jefferson Junior's room, still arguing about how much time he spent away from home. He tried to quiet her, taking her out of their son's bedroom. Felicia continually nipped at him while he went to the kitchen to make a sandwich.

"You were with some bitch, weren't you?" she had railed.

"No, Felicia, you know where I was. You called the library every hour and spoke to me."

"Probably had the cunt with you, fucking her in those precious library stacks you find preferable to being with me!"

"Felicia, please, I haven't been with anyone."

"The hell you say! That little bitch came looking for you. Said she wanted to thank you for getting her an A on her mid-term! I know what's going on between you and that Marcia Childs!"

"I'm her tutor, Felicia. That's all that's 'going on' between us. I'm glad she's progressing well in her studies. She's only a kid, a freshman, and away from home for the first time. She's a little lonely and a little afraid, but I'm not having an affair with her or anyone else! Now, can we please drop this? I'll make coffee for us and then we can relax together."

"Relax? I don't want to 'relax'! I want you to fuck me the way you've been fucking that cunt! You're mine, not hers!" she had yelled, grabbing a knife from the wooden holder and jabbing it at him.

When the shock cleared, he successfully dodged the blade. He grabbed her arm and wrestled the knife from her hand. Just then, he noticed Jefferson Junior standing in the doorway of the kitchen. The boy was hysterical, screaming not to hurt his mommy. He had gone to his son and scooped him up in his arms. Jefferson Junior was crying and beating him in the face. Again, Felicia attacked him with a knife. He had put up his arm to protect himself and Jefferson Junior from her, but he wasn't fast enough with a hysterical boy in his arms. Before he could get Jefferson Junior to safety, the knife had logged in his son's leg and blood was everywhere.

Jefferson snapped himself back to the present. His boy was asleep and safe now. The memory of that time, he hoped, had gone.

"I love you, son," he whispered, as he kissed his son's head. Then he closed and re-locked the bedroom door.

***

A week later, Dakota was pulling groceries from her car when she heard the yelping of the pup she had rescued. Following Hercules was his owner, the little boy who was not lost.

"Not you again," she said to the frisky pup, prancing and dancing at her feet. She lowered to her haunches to pet the puppy that turned his belly up for a rub. She accommodated the pup and briskly rubbed him, sending him into visible pleasure.

"Hi." A bright smile greeted her.

"Hi," she said back to the little boy. "I see Hercules has a leash now."

"Yes," Stevie said. "We bought it to keep him from running away."

"Leashes don't stop you when you want to leave. Teach Hercules to walk with you."

"How do I do that?" he asked, smiling quizzically. "Will you help me?"

Dakota smiled at him and, hearing the approach of others, looked up. Her breath caught. She rose to her feet. Coming up the gravel rise toward her cabin was Jefferson Logan flanked by two other young boys. She looked from the boy at her side to the two with Logan. They were clearly his sons. Except for the boys' lighter complexions, all three boys couldn't have looked more like Jefferson than if they were cloned. Feeling a small hand in hers, she looked down into the big, doe eyes, sadness still lurking behind them.

"It's okay. You don't have to be afraid. The Ambassador is just very tall, but he won't hurt you," Stevie attempted to reassure her.

Dakota wasn't at all sure of that.

Jefferson nearly dropped in his tracks when he saw Stevie standing beside Dakota Sinclair and holding her hand. She looked so beautiful with her hair pulled back in one, thick, long plait, and a Native American headband around her head. She wore what appeared to be a Native American talisman around her neck and no bra under her bright orange spandex, with short, black warm up running shorts below her narrow waist and covering the firm thighs and legs. . His eyes locked on to hers, as he approached.

"Father, this is the pretty, angel lady who found Hercules," Stevie said, looking up at his father.

"Dakota Sinclair is her name, Stephen," Jefferson said, his heart pounding against his chest.

"Chandler," she smoothly corrected. "Dakota Sinclair-Chandler."

"Oh, yes, my mistake, Mrs. Chandler. Congratulations on your marriage. These are my sons. Stevie, you've already met. This is Miles and Jefferson Junior."

"J. Montrose," Jefferson Junior corrected, stepping forward and extending his hand to Dakota.

"Gentlemen," Dakota said, shaking first Jefferson Junior's and then Miles' hand.

"Visiting?" Jefferson asked.

"Uh, no, I live...I mean, Billy and I live here. It's easy for me to work from here when he's away," she said hastily, noticing Jefferson glancing around for another car.

"Oh, I'm sorry to hear that," he said, warming to the lie. He was thrilled to find her alone, without Bill Chandler to run interference. "I enjoyed dinner with him a few weeks ago. You were 'unavailable' he said."

"Uh, yes, I had business out of town. Billy told me he enjoyed the meal."

Jefferson noticed his sons were apparently as awed by her beauty as he was. Miles' mouth was hanging open, Stevie had a big smile on his face, and Jefferson Junior's eyes were dancing. His own body was fighting the vision of her loveliness, but, even in his rapt attention to her, he noticed she had no tan on her shoulder and, more telling, no rings on her fingers. If she had spent any time in the tropics on a honeymoon, she should have had a tan.

"Uh, boys, why don't we give Mrs. Chandler a hand with her groceries?" he said, taking the bag from her car.

"That's not necessary," she said quickly, but not before the boys retrieved her other bags.

"We insist," Jefferson said, grinning. "It's the neighborly thing to do. Besides that, I owe you a big debt of gratitude for finding Stevie and Hercules."

"Neighbors?" she asked. "You live up here?"

"My sister, Savannah, has a cabin on the other side of the lake. We're spending the summer here until school starts."

"The summer," she echoed, fighting her rising anxiety.

The sight of him in a T-shirt, walking shorts, and climbing boots caused something within her to constrict. She could barely breathe normally. She had seen fine physiques before, plenty of them, but none had caused this strange reaction in her. Jefferson was a masterpiece in a tuxedo, but he was ruggedly magnificent in his sportswear. Absently, she thought, he'd be unparalleled in the buff.

"Yes, the summer. After you, Mrs. Chandler," he said with a courtly bow.

Jefferson was surprised at the sparseness of her abode. He had no doubt now that Bill Chandler didn't reside in this house. Chandler was accustomed to the finer things in life, and he would have transformed the bleakness of the cabin into a harem for Dakota, if he had been in residence for any length of time. The cabin, although unadorned, was spotlessly clean. Nothing was there to be out of place, however. Not a book or a magazine. No television or radio. No pictures on the walls or on the mantel of the fireplace. No pots or pans in the kitchen. *Who is she?* The question nagged him. He began unloading the groceries. Only fresh fruits and vegetables, a few toiletries, and sundry items. Staples, like rice, dried beans, and peas were in the bags. Equally unrevealing. Yet there were fishing poles in the corner by the lakeside door.

"Healthy," he said, looking at Dakota.

"Uh, yes," she stammered. "Uh, thank you for your help," she said, trying to bring her guests' impromptu visit to a close.

"Have you lived here long?" Jefferson asked, aware she wanted him to leave, but unwilling to let her push him away so soon.

"Yes. I mean, it's a retreat. I owned it before Billy and I...well we're not here often. Billy has a place in town. We live there most of the time," she said, finally gaining some semblance of composure.

Lying didn't come easily to her, he noticed. In fact, she was having great difficulty with it. That pleased him. He was now convinced he had to know the reasons for the subterfuge. He would get to the bottom of it.

"We'd like it if you'd have dinner with us tonight. It's the least I could do for you coming to Hercules' rescue," Jefferson said, leaving no opportunity for her to refuse. "Seven o'clock? The boys will cook, so bring your appetite." He smiled looking at her long, firm legs in leather boots. "Casual attire."

His sons all looked at him, as if he had lost his mind.

Jefferson couldn't wait for seven o'clock to come. All the preparations were made. Even Jefferson Junior was cooperating in the effort, he noticed. His cell phone rang taking his attention away from his boys.

"Yes," he said.

"Mr. Ambassador, I have the information you requested."

"What did you find, Yates?"

"The property and cabin are titled in the name of Sinclair House. It is an orphanage in North Dakota on the edge of a sparsely-populated Native American Reservation. Dakota Sinclair purchased the orphanage approximately six years ago, according to the county records, and changed the name from Sinclair Home for Wayward Children to Sinclair House. It's over a thousand acres in a remote area.

"She bought the land in Maryland and built the cabin several years ago, too. She paid cash for the purchases, so there is no mortgage in her name. Then, she deeded her cabin to the orphanage. All of her holdings are in the name of the orphanage. A Native American woman, a Ms. Rainwater, manages the orphanage property. Ms. Sinclair is the biggest benefactor of the orphanage, but apparently hasn't visited there in quite some time. Or that appears to be the case. There's another entrance where native residents report some type of survivalist camp exists. No one has seen it though. It's included in a no-fly zone."

"Is this Ms. Rainwater a relative?"

"No, there's no evidence of that. Apparently, Ms. Sinclair was once a resident of Sinclair House. She grew up there. There's no birth certificate and no known relatives that I've been able to find so far. Shall I continue the investigation, Sir?"

"Yes, Yates, and keep me posted."

"By all means, Sir."

They hung up and Jefferson steepled his fingers, as he sat reflecting on what Yates had found. He was still confused, particularly about the no-fly zone in what was apparently a wilderness area, but beginning to connect the dots.

Dakota opened a briefcase, pulled up an antenna, and pushed one number. When the digital numbers connected across the green screen, she placed her hand over the screen and her eyes to a viewer.

"Identify confirmed, Wind Breeze. Go ahead," a digitized voice said on the other end.

"The Stallion," she said.

"Connecting," the disembodied voice replied.

Shortly Bill answered. "What's happened?"

"Logan. He's here. He's staying across the lake. Apparently, something was missed in the research."

"You sound edgy. That's not like you. He gets to you, doesn't he?"

"Of course not," she said, but her words lacked conviction.

"Check the length of your nose, Dakota. It's growing."

She dismissed his comment. "I can't leave. When can you get here?"

"Oh, so now you want me around?"

"Well, you are supposed to be my husband, aren't you?"

"This could get interesting."

"What's your ETA?"

"Forty-eight hours. Put a candle in the window and wait up for me."

Dakota disconnected the call. She rubbed her temples. Forty-eight hours was a long time to have to wait. She tried to think of a strategy, but the thoughts of Jefferson Logan kept getting in the way. The silent phone blinked and she answered.

"Honey, I like powdered silk sheets, warm fluffy towels, brandy by the bed, and, uh, don't forget to wear your rings," Bill said.

"Right," she said, snorting.

"Hold the thought, lover." He hung up.

Bill was right about one thing, she thought. She might have forgotten about the rings.

CHAPTER 18

Nathan smiled contritely as the volley cleared the net and whizzed by him.

"Game, Conway," he said and smiled. "You know, if I didn't know better, I'd think you were a ringer." He went to the net and Gail approached from the opposite side.

"Really, Nathan, I've never played tennis before." She giggled.

"Then why did you suggest we play?"

"Because you're usually so pent-up, almost anal retentive." She laughed at his mutinous expression. "I thought you needed someone to beat up on. Let out some of that energy."

"Oh, really? Is that the only reason?"

"No," she said coyly, "you look great in shorts."

Nathan just shook his head. "The things you say, Ms. Conway. Are you flirting with me?"

"You finally noticed." She smiled. "For a person who makes his living knowing what the other person is thinking, I'm surprised you're as successful as you are. I've tried in every way possible to send out signals that I find you very attractive—" her eyes raked over him, "all of you. Very attractive, indeed."

Nathan blushed. "I've noticed, but Gail, you understand—"

"That you haven't gotten over what's-her-name. I do understand. I'm not completely over my ex, but I don't want to be sad anymore and I don't want you to be either. Life's too short to wake up with regrets. Let's just enjoy our newfound friendship and leave it at that."

"You make it sound so easy, and, believe me, I want to move on with my life—"

"You will. It's only a matter of time before the pain will decrease. I know. I'm an expert at it. Remember? I've made a career out of being dumped by men I cared about. Now, because of you, Nathan Flack, I have a new attitude."

"Another game?" he asked.

"Only if you continue to play with blinders on, one hand tied behind your back, and a shackle on your ankle."

"That puts me at a competitive disadvantage."

"Now you know how I feel about Ms. What's-her-name." She giggled, kissing Nathan quickly on the cheek, and trotting to the other end of the tennis court.

Nathan shook his head in amusement. Gail Conway had a vibrant smile and easy disposition. She was uncomplicated and simplistic. He enjoyed being with her, he thought. Even if nothing came of it, his ache for Savannah was still real and deep. He wanted, no, he *needed*, actually craved Savannah. As complex as the relationship with her was, he still loved her very deeply. He knew it would take him a very long time to get over what they shared. He looked up at Gail. Maybe, he thought. Maybe loving would be easier the second time around.

After Nathan showered, he stood in his kitchen wearing a bathrobe. He uncorked a bottle of wine he had chilling in the wine cooler to let it breathe. The soulful sound of Kemistry's latest CD wafted through his condo.

"Dinner is ready," he called out.

Gail came out of his bedroom wrapped in his terry cloth robe.

"Mmm," she hummed in her throat, sniffing the air. "When you said you could cook, I frankly didn't believe you." She smiled at him while drying her hair with a towel.

"What is a man to do when he makes a bet and then loses?" He shrugged. "It's tough enough when you get beaten that badly at tennis, and by a novice, of all people."

"You let me win and you know it, Nathan." She giggled. "You just wanted to make me feel better for falling flat on my butt when you hit that ace by me." She laughed. "You're just an old softy."

"Scouts honor," he said, holding up three fingers, "you won fair and square."

She tilted her head to the side slightly and smiled. "I could believe you were a Boy Scout. Is that why you're in the diplomatic corps, because of a pledge to Mother Country?"

"Actually, I've never been a Boy Scout. I joined the diplomatic corps after I heard Dr. Jefferson Logan speak at a National Bar Association dinner.

"I was practicing corporate law at the time and doing quite well, but liking it less. The things Jefferson said made me realize he was living with a sense of purpose and commitment to something bigger than the size of his bank account or the model car he drove or the designer clothes he wore. He had a sense of purpose to be accomplished to honor the ancients of our people and all people. When he spoke, it was with conviction and courage to gain human rights and full citizenship for all, not just the privileged few. He was vehemently opposed to what other cultures and countries had suffered at the hands of America, and he made no bones about how people of color in this country had been treated. He wasn't on any soapbox trying to play Moses and lead our people out of our condition. He was already a free man, unshackled by how society viewed him. He made no apology when someone accused him of living in the lap of luxury with a rich wife who was not Black. He said *I abhor racism and I don't practice it publicly or privately*.

"After that dinner, I sought him out, we talked for a while, and I realized he didn't just speak the words, he lived the reality. We shared a vision for a better world. Not just a better life.

"The next day, I resigned my position at a top New York law firm where I was a senior partner and joined the Civil Service. I went back to college to get a master's Degree in psychology. Several years later, I ran into Jefferson again at a State Department function. He asked me whether I wanted to work harder than I ever had before and I said yes. He made good on that warning and I haven't regretted it a day in my life."

"He's very important to you, isn't he?" Gail asked, threading her fingers through the folds of his bathrobe, stroking his bare chest, and looking up into his eyes.

"We're friends—good friends," he said, stepping back.

"Nate, please, don't run away from me," Gail said softly.

"I have to, Gail. One of us has got to keep his or her head on straight."

"I know what I'm doing." She moved closer to him and rested her head on his chest. "I want to make love with you, even if you can't make love to me."

She looked up into his eyes again and licked softly at his lips. Nathan closed his eyes, trying to dispel the vision of Savannah. Why couldn't he just let go? Let go of Savannah, and, for once in his life, throw caution to the wind. Gail dropped her robe and folded herself inside his bathrobe against his nude body. He didn't want to hurt her, but his need for sexual release was building, as was his vision of Savannah. If only Savannah were the one in his arms instead of Gail Conway. Maybe he could pretend. Gail slipped her arms around his neck and deepened her kiss.

Finally, the heat of her passion kicked in and he enveloped her, pulling her deeper into his embrace. She slipped him out of his bathrobe, tracing feathery kisses across the broad, firm plane of his chest. He was about to take her into his bedroom when they both heard a door slam shut. Startled, they broke off their passion and turned to see Savannah Logan glaring at them and seething with anger.

"Excuse me, uh, did I come at a bad time?" She asked too calmly for Nathan's comfort.

"Uh, yes, Savannah, you did." He tried to recover, but Savannah, under ordinary circumstances, made his heart rate quicken. When she was angry, she was so beautiful it made his heart stop. She took his breath away, the way she stood her ground with one hand on her hip in an impressive pose. "You should have called," was all he was able to say.

"Which call would you have answered or returned? The tenth? Twentieth?" She flung the words at him through gritted teeth.

"Uh, maybe I should let you two talk," Gail said, slipping back into the terry cloth robe. "I'll be in the kitchen, Nathan. I'll make the bread."

"Fine, Gail. I apologize. This won't take long," he said, putting on his robe and tying the sash tightly around his waist.

Gail left the room and Nathan folded his arms across his chest. He and Savannah glared at each other.

"Practicing?" Savannah asked cryptically, sauntering toward him.

"Practice time was over," he clipped.

"You can send the second team home. I'm here now," she said flippantly.

"What, bored with Jacob Hawkins so soon? Gee, he didn't even last a year." He snorted.

"Through with him is more like it," she said, her nose in the air.

"Tough. He seemed like such a nice guy," he said facetiously.

"Well, maybe he and Ms. Muffin-in-the-kitchen will get together. How's her baking?"

"I do the cooking, remember?"

They were standing a breath away from each other.

"Then tell her to get her hot buns out of my robe and hit the road."

"I've developed a taste for hot buns and that's not your robe. It's mine."

"I bought that robe for you last Christmas."

"You've worn it every time you've been here."

"You loved me in it, and out of it, too."

"Take it with you when you leave. I'm sure I can find another one for her. One I don't have to share."

The double entendre was biting and right on the mark, but Savannah felt like she was fighting for her life.

"There is no other one. It's one of a kind and so am I. Negotiate on that when you hold Ms. Hot Buns in your arms tonight. Remember clearly how you made love to me in that robe and out of it. In your bed. On the floor in front of the fireplace. In the shower against the wall. There isn't an area in your home we didn't christen several times over.

Remember how I felt and how I made you feel. How I touched you and you called out *my* name."

The heat between them was searing. Savannah was kicking butt and taking names. God how he wanted her! Still, he couldn't let her commit erotic terrorism on him any longer.

He held out his hand. "My keys," he said, surprised his hand was steady. Inside he was vibrating like a plucked bow just being within close proximity to her.

"On my body. Find them yourself."

Nathan backed away and put up both hands. Touching her would have been his undoing. "Fine. Keep the keys. I'll have the locks changed tomorrow. Now, if you'll excuse me, I have something baking in the kitchen. You know your way out."

Savannah was so angry she could have taken the Watergate apart, brick-by-brick, but she knew Nathan loved her. She could feel it in his heat and see it in his eyes when he looked at her. She had to have him back though. Ms. Hot Buns was no slouch and she clearly had eyes for Nathan. She felt strangely triumphant and turned on the music in her Lexus, singing, *"I'm Every Woman,"* at the top of her voice.

Nathan was shaken, as he leaned against his leather sofa, legs crossed at the ankles and arms folded across his chest. Just being in the same room with Savannah made his member thick and hard. He lowered his head, pinching the bridge of his nose between his eyes, her perfume still drawing on his senses. He closed his eyes and exhaled.

Then the aroma of something else teased his senses. He opened his eyes to see a piping hot bun under his nose.

"I do know how to bake," Gail teased.

She pulled him back onto the sofa and straddled him.

"You whipped these up yourself?" he asked.

"Yep." She smiled coyly, feeding bits of the warm bun to him. "That's not all I can do."

"I'll bet."

"No, you'll see," she answered seductively, as she removed the bathrobe and covered his mouth with hers.

CHAPTER 19

That's all the rocks I need," Dakota said, as she finished building the temporary fire pit in the soil.

"How about these twigs?" Miles asked, holding them up to her.

"Very good, but we need more than that to bake these fish," she said, sending the boys off to forage for more wood.

Jefferson watched with rapt pleasure, as Dakota worked her magic on his sons. She gave them guidance, as they built the fire pit in no time flat, the expensive gas grill standing idle and unused. He sipped his beer and marveled at the sight of her sitting flat on the ground, legs crossed Indian style beneath her, pawing in the dirt.

She wore no makeup. Her hair plaited in a single braid from the crown of her head that hung down her back between her shoulder blades. No bra straps were imprinted on the clean, white T-shirt she wore. No insignia on the gray warm-ups or the socks with ankle boots. No perfume or other manner of intoxication, except her clean, fresh, natural scent.

In short order, she started a fire in the pit and one in his heart. Earlier they went fishing in the lake and caught six fat trout. She laid the stuffed fishes out surrounded by unpeeled potatoes, unshucked corn, and berries they picked. He thought she was masterful in the ways she let the boys help her. She sliced fresh fruit and laid it on a bed of fresh spinach, giving each of the boys a piece to chew on while the remainder of the dinner cooked. They talked with her without holding back, marveling at the stories she told about her childhood growing up in the mountains, what berries were the sweetest, and how to tell the difference in the pine trees from the needles they shed. How to pick mushrooms and distinguish the safe ones from the poisonous. She was a naturalist and he wondered at the dichotomy. Sophisticated businesswoman and Indian Princess rolled up into one package that still spelled mystery.

That's how he would always think of her. Sitting on the ground as the sun started its decline behind the hills of Western Maryland. His sons gazing at her with Hercules curled comfortably in her lap, pleasantly accepting her gently stroking hand. She talked with them easily and they listened almost as if in a trance. Yes, that's exactly how he would remember this unexpected, wondrous day.

Dakota found herself caught up in the wonder of the three Logan boys. They were all as different as the seasons, but each very intelligent and inquisitive in his individual way. It was a pleasure talking with them and she found it easier than she had expected. Far easier than talking with their father who she knew was watching her every move. His gaze was disturbing and heated her to her core. Making eye contact with him was problematic. She could not look at him directly. His eyes seemed to look into her soul. She felt a sensation, a blush when their eyes met, so she continued to direct her attention to the boys.

All through the evening, she noticed the distance Jefferson Junior put between himself and his father. Miles was less antagonistic and Stephen was even friendly to his father. She could see this distance hurt Jefferson, though he tried to hide it. He was there for them; they only had to realize how much he cared, she thought. Whatever had caused the breach between father and sons was deep and galvanized. She wondered about their mother. She had not read Jefferson's dossier lately, but the sorrow in his eyes gave her reason to be curious.

Dakota's head snapped up sharply, as if sensing danger. Jefferson tensed at her movement and looked around, peering into the darkening woods. He saw nothing, but instinctively knew she did. Following her line of vision, his eyes settled on Jefferson Junior as he raised his camera to his face to take another series of pictures.

How foolish! Dakota chastised herself. She was so engrossed in the Logan boys and their father she had dropped her defenses. She hadn't noticed when Jefferson Junior brought out a camera and started taking pictures. She had no idea how many pictures he may have taken before she heard the nearly imperceptible whine of the camera motor advancing the frame. Somehow, she had to delete the photos without raising anyone's suspicions.

"That was delicious, Dakota," Jefferson Senior said, sitting on the ground across the campfire from her. He noticed she shied away from Jefferson Junior's attempts to get a clear shot of her.

"Yes, Mrs. Chandler, that was very good. The Ambassador, uh, I mean, Mr. Logan cooks with oil in a pan on the stove. Our cook at home in Boston uses butter in everything, and we've dined in some of the best five-star restaurants around the world, but I've never tasted anything as good as that," Jefferson Junior admitted.

"Did you like it, Miles?" Jefferson Senior asked.

"Yes, what are you going to cook for us tomorrow, Mrs. Chandler?"

The smile that bloomed on Dakota's face rose to her eyes and the firelight lit her beautiful face.

"Uh, fellows, we invited Mrs. Chandler to have dinner with us, and she ended up doing almost all the work," Jefferson said.

"I helped, Father," Stevie added defensively.

"Yes, Stevie, you did. All of you did a very good job," Dakota said, "but now it's time for me to go. I'll help you to clean up and douse the fire," she said, thinking that, in the rush to clean up, no one would pay attention while she deleted the photos of her in the camera. She would appear to be taking pictures of the boys while she deleted any pictures of herself.

"There's not much to clean up, Mrs. Chandler. We've managed to devour everything edible," Jefferson Junior said, while he picked up his camera and hung it securely around his neck.

"Uh, I guess you're right. Then I'll be going," she said, rising to her feet. She wasn't going to be able to get to that camera now.

"We'll walk you home, Mrs. Chandler," Miles said.

"Uh, that's very kind, but I'll be fine. You needn't bother—"

"Please, Mrs. Chandler," Stevie begged.

Dakota smiled at Stevie. He needed female contact, she surmised.

"All right, if you'll hold my hand," she agreed.

They made sure the fire was out and then took the long way around the lake, walking slowly to Dakota's cabin. Stevie never let go of her hand during the entire distance. She noted Jefferson Junior kept snapping pictures, not of her necessarily, but of the scenery and the wildlife. Clearly, the camera was equipped to take shots in the near darkness using only the light of the moon and stars. When they arrived at her cabin, Stevie beckoned her to stoop and when she did, he planted a kiss on her check. Dakota was surprised by the gesture and then hugged Stevie in return. Again, she heard the camera whirl. Jefferson Junior was taking more pictures of her. She had to get the SIM card from that camera!

"Good night, Dakota," Stevie whispered to her with a big smile.

"Good night, Stevie," she said and smiled back at him.

She turned to Miles and then Jefferson Junior who both shook her hand. She gave Hercules a tussle and his little tail wagged frantically. Then she turned to the all-engulfing Jefferson Senior. She extended her hand and he took it, raising it to his lips.

"Like son, like father," he said and smiled at her.

Dakota felt a tingle peppering her body when Jefferson's lips touched the back of her hand. Her nerve endings went haywire and her breathing quickened. She felt like she had been capsized in a boat when the wave hit her. *Whirl. Whirl. Keep your mind on business!*

"Good night," she murmured around a large lump in her throat and swiftly walked away.

Stevie reached for his father's hand and Jefferson's heart leaped.

"Smooth move, Dad," Stevie said, as they walked.

Jefferson stopped in his tracks and looked at his youngest son. Then he swept the boy up in his arms and smiled.

"Think so, huh?" he said, holding Stevie in one arm.

Stevie gave him the thumbs up and then buried his face in Jefferson's neck, giggling.

Jefferson roared with laughter as he carried Stevie perched on his shoulders while he and his sons walked back to their cabin with Hercules leading the way. His mind was on Dakota's uneasiness around having her picture taken. It seemed innocent enough to him, but he'd have to make sure he had the pictures stored on his computer and printed as soon as possible to determine what was causing her so much concern.

As the boys prepared for bed, brushing their teeth, Jefferson chanced to overhear their conversation.

"She's a fox!" Miles said emphatically.

"No, she's an angel," Stevie interjected earnestly. "When she came to help me find Hercules she moved so quiet I didn't even know she was there. Her feet never touched the ground. She must be an angel."

"Not that kind of fox, Stevie. I mean, she's hot. Like a honey, a babe. You know?" Miles tried to explain. Stevie still looked confused. "Never mind that now. I'll explain it to you when you're older." Miles sighed. "Wonder where her husband is?"

"Probably dead like our mother. That's why she's fair game and I'm just the man to handle the situation," Jefferson Junior asserted.

"Man, she's old enough to be our mother. Besides, did you see how Father was looking at her? I think he's got a serious jones on."

"He's not our father!" Jefferson Junior railed. "Our father is Tyler Montrose, not that Logan person. He was just the sperm donor! Don't you go soft on him. Tyler is going to get us back, he promised, and the sooner the better!"

"I'm not sure I want to go back," Stevie meekly interjected.

Both boys turned and looked down at him.

"We've got to go back, Stevie. This man doesn't care about us. Remember our real father told us he would try to turn us against him. He told us to be strong and he would take care of everything," Jefferson Junior tried to convince Stevie.

"Lay off of him, Jay. He's only a little kid," Miles said sternly, "but he has a right to his own opinion."

"You going back on your word, too, Miles?" Jefferson Junior asked bluntly.

"I don't know, but I won't let you make up my mind for me either. I can think for myself."

"I don't like the way you're acting."

"I don't like the way Grandfather is always putting Mr. Logan down. Calling him a low-life N-word from the country. Saying he raped and murdered our mother. If he did all that, why is he an Ambassador and why isn't he in jail?"

"Father is working on that. He told us so, remember?"

"Jay, our mother died four almost five years ago. If Grandfather could prove that Mr. Logan did it, what's taking him so long? I've got newspaper articles on my iPad about Mr. Logan. Nobody ever said he killed our mother. He wasn't even in the country when she died. There are a lot of articles about our mother too. She died in a car accident with some German man. They say he was her boyfriend. Besides, have you looked in the mirror lately?"

"What are you talking about?"

"We look like him—like Mr. Logan, I mean. We don't look like Grandfather."

"What's that got to do with anything?"

"Every time Grandfather calls Mr. Logan bad names, it makes me angry. Sperm donor or not, he's still our father and he's no..." he stalled. "Neither am I, and neither are you and Stevie."

Jefferson didn't know whether to be pleased or disheartened by what he overheard. His fist clinched when he thought of the venom Tyler Montrose imbued in his sons. At that moment, he could have gladly broken Tyler's neck and followed him to the grave, but he had his sons to think about and time to try to heal the wounds.

"Ready for bed yet, fellas?" Jefferson Senior asked, clearing his throat.

"Did you rape and murder my mother?" Stevie innocently asked, looking up at Jefferson.

Jefferson lowered himself to Stevie's eye level.

"No. I did not rape or murder your mother, son," he said, as calmly as he could.

"What does that mean anyway?" Stevie asked, confused.

Jefferson explained it as best he could for his son's young age while the older boys listened.

"You wouldn't hurt somebody, would you, Father?"

"No. I wouldn't. Especially not your mother, Stevie. I swear."

"I didn't think so, but Jay thinks you did."

Jefferson looked up at his other sons. "I would gladly give up my life before I would hurt any of you or let anyone else hurt you. That's what I felt about your mother, too.. No person, especially no man, can claim to be a man if he hurts a woman in that way. I am a man. I'm not perfect in many ways, but I never hurt your mother.

"I am your father. Your grandfather and grandmother, my father and mother, built my foundation. They were clear about the foundation they laid for me and your Aunt Savannah. It was not weak; it was strong like the foundation laid by their ancestors back through the generations to Africa and for generations to come. We come from a long line of teachers who gave themselves to truth no matter how distasteful the truth can sometimes be. I never lied to my parents and I'll never lie to you."

"I believe you, Dad," Stevie said, hugging Jefferson's neck.

Jefferson didn't realize that tears were in his eyes until he felt them against Stevie's cheek.

***

Dakota rolled to her side and stretched her body fully until she felt all of her muscles respond. She wondered why her stomach took a dive off a high perch whenever she was in Jefferson's presence. It wasn't normal or natural behavior for her. Perhaps she was coming down with something, she thought, but except for her injury, she had never been sick a day in her life. Maybe she was allergic to him or something he wore on his skin. Foolish thought, she chastised herself.

She had seen him and his boys every day since their first cookout together, and every day they had done something different together.

Today they were going swimming in the lake. The water was warmer and the nights were not as cool as before. She rolled to her other side and stared out of the balcony door at the lake and toward the Logan cabin on the other side. *What am I doing? Why does this man cause me to react like this, almost giddy and silly? Foolishness,* she huffed, and rolled out of bed.

Then she heard a familiar sound in front of her house. She knitted her brow, slipped into a shirt and went to the alarm to disarm it. When she opened the door, Bill stood leaning against the frame, lasciviously eyeing her. He had a few days' growth on his smooth, handsome face, his cheeks more hollow, his skin tanned, his blue eyes sharp and clear.

"Well, hello, Mrs. Chandler," he said lowly, sensuously. He eyed her bare feet and legs to the top of her head. "If I had known you looked as sexy as this in the morning, I never would have left home."

"It's too early in the morning, Bill. What are you doing here?" she asked without emotion.

"You called me, remember? I'm sorry it took so long. I finished up as early as I could and then caught the fastest jet I could find." His eyes raked over her again. "How are our powdered sheets coming?"

Dakota rolled her eyes, shook her head, and walked away from the door. Bill followed, eyeing her rear. His complexion flushed.

"How did it go?" she asked, her bare feet silently padding across the floor to the kitchen.

"Uh, Dakota, give a man a break, would you? You look like every man's wet dream and you expect me to talk about business? I'm good, but you'd give a saint a hard on."

"Business, Bill," she said laconically. "I'm in no mood for your jokes this morning."

"What you fail to realize, my lovely wife, is that I'm not joking. I'm as serious as a heart attack, which I'm about to have if you reach up any higher for whatever it is you're looking for in that cabinet."

"Coffee," she said, still reaching.

Bill went to her side and pulled the box of Keurig coffee containers from the shelf.

"See? There are advantages to having a tall man around. Why don't you let me show you a few more things you can use me for, Mrs. Chandler?" he asked with a sexy grin.

"Yes, I will. You can make the coffee. I'm going to shower. Maybe when I get back you'll be in a better frame of mind and we can do some work."

"I wouldn't count on it, but I can work wonders in a shower. I could make a career out of holding your soap," he said, watching her climb the steps to her loft.

Dakota didn't answer him. She smiled to herself. *Bill certainly is in rare form*, she mused. *Jefferson wouldn't say those things to me*, she thought. Then she stopped in her tracks. *Why the hell am I thinking about Jefferson Logan? Humph!*

Twenty minutes later, Dakota came down the steps fully dressed, her straight black hair still damp and combed away from her face. The coffee was ready and Bill was still shamelessly eyeing her. Then she heard a truck pull up and stop. Bill looked at his watch and put down his coffee mug.

"It's for me," he said, rising smoothly from his seat and going to the door. "Right on schedule," he said, as men came in and began removing what little furnishings she did have.

"What the hell are you doing?"

"A little redecorating," Bill said, as the commotion began.

"Redecorating? Why?"

"The Ambassador is no fool, Dakota. He'd take one look at this place and know immediately it's not exactly a love nest—at least the nest part is right."

"Logan has already seen this place. He didn't say anything."

"He didn't have to, but I'll bet he thought about it. Now I'm giving him something else to think about."

"Bill," she started.

He took her in his arms. "Do you trust me?"

"Of course, I trust you, but this is insane."

"We'll see."

Jefferson noticed the black convertible Mercedes Benz 500 SL parked in front of Dakota's cabin with plates that read: RISQUÉ. Then he noticed the potted flowers lining the porch and walkway. Furrowing his brow, he and his sons approached the cabin. He braced himself for the performance he knew was about to unfold.

Bill opened the door, wearing his swimming trunks, and smiling broadly.

"Mr. Ambassador," he acknowledged, shaking Jefferson's hand. "These must be the young men Dakota's been talking about."

"Yes, these are my sons, but as is our custom, Bill, let's dispense with the formality, shall we? Call me, Jeff, and this is my eldest son, Jefferson Junior who prefers to be called Jay, Miles, and this little man is Stephen Christopher, Stevie for short."

"A pleasure to meet all of you," Bill said, shaking each boy's hand.

"Are you *the* William Chandler?" Jefferson Junior asked. "The owner of *Risqué*?"

"I am, indeed," Bill said, his brow drawn together in concern. "Uh, you've seen my product?"

Jefferson Junior blushed. "Uh, not really, but my grandmother took us to the Festival de Cannes last year. One of your movies won a prize, but we weren't allowed to see it."

"*Whew!*" he said, demonstratively, and then smiled. "I'm glad to hear it. My films aren't of the Walt Disney genre."

"I'm thirteen," Jefferson Junior announced defensively.

"Going on thirty-three, I can see. Well, have a seat. My wife will join us in a moment."

"Uh, nice place," Jefferson said, tongue planted firmly in cheek as he looked at the harem that had suddenly materialized in the cabin. It had been transformed into a true love nest, complete with wedding pictures suitably framed, flowers and plants properly placed, furniture carefully selected, along with books, magazines, an ultramodern entertainment center, candles of all types and descriptions, and real kitchen utensils hanging from a ceiling rack near the range top. He thought the empty champagne bottle turned upside down in the bucket and the fresh strawberries in whipped cream was a little over the top. Nevertheless, it was a credible effort at staging. Hollywood couldn't have done it better or in less time.

Dakota descended the stairs and Jefferson's eyes locked on to her. The swimsuit was straight out of Victoria's Secret, very revealing, but offering not a whisper. She took his breath away, but somehow he knew she would be just as happy in the buff instead of in the hot little—emphasis on little—number she was wearing. He swallowed hard and heard his sons all gulp as well. The game was afoot and Jefferson was ready and eager to play.

CHAPTER 20

Who won?" Savannah asked.

Georgetown Medical's softball team dejectedly filed into the doctors' lounge, following the game.

"They did," Chuck Montgomery huffed. "We almost had them, too. It was the bottom of the ninth and we were tied six all. Then Nathan steps to the plate, with the bases loaded, and hits one out of the park. The man was zoning all afternoon!"

"I would have been zoning, too, if I had a babe, like Gail, rooting for me!" Keith Monroe, a lab technician, chirped up before he thought about it, but it was too late. The words hung in the air more poignant and pungent than the smell of hospital solvent. Silence filled the room.

Doctors, nurses, and hospital staff started easing their way out of the way. Savannah noticed. She pretended she didn't and continued writing notes in the medical charts stacked in front of her on the table. Then she looked up and slid her eyeglasses to the top of her head.

"Tough loss, huh?" she nonchalantly asked of no one in particular in the quiet room.

"Uh, yeah, real tough," Keith meekly commented.

"Don't take it too hard, Keith. Nathan is a real hardball player. He's tough up in the cut," she said, amused, and smiled weakly.

Rising, she gathered her patients' charts and walked out of the lounge amid a hanging silence. She heard the audible sounds of relief as she left. That's what comes of dating a high-profile man, like Nathan Flack, and being seen as a couple. Everyone was walking on eggshells around her now that Nathan and Gail were being viewed as the couple *de jour*. They were on the social scene and constantly bumping into her friends, acquaintances, and coworkers while she had buried herself in her work. However, her work wasn't enough anymore. She ached to be with Nathan, but unlike arguments they had in the past, he wasn't trying to reconcile. Instead, he seemed to be putting his life back together with Gail as the object of his attention.

***

"You played great today, Nate," Gail swooned, as they arrived at her condo.

"Thanks, I enjoyed having you come with me."

"Next time, why don't you ask me to come, instead of my having to invite myself along?" she teased.

"I have to be completely honest with you, Gail. The situation today was somewhat awkward for me."

"Oh and why was that?"

"The team we played, Georgetown Medical, well, Savannah is a doctor on the hospital staff, and we've socialized a lot with many of the people from the hospital—"

"Seeing you with another woman, the word would get back to Savannah, and her feelings would be hurt? Do I have the scenario right?"

"Uh, you do, yes."

"The last thing you want to do is to hurt Savannah, right?"

"I haven't tried to deceive you, Gail. I still love her very much. I'm trying to get over it, but it's going to take time—a lot of time. I don't want to hurt you either."

"You haven't hurt me, Nathan. One of the things I think is so special about you is that you're honest. After Savannah found us together and you couldn't make love with me, I thought it was me. That I wasn't sexually appealing to you."

"Nothing could be further from the truth, Gail. I find you very appealing, but—"

She silenced him with a kiss, stroked his face, and smiled into his eyes. "I'm a very patient woman, Nathan, and you're worth waiting for.

Until you're comfortable with making love with me, I'll simply have to lust after your body in my heart."

Nathan chuckled. "Thanks, Gail. You're a very understanding woman. If I met you before I met and fell in love with Savannah, things might have been very different."

"I would have made sure of it."

***

Jefferson laid his towel across his lap to hide his arousal. He had taken several dips in the lake, but nothing seemed to stem the urgent need that played havoc with his loins. Dakota doing the backstroke was tempting, the breast stroke was teasing, but stretched out on the dock with the sun dancing on the beads of water caressing her skin was downright unfair, he thought. Her long, jet-black, thick hair looked even heavier and curly when wet, he noticed. He also noticed she seemed to be walking with a slight limp, which she claimed was a Charlie horse. That didn't wash with him either. He had noticed it before, but, of course, there were many things about her he was learning every minute of every day they spent in each other's company.

She seemed always very alert, watchful. Her senses were attuned to the slightest change around her. The most important thing he noticed about Dakota was she was not in love—not with Bill—in any event. Yet, this marriage charade still had him confused. Bill was living at the cabin with her, but if they were blissful, her eyes never showed it. Bill's eyes, on the other hand, reflected a deep yearning matched only by his own developing feelings for Dakota. However, Bill was a professional actor. He could be easily faking. His sons were also in rapt attention to her and she made them all feel very special.

"Beer?" Bill asked, rising from his seat.

"Uh, yes," Jefferson said, snapping his ceaseless attention away from Dakota to watch his boys swimming.

Shortly, Bill returned carrying a small cooler filled with ice and expensive, imported beer. He handed a beer to Jefferson who accepted it with a quick "Thanks." Then Bill sat on another chaise lounge next to Jefferson. Bill and Jefferson each took a quick swig of their beers and continued to look out over the lake and the increased population enjoying the warmer waters and weather. Both men could not avoid the sight of Dakota lying on her back a few feet away from them. Sunshades covered her eyes against the bright, hot, summer sun, but the rest of her body was only scantily clad. When Dakota shifted onto her stomach, both men uttered an audible sigh almost simultaneously. They knew, almost instinctively, what the other one was thinking. Neither admitted it.

"You know, Jefferson, you're not at all what I expected," Bill commented.

"Oh, what did you expect?"

"The usual profile of a diplomat: distant, erudite, scholarly, intellectual, generally a stuffed suit."

"Oh, I see," Jefferson said, amused. "It's a common misconception."

Bill laughed. "That's not to say you don't have all of those qualities—except the stuffed suit business—but you're a regular guy, as well as a well-respected statesman. Rare quality to find someone so grounded, yet so well prepared to deal on a global basis."

Jefferson laughed. "I understand your meaning. Something like you and Dakota: a mirage. Something you think you see isn't really there."

"What, because she's Black and I'm not? I understand your wife was not Black. I would have thought the liaisons between people of different backgrounds would not have affected a statesman who deals regularly with people of all colors."

"It's not the ethnic or racial difference between you that surprises me. Dakota is a very beautiful woman. Any man, regardless of his ethnicity, would find her captivating."

"Then what is it about our marriage you find hard to fathom?" Bill asked just as his cell phone rang. He looked at the numbers displayed on the screen and took the call. "Uh, yes, I'll be there in three hours," he said, then closed the phone. "We'll have to continue this conversation at a later date. The State Department has cleared our mission to the Middle East."

"Sorry to see you have to leave so soon," Jefferson said.

"Duty calls," Bill answered smugly. "You know how that can be, don't you, Jefferson?"

"All too well," he said, pleased Bill would be out of the way for a while.

Bill hovered over Dakota and woke her gently with a kiss on the back of her neck. She turned on to her side, cleared her mind, alert to Jefferson's presence.

"Have to go, honey," Bill said, sitting alongside of her. He bent and kissed her lips. "I'm going to miss you."

"Do that again and I'm going to break your neck," she hissed lowly through a clinched-teeth, sweet-as-syrup smile.

Just for spite, Bill bent to kiss her again in a sensuously searing kiss. "Remember, darling, the Ambassador is watching," he whispered against her lips. "Now, this time put your arms around my neck, pull me close, and kiss me like it's him in your arms."

"Oh, honey, do you have to go so soon?" she whined, moving to a sitting position and avoiding his kiss.

"Uh, yes. I just got the signal from the State Department."

"Well, I'll help you pack." She rose to her feet.

"Please excuse us, Jefferson," Bill said.

"Certainly," Jefferson said.

Bill put an arm around her shoulder as they went into the cabin. As soon as they were inside, Dakota put a hard elbow in Bill's solar plexus. He buckled and went down on his knees, gasping for breath.

"It was worth it," he said, choking through the pain. "I can't tell you how long I've wanted to do that," he said, struggling to gain his breath and his composure.

Dakota's fists jabbed into her hips. "That's the last time you'll do it, too!" she raged.

***

Nathan knew when he walked into the restaurant what he would find and it wasn't on the menu.

"Ah, Ambassador Flack," the maître d' acknowledged and smiled broadly. "It's good to see you, but Dr. Logan didn't indicate she was expecting you. I'll show you to her table."

"François, Dr. Logan isn't expecting me. Would you seat me somewhere near where she's sitting?"

François raised an eyebrow and Nathan noticed. He reached into his pocket and palmed a generous gratuity.

"I'm sure you understand, don't you, François?" he asked, shaking the man's hand.

François peeked at the gratuity and smiled broadly.

"Of course, Mr. Ambassador, right this way," he said, lifting a leather-covered menu and bowing slightly.

Savannah was pouring over a medical journal while she devoured her chicken salad. She didn't notice the man sitting at a table near her. Nor did she notice other eyes furtively watching her. Her thoughts were on the article concerning the number of hospitals that were defying the insurance industry and permitting new mothers to be hospitalized beyond the customary one-day stay. She made a note to write a letter to the editor, praising the efforts of the medical profession and the hospitals.

"More tea?" her waitress asked.

Savannah looked up and smiled. "Yes, thank you, Berna."

As Berna moved away, Savannah saw Nathan looking over his menu. Her heart nearly stopped. *What's he doing here? This couldn't be a coincidence.* Nathan knew she generally ate lunch in this restaurant. They had often eaten lunch there together. She returned her attention to the article, but the page was a mass of confusion. She couldn't think, much less read. Briefly, she closed her eyes, trying to inhale normally. Letter to the editor, she prompted herself, as she attempted to refocus. Refocus. She had tried so often to refocus, but thoughts of Nathan kept getting in the way. She missed him terribly, but apparently, he hadn't missed her.

She and Nathan had many friends in common. He was seen on numerous occasions with Gail, her friends reported. He had moved on, she sighed, but she was having difficulty doing the same. She turned down dates, invitations to parties and receptions, and opted to stay at home or visit with her brother and nephews rather than chance running into Nathan and Gail together on the social scene, but she found no solace there.

Everywhere in her town house reminded her of Nathan. Sitting on her back deck overlooking the Canal. Going out alone proved to be just as disconcerting. She always ended up going to places where she and Nathan had gone. Maybe she needed a change of scene; somewhere she and Nathan had not been together. Aruba, she thought. No, that wouldn't do. They had planned to go there in the fall. Maybe she would take a cruise on one of those floating bordellos that stopped at several islands. Yes, they had not been on a cruise together nor had they talked about it. In fact, Nathan hated cruises. They had gone out on a private yacht for an evening with people from the State Department. Nathan was never comfortable on the water. He was a great swimmer, but boats made him nervous. Perhaps a cruise was the answer for her. She would certainly meet new people and....

"Savannah," Nathan's low, melodious voice broke her consentration.

Her heart tripped, as she looked up at him standing next to her table.

"Good afternoon, Nathan," she said, covering her anxiety with a cool response. She looked around him, scanning the area.

"Waiting for someone, were you?" he asked, noticing her motion.

"No, just looking for Ms. Hot Buns," she said. "If you're here, she must be somewhere in the vicinity."

Nathan smiled. "Uh, you mean Gail. No, not that I know of. Mind if I join you?"

Savannah shrugged. "Suit yourself."

Nathan sat across from her. He had waited as long as he could before approaching her. She was so much a part of him, he felt disconnected when they were not together. That's what prompted his visit to find her. Now, sitting across from her, he knew he made a mistake. Seeing her, but not touching her, not even for a kiss, was wrenching his gut.

"I haven't seen you around with the old crowd lately. You must be keeping busy."

"Yes, my practice has grown considerably."

"You were thinking about bringing on another partner to share the load. Have you thought more about that?"

"Yes, I've considered it, but I haven't made a decision yet. Vivian Alexander Montgomery offered a full partnership opportunity with her former husband's medical practice."

"What are you waiting for, Savannah? That's a great opportunity. You would be at liberty to bring on junior partners to help with your patient load. You know you spend too much time working as it is. You need to make time for yourself and for—" Nathan cut off his thought. There he was, right back where they started. Her schedule at the hospital and his schedule in high-level negotiations rarely left them much time to be together.

"You were about to say?" she quizzed.

"I was about to say you should make more time for yourself and your family," he covered diplomatically. "Now that Jefferson has his sons, I suspect he'll need you to help him with them."

"Jefferson is capable of handling his family, but I do enjoy spending time with them. In fact, my nephews have conned me into taking them to Disney World for a week. Jefferson is not going with us. He's going to start work on his next book."

"Disney World," he mused. "We were there, when? Two years ago, was it?"

"Yes, then we flew to Cancun for the weekend. We rented that little villa on the—" Savannah cut off her thought. The recollection of that time caused a lump to form in her throat. Any moment she felt like she might burst into tears. She felt that way many times since she and Nathan called it quits. Especially when she found him in Gail's arms. The vision was still jarring. She shivered slightly, rubbing her arms briskly and looking down at her notes. She couldn't look up into Nathan's handsome face without wanting to touch him, to kiss his mouth, and let their tongues dance together.

Nathan's heart was pumping so strongly in his chest he didn't immediately register the vibration of the device on his belt. Then he checked the message and knew today was perhaps the last time he would see Savannah for a very long time, if ever again. The thought registered in his mind, but not in his heart.

"Uh, I have to go," he said blankly. He looked into her eyes and nearly crumbled. "Savannah, I wanted you to know I still—"

"Good afternoon, Savannah," a voice came breaking into their concentration on each other.

They both turned to see Jacob Hawkins standing by the table.

"Your nursing assistant told me I would probably find you here, but she didn't mention you were lunching with Mr. Flack."

"Hawkins," Nathan acknowledged, as he stood and shook Jacob's hand. "Savannah and I bumped in to each other and I was just leaving," he said, looking at Savannah.

Savannah wanted to leap out of her seat and fly into Nathan's arms, but she sat rooted to her spot.

"Savannah, take care of yourself," Nathan said.

"I'll take care of her," Jacob interjected.

Nathan looked at Jacob Hawkins with a focus that could kill. He didn't comment, but looked at Savannah one last time. He loved her, but he had to leave her.

When Nathan departed, Savannah's emotions were in turmoil, but one emotion was very lucid—anger. "How dare you tell Nathan that 'you'll take care of me'!" she raged. "I've told you Nathan is very important to me and I won't tolerate you trying to belittle him!"

"'Important to you?' Ha! Is that what you call it when you can't call it love? Are you in love with him, Savannah? Do you see yourself married to that stuffed shirt? Raising little stuffed shirts? No, I doubt that seriously. You're a passionate woman, my dear. You have an unquenchable thirst for life, love, and adventure."

"You're wrong, Jacob! I do love Nathan, very much!"

"Really," he said, snorting. "Then go to him. Profess your undying love—and your desire to be his bride or—"

"Or what?"

"Or stop the charade of this pretend love and come with me to Greece for the week. I have some business to take care of there."

"No, I'm busy," she said, but the idea appealed to her. She was still basically a country bumpkin. Seeing exotic places with those who could afford to use it as a playground was fascinating.

"Too busy to marry Flack or too busy to come to Greece?"

"Both or either!" she fumed, stacking her papers and preparing to leave.

"My car will pick you up at nine in the morning. Pack nothing. I have a yacht there. We'll cruise the Greek Isles," he said confidently.

"Go to hell, Jacob!" she snapped, as she rushed out of the restaurant.

Jacob pulled a cell phone from his pocket and pushed one button. A voice answered.

"It begins," Jacob said and then hung up. Looking at a man seated a short distance away, Jacob motioned with his head. The man nodded, got to his feet, and followed Savannah out of the restaurant.

CHAPTER 21

Jefferson read over his notes, and then picked up the microphone to begin dictating another chapter for his most recent manuscript into his laptop. He had been working for two days straight and frequently lost track of the time. He hadn't remembered how tiring writing could be. His neck muscles were tense and his body needed to stretch. He shut down his computer, stood, and stretched. The clock on the wall said he had missed lunch and the dinner hour had come and gone. The cabin was too quiet with his sons away with Savannah for the week. He wanted to go with his boys, but Savannah wanted to have them all to herself. She thought his sons might relax and talk more freely if he weren't along. Perhaps she was right, but having idle time was something Jefferson was totally unaccustomed to, and the walls of the huge cabin were beginning to close in around him.

He decided a walk might be what he needed to flex his muscles and shake off the cabin fever. When he left the house, he had no set direction or purpose in mind, but like a magnet, he was drawn to walk around the lake past Dakota's cabin. It had been a week since he last saw her. Just after Bill left, she made herself scarce. It bothered him not to see and be with her. He enjoyed their talks together and his sons were still captivated by her. He wondered what she was doing and decided it would not be inappropriate for him to simply stop by.

Before he reached the house, he saw her swimming alone in the lake. He walked through the woods beside her cabin and stood on her dock, watching. Then he stripped down to his shorts and dove into the water.

Dakota heard someone coming through the woods, then saw Jefferson standing on the dock. Their eyes locked and she was helpless to turn away.

The thrill that went through her when she watched him peeling off his clothes was like electricity, a jolt that came hard and unexpected. He was a magnificent specimen of a man. Strong and virile. Too much man for her, she thought, but something about him sparked more than a few dreams and emotions. Dreams she never experienced before and emotions she didn't know what to do with.

Jefferson didn't know or understand what instinct told him to swim to her, but the warm water over his tight muscles didn't cause his body to relax. His heart rate quickened and his breathing deepened. He reached her in what seemed like an eternity, but was only a matter of seconds.

"You shouldn't swim alone," he said, as they treaded water and he wiped the water from his face. "Especially this late in the day."

"I'm a good swimmer and I'm not afraid to swim alone."

"You said you sometimes get a cramp or a Charlie horse. What would happen if you experienced that when no one was around?"

It surprised her he remembered her ruse to cover the limp she was developing, but then it shouldn't have. Nothing much escaped scrutiny where Jefferson Logan was concerned. She hoped he didn't notice how much his mere nearness intrigued and fascinated her.

"I can take care of myself."

"No doubt you can, but while Bill is away—"

"So you think I need a man to watch over me?" If only he knew, she thought privately. However, she couldn't tell him she led highly-skilled agents.

"I'm not being chauvinistic, just cautious. Look, I like to swim, so why don't we make an agreement to swim together? That way you can look after me and I can look after you. That's fair, don't you think?"

"What happens when one of us is unavailable?"

"Then the other one agrees not to swim alone."

Dakota smiled. "Is that how you diplomatic types handle your negotiations? Having it your way regardless of the opposition?"

"Basically," he said, "but we do it diplomatically. Unlike you business types who razzle dazzle your customers into agreeing to buy products they don't need."

"Yes, but we do it with showmanship."

She found herself more intrigued with their easy reparteè, his company, a new emotion—enjoyment—she thought.

"You've successfully avoided my suggestion."

"I'll consider your offer."

"We should set a time limit on these negotiations. Say until we reach the dock."

"Further setting the perimeters of the negotiations, I see," she said, as she began to swim toward the dock.

Jefferson followed and kept pace with her long, smooth strokes. When they reached the dock, they both hoisted themselves aboard and sat on the edge, dangling their feet in the water. Jefferson was feeling something he never felt before, something akin to an awakening. A revival of his spirit and soul. Just talking with Dakota alone and quietly without pretense or purpose, short of getting to know her better, was unmatched with other women he had known.

With other women, the pretense was often less important than the purpose. They wanted sex. Sex without feeling or emotion. That's what Felicia had wanted from him, too, and he had given it to her amid her threats she would do bodily harm to herself or to their children. Emotional terrorism, he called it at the time, but sitting here with Dakota, all of his prior life with Felicia, except for his sons, seemed inconsequential. For his sons, he blessed the days she had borne them.

He looked at Dakota, her long, thick, black, slick hair dripping streams of water down her back. Droplets streaming down her face onto her full, round bosom and disappearing beneath the unadorned, black, one-piece bathing suit. He reached out and tucked an errant strand of hair behind her ear while she twisted her hair to wring out the lake water.

"Now, to bring closure to these negotiations," he began.

"I didn't agree to any of the terms or conditions you set, Mr. Ambassador. From my perspective, we have no deal to close."

Dakota shifted slightly and shivered.

"Cold?" Jefferson asked, his voice low and warming.

"No, I'm fine," she said absently, flipping her hair over her shoulder and looking away from him to sights of other people who were now coming to boat on or swim in the lake. There was a group of young women crewing. The coxswain's shouts clear on the quiet lake.

Dakota couldn't imagine what came over her. She never felt the agitation growing inside her before. The sensation that sprung from her loins hardened her nipples into peaks. Her core contracted, fighting off the sensuousness of his gesture. He had acted so quickly, her reflex did not engage, but her breath became labored. She was trembling, but not from a chill. She had to move quickly. She started to get to her feet, but as she stood up her left leg buckled her.

Jefferson was on his feet in a flash and caught Dakota before she fell.

"What is it?" he asked, as he hooked his powerful arm around her.

"A Charlie horse," she answered, while attempting to ease out of his hold on her. "As you know, I sometimes get them. It's just muscle tension."

She tried to walk, but could only limp; the burning sensation in her leg was excruciating.

"A Charlie horse, huh?" Jefferson easily lifted her into his arms. For a tall, well-built woman, she felt lightweight. He looked into the surprise on her face. "Put your arms around my neck," he ordered.

"Put me down. This is not necessary," she said, squirming. "I can walk."

Jefferson lowered her to her feet, stood back with his arms akimbo and waited. "Okay, then walk."

Dakota sucked in a deep breath and tried to take a step. Again, she began to fall, but Jefferson had her in his arms, holding her against his massive chest.

"Uh huh," he intoned. "No more argument. Put your arms around my neck and hold on," he said, as he easily lifted and carried her to her cabin.

Dakota complied and moments later, they were inside. Jefferson carried her to her loft and laid her on her bed.

"Where's the telephone?" he asked.

"Telephone?"

"Yes, the thing that Alexander Graham Bell invented," he remarked with no small amount of sarcasm laced in his voice.

"I don't have one," she fussed.

"You mean your husband leaves you alone in this isolated area without a telephone? I don't think so. Besides, you work for a high-tech communications engineering company."

Dakota exhaled in exasperation. "In the drawer," she said, nodding toward a nightstand.

Jefferson opened the drawer and retrieved the cell phone. Quickly, he punched in a number.

Hours later, Jefferson closed the front door of Dakota's cabin behind the doctors who he summoned. He slowly climbed the steps, deep in thought. The doctors told him she likely had a severely pinched nerve in her spine or hip and needed complete bed rest for at least a week. They could not offer more information without a series of tests, which Dakota refused to take. He looked up as he climbed the spiral staircase to her loft and noticed Dakota wrapping herself in her robe.

"You're not supposed to be on your feet," he said, as he reached the top step.

"I'm much better now. It wasn't necessary for you to call in all of those doctors. I told you it was nothing."

"Nothing is when you have a slight ache or pain, but you, my dear, Mrs. Sinclair-Chandler, have far more than an ache and you know it. Now why don't we get down to the facts? You have a very serious condition. I think I should call your husband, don't you?"

"My husband...uh, no. This mission is too important. I'll call someone else to stay with me."

"Who? Who are you going to call, Dakota?" he asked, holding the cell phone out toward her.

Dakota couldn't think of anyone to call. She had no close friends and, certainly, no family she knew of. Her team was on various missions with less than a third bivouacked nearby on R&R. She couldn't call her handler or her superior. To do so would be an admission her condition was not improving. She stared at the cell phone and then turned away.

"I'll think of someone. You needn't stay here. The boys will be worried."

"My sons are in Florida with Savannah. So, I'm staying," he said, looking into her eyes.

Dakota knew in an instant Jefferson Logan was not a man who could be dismissed. His jaw was resolutely set and his mesmerizing gaze inflamed her.

"The doctors said you need to keep your muscles toned and I'm just the man to do that. Lay back," he said, sitting beside her on the bed.

Dakota followed his order and stretched out on the bed. Jefferson took one leg and massaged it, stretching, bending, and flexing as the doctors instructed. Then he began on the other. He soothed her with calming conversation until her eyes began to close. Once she was asleep, Jefferson stood and looked down at the sleeping beauty. Her flawless earthy, reddish-light brown complexion looked so smooth, soft, and supple. He inhaled, fighting the want of her, and walked down the steps and out the door.

Dakota waited until she heard the door close behind Jefferson before she moved. She couldn't let him stay. All she feared would have been lost. His touch was too warm, too tantalizing, and too erotic. She knew him to be a gentleman. He would leave only if he thought she was asleep. Yet, how could she sleep? His touch had inflamed her.

She thought that now, as she recalled the night when she stole into his cabin in search of the camera. When she couldn't find it in the boys' rooms, she searched everywhere, including Jefferson's room while he slept. She stood over his prone body, but for a brief few seconds, wondering whether he sensed her uneasiness about having her picture taken and then hid the camera. Dismissing that thought from her mind was relatively easy, but dismissing the finely chiseled outline of his physique from her thoughts was a wholly impossible task. Her mind wondered what it would feel like to have him atop her, touching her, kissing her.

With monumental effort, she pulled her thoughts away from him and continued her thorough search, but turned up nothing.

Jefferson was only gone long enough to shower, change his clothes, and eat a sandwich. He knew with his sons away, being near Dakota was his top priority. Reentering her cabin, he took up his position on the sofa. Above him, she lay sleeping, he thought, as he continued to put chapters of his manuscript into his laptop using the new Dragon app. The hours grew into night and darkness descended. He had completed three chapters, but all the while Dakota was still on his mind.

Instinctively, he looked up to find her staring down at him from her loft. For a humming moment, they simply stared at each other without a word passing between them, but something was communicated.

"You're not supposed to be out of bed," he finally said, rising from his seat and slowly climbing the stairs, two at a time. His eyes never left hers. They stood, scrutinizing each other.

"I cannot lay there like a lump on a log," she said unemotionally. "I have a lot of work to do in preparation for the upcoming trip to the African continent."

"Doctor's orders," he said, helping her while she limped back to her bed.

"More like Logan's orders," she muttered, frustrated.

Jefferson laughed. "Yes, that, too."

His laugh was infectious and Dakota smiled. Jefferson's heart nearly burst.

"Now that wasn't so bad, was it?"

"What?" She quizzically tilted her head to one side.

"The smile. You smiled at me."

"Oh," she said, embarrassed by her momentary lapse. His gaze was so penetrating she looked away.

"You know, you always do that," he said, craning his neck to find her face.

Dakota dropped her eyes, not wanting to look up into his, but her focus settled on the hard plane of his muscular chest under the sheath of his white T-shirt.

"Do what?" she asked, not looking up.

Jefferson put a finger under her chin and raised her face until her eyes met his. "You try not to blush when I look at you. You always look away from me."

"I, uh, guess it's a learned response."

"From what?"

"My childhood."

"Oh? Tell me about it."

"What's there to know?"

"That's what I'm asking you."

"That was a long time ago. It's of no consequence now."

"A long time ago? You're what, late twenties, early thirties?"

"I'm not as young as I used to be." She smiled slightly, massaging the cramp in her leg.

"Nor are you as old as you will be." He smiled back at her. He moved her hands away and began his own ministration. "Now start at the beginning and bring me up-to-date. You were an orphan, am I right?"

His question startled her. "It's not important," she said, anxiety edging her voice. His hands were strong, firm, but soft on her skin.

"Apparently, it is. You still—"

"Perhaps you should get back to whatever it was you were doing," she suggested, again removing his hands from her skin and turning away from him. She remembered all too vividly the lack of tenderness or touch that was her childhood. Suddenly, she wanted someone to hold her. To ward off the pain and hurt that was present in years gone by and creeping into her consciousness all too often now. For too many reasons, none of which she could talk about, that person could not be Jefferson Logan.

Jefferson saw the flickering hurt and something more in Dakota's eyes. Suddenly, he swept her up in his arms and, before he knew what he was doing, his mouth covered hers. Dakota pushed back against his chest, but he held her fast. His kiss was soft, yet possessive. Urgent, but tender. Never before had her heart beat so fast and furiously in her chest. Her breathing quickened when his tongue beckoned at the entry to her mouth. She began to relax, caught up in the fascination of the feel, texture, and taste of his mouth.

Jefferson was so deeply caught up in the moment his mind blanked while his senses took over. Then he felt her relax and nearly go limp in his arms. Confusion edged his senses, but his urgency was in the velvet-soft recesses of her mouth. He felt her flinch when he caressed her face. Slowly, he lifted her arms to his shoulders, stroking the length of them lightly.

Dakota didn't understand what was driving her—an instinct or an emotion—but she melted into it. It felt good and strangely right. She allowed him into her mouth and vaguely heard and felt a groan. She couldn't distinguish whether it came from her or him.

Jefferson knew he wanted more from her. More than he had wanted from any woman, but he sensed Dakota had already gone too far for her own comfort—and there was still the question of Bill Chandler. Felicia's infidelities during their marriage came back to him. He was faithful to her, although he was not in love with her. After her death, he never took another man's wife to his bed. He wanted Dakota more than he ever wanted any other woman, but he would not take her until he knew what was going on between her and Bill Chandler. What was clear in his mind was he would have her. He would make her his or severely suffer trying. He didn't want to let her go, but he knew he had to do it or his mind would not take control of his body. He struggled with his decision, but discretion won.

Dakota felt strange when Jefferson released her. Like a million little electric shocks were prickling her skin, causing goose bumps to form. She drew in a ragged breath, looked down at her hands, and tucked her lips inside of her mouth. She could still taste him, but she didn't know how to react—what to do with what she was feeling, then he spoke.

"I should apologize for kissing you, but I won't. It would be a lie if I said it and I don't want to have lies between us." Now it was his turn to look away. "I've wanted to do that from the first day I saw you in London several years ago."

"Then, if you won't apologize, I'll settle for your pledge that it won't happen again," she said, gaining some sense of composure.

Jefferson shook his head. "No, that would be another lie."

"Jefferson, I'm married to Bill, remember?"

"I've said I want no lies between us, Dakota. For whatever reason you and Bill want to carry on this charade, go ahead, but you haven't convinced me there's anything between you two except friendship."

"Marriages have been built on far less than that," she said defensively.

"Of that, I'm well aware."

"Perhaps your marriage would have lasted longer if you hadn't kissed every woman you met after knowing her for only a month," she said, still looking away.

That statement cut deep. Jefferson was aware the tabloids had painted him as some sort of Casanova or Don Juan, but the truth be told, his conquests, if they were that at all, he could count on one hand. The women in question had, for the most part, used him for their own purposes—to make their husbands or men friends jealous, to kiss and tell for the momentary notoriety that such liaisons garnered, or for more nefarious reasons, like to gain what they perceived as valuable information for their political or business interests.

No woman truly loved him, not even Felicia. The type of loving and caring relationship his parents shared escaped him for his entire adulthood. He had a lot locked away, waiting for the opportunity to show a woman how deeply he could care, but none of the women in his life wanted to unlock or unleash his tide of affection. He knew that going into each liaison. It did not matter as much then as it did now. With Dakota, it did matter for some reason that was not clear to him at the moment, it mattered a hell of a lot.

"Apparently, you've been reading the tabloids' accounts of my life. That's unfortunate. It's true my life has had its blunders. Making mistakes is a part of life and living, and I've learned from those missteps. I never repeat the same lapses twice."

Jefferson rose from his seat beside Dakota and walked down the curved staircase to the sofa below. Dakota could see the pain in his eyes, although he tried to hide it. She leaned her head back against the headboard, closed her eyes, and gritted her teeth. *Why did I do that? Why did I dig for something to ease my anxiety about someone wanting to comfort me, hold me, or even touch my life? It was how I dealt with every man who had shown me a modicum of kindness—especially Bill, and now Jefferson. Emotions! Me and Mr. Spock must have come from the same gene pool.*

CHAPTER 22

S ir, we have what we think you've been waiting for," Jeremy, the attorney said, confidently handing a stack of photographs to his boss. "These photos demonstrate that Logan is of low moral character. Surely the court will acknowledge—"

"You call this *incriminating*?" he shouted angrily, flinging the pictures in the man's face. "Damn you, you moron! I pay good American money, and a lot of it, for you to bring me pictures of Logan swimming with the Sinclair woman? In an open lake? In broad daylight? The boys weren't even there! Idiots! The whole lot of you are idiots!" He grabbed Jeremy's shirt near the collar and jerked him forward. Then he lowered his voice to a guttural growl. "Now you go back and get me something I can use! Pictures of them in bed together in some perverse sex act! Preferably with animals in the act with them!" He pushed Jeremy away and the man stumbled backward, attempting to gain some poise.

"Sir, Logan hasn't done anything 'perverse' that we know of. He's even been circumspect with the relationships he has had since—"

"He's Black! All Blacks revert to their animalistic instincts sooner or later! Get me something on him or you won't be able to find a job chasing ambulances! Don't fail me again!"

"But, Sir…" Jeremy tried to protest, but saw the rage building in his boss' eyes. He made a speedy retreat. We didn't want to get slapped again.

"TM, you're going at this from the wrong angle," another man sitting in the room said calmly, as he rolled a cigarillo between his fingertips.

"What do you mean 'the wrong angle'? I'm going at this from *every* direction! You want to do business with me, you'll do as I said! I don't take kindly to some half—"

The man rose menacingly from his seat, narrowed his eyes, and pointed his cigarillo at Tyler Montrose. "You're a racist pig, old bastard. Remember who you're talking to before your mouth writes a check your body can't cash. You came to me, remember? I don't like you, nor do I need you. There are twenty other companies I can use to get what I want."

"The hell you say!" Montrose bellowed.

The man flicked his ash on the rich, ankle-deep, Aubusson carpet and grinned menacingly. "In fact, when that oldest boy turns sixteen, Logan will have you by the balls. I may have to reconsider my position and perhaps strike a deal with—"

"It'll never happen! I'll kill Logan first before I'll let that happen!"

The man stuck the cigarillo between his teeth, grinned, and turned to leave. "That's what I thought," he said, as he reached the door. "And you call your flunky an idiot," he said, laughing.

"You just do what I tell you!" Montrose bellowed to the closing door. He then moved toward a telephone on his desk and dialed one number. Shortly a voice answered.

"Yes, Sir?"

"What's the delay?"

"These are delicate matters, Sir. Maneuvering Logan into a trap isn't going to be as easy as we thought. Flack is doing a credible job. He's no lightweight when it comes to negotiating."

"Then put Plan B into operation!"

"It's too soon, Sir. Someone is already suspicious about our opposition to Flack in the first place. That's why the mission was delayed. We can't have a hint of involvement if we're going to be successful. Plan B has to appear to have been executed by terrorists."

"I know what Plan B is, you fool! I'm tired of waiting! Now get me some action!"

"Yes, Sir, but it's not you who could end up in prison for the rest of your life, if anything goes wrong. I've got a wife and family to think about."

"You won't have anything if you fail me!"

CHAPTER 23

Jefferson moved around the kitchen, confidently putting the finishing touches on the breakfast tray he made for Dakota. He tried to keep his attention on what he was doing, but thoughts of her plagued him the entire night. He had gotten very little sleep after reviewing his notes and attempting to begin another chapter. Something was nagging at the edges of his consciousness. *Innocence*, he thought. That was what he couldn't quite reach in Dakota's reaction to his kiss. She did not respond, as other women would have. She didn't push him away with indignation or lace her retorts with sarcasm. Rather she seemed *unschooled* in the womanly wiles.

He stopped his work and thought back on his previous encounters with her. Clearly, she was totally oblivious to the effect she had on men. She didn't carry herself as if the world should bow to her beauty. She was more guileless in her behavior than calculating. *How could that be?* She was a devastatingly beautiful woman and didn't wear a speck of makeup to enhance her looks. Certainly, men dropped at her feet. Bill was obviously one of them, although his apparent sexual proclivities would mitigate against that possibility. Yet, there was still something that didn't compute. He rolled the thoughts around in his head, and then dismissed them.

Picking up the tray, he climbed the steps to the loft. Dakota was still sleeping. He stood a moment, gazing at her and wondering what to make of her behavior. Then she moved and her eyes opened. She stared at him and then sat up, confusion on her face.

"What are you doing?" she asked, as the sleep cleared from her head.

"Serving breakfast to you in bed," Jefferson said, as he sat the tray down across her lap.

"Breakfast?" she asked still confused. "Why did you do that?"

"It's morning. People usually have breakfast in the morning, but if you'd prefer lunch or dinner..."

"Jefferson, I—"

"I hoped that you'd call me Jeff. Most of the people I serve breakfast to in the morning call me Jeff."

"You're in the habit of serving people breakfast in bed?"

"I've been known to do that. Lunch and dinner sometimes, too. Rarely all three with the same people. You'll be my first."

"First? You mean you intend to stay here? With me? In this cabin?"

"Gets a little awkward serving breakfast, lunch, and dinner to you in my bed, in my sister's cabin, wouldn't you say? However, if you'd prefer that—"

"Your bed?" she asks suspiciously.

"That's usually where people are served breakfast in bed," he said, thoroughly enjoying teasing her. She was absolutely delightful.

She was so refreshing, he thought. As if this had never happened to her. Surely, with other men she's had the occasional breakfast tray. Oddly enough, though, nothing he found out about her so far gave any insight to the men she had been with. She was never married, at least, not under her name—except for this camouflage with Chandler. At the moment, however, he didn't care to know about the other men in her life. He was enjoying her innocence and remarkably taken with her sensuousness sitting in bed. He was beginning to feel his nature rise. Nothing he would have enjoyed more than slipping between the sheets with her in his arms, but he knew she would be out of that bed in a flash, if he made that type of move on her. In fact, as much as he wanted to sleep with her, he wanted something more. He wanted to know her—completely.

"*Bon appétite*," he said. He started to rise to walk away and then turned back to her. He kissed her gently on the forehead, and then smiled. "Good morning." Then he kissed her nose and her mouth.

When their lips parted, Dakota felt her breasts tingling and the hardness of her nipples surprised her. When she felt the current throbbing between her thighs, her eyes widened. *What was happening to her?* When he kissed her last night she could have sworn the earth suddenly moved. Now her head was spinning and her heart was beating like Sioux war drums against her chest. She began to tremble and took a silent deep breath. Maybe she was coming down with something, she thought, although she never remembered ever being sick before. She looked up into his eyes, then quickly away.

"Good morning," she mumbled and pretended to be interested in the food on the tray. Actually, she had no appetite whatsoever.

Jefferson was always around over the next three days, as Dakota struggled to get her body to respond to exercise. Now, though, Jefferson watched over her, not letting her work too long or too hard at any time. Although he was often in close proximity to her, he did not attempt to touch her as he had before. She became accustomed to hearing him moving around in the cabin both day and night. There were periods of time when he would leave the cabin to take a long walk with Hercules, go to his cabin to shower and shave, or to the country store for more groceries, but he always returned in no time. He wasn't a bad cook, she thought to herself. Those times seemed strange because, although she cherished her quiet domain, his presence added a dimension she missed when he was away.

Dakota heard Jefferson coming before his foot hit the porch. She quickly picked up the book and pretended to be reading when he entered the cabin. She looked up briefly at him as he shifted the logs he carried in a sling from one hand to the other.

"How are you doing?" he asked, as he moved toward the fireplace. He dropped the wood on the floor and shook off his coat. Rain pounded on the standing-seam roof of the cabin and the night was pitch-black.

"I'm fine, but what is that for?" she asked, nodding toward the wood.

"It's cold in here. It's summer, but it feels like a fall chill."

"It's not cold. It's just dry air. These mountains are like that even in the summer. In the Siouan, in the Rocky Mountains, no one would notice the temperature."

"Is that where you grew up?" he asked, as he stacked the wood in the fireplace.

"Yes," she said, aware she said more than she should.

"Tell me about it."

"Some other time," she said, returning to her book. "I'm reading now."

As he stacked the wood in the fireplace, he stopped and looked over his shoulder at her. She seemed nervous to him. Probably cabin fever, he surmised. He sensed she was not a woman who spent a lot of time indoors. Hard to do for someone who was supposed to be a Vice President for a telecommunications company. Then he noticed the book.

"What are you reading?" he asked.

"J. California Cooper's *Some—*" she caught herself. "A book by J. California Cooper."

"I've read her before. I like her work," he said, as he lit the kindling he had stacked before he left. Then he stood and walked over to her, lifted the book from her hands and turned the book right side up. "But I don't have the skill it takes to read her work upside down." He handed the book back to her.

Caught, she thought. How foolish! The nervous tension she seemed to feel whenever he was around made her do things she had never done before. Why, she didn't know.

Jefferson took the book from her hands again and put it on the sofa table.

"Dakota, I'm about to do something and I want you to know it before I do it."

"What?" she asked, looking up at him quizzically.

He bent and kissed her mouth and then backed away.

"I'm going to kiss you."

"You already have, it seems. I thought you weren't going to do that anymore."

"You *hoped* I wouldn't, but I never promised you that I wouldn't. In fact, I told you I would. I'll tell you something else."

"What's that?"

"I'm going to do it again."

Jefferson's passion rose as he kissed Dakota. He knew he was in trouble and started to move away, but tentatively Dakota put her arms around his neck and he groaned deep in his core. Slowly, he laid her back on the wide divan and slid in beside her. Her mouth opened to him and he was totally lost in the feeling. Gently, he pulled her to him, stroking her back. She arched like a sated cat and her breast teased his chest. He pulled her leg over him and felt her trembling. He pulled away and looked into her eyes.

"What is it?" he asked, searching her face and still stroking her leg comfortingly.

"I don't know what I'm doing. I don't know what you're doing to me... but, I, uh. I, uh, like it."

Jefferson smiled. "I kissed you. That's all."

"You've done this before, haven't you?"

He grinned. "Yes, from time to time I've kissed a woman."

"I mean you've seduced women."

"It generally hasn't been classified as a seduction. It was by mutual consent."

Dakota raised her eyes to him slowly. "Would you seduce me?"

The question was surprising, but Jefferson didn't think she was joking with him.

"You've seduced me every day since the moment I first saw you and now you want me to seduce you?"

"If you don't want to, I'll understand," she said, dropping her eyes to a spot on his broad chest. Anything was preferable to looking into his eyes.

Now Jefferson was really confused. He was beginning to feel like a teenager. Refreshed and alive. His phallus was straining against his jeans and she was questioning whether he wanted to seduce her? He didn't want to think about it. He needed her. He wanted her. Damn it, he craved her. He loosened the rawhide that held her hair together and let it fall to her shoulders and down her back. Then he stroked her face.

"I want to and I will, but you'll have to be patient with me. I haven't seduced a woman in a lot of years."

He began to kiss her again. Dakota melted into him. She knew that she was out of her element, but didn't know what universe she was spinning in. He held her so gently, so possessively, she moaned involuntarily. She had always been in full possession of her faculties, never permitting herself to be off center, but Jefferson's quiet strength had her teetering on the brink of an abyss she had never felt or known before.

Jefferson wanted her more than he wanted his next breath, but he wanted answers before he would let his passion loose. First and foremost, he wanted the truth. He wanted to know whether she was truly another man's wife.

CHAPTER 24

At the end of the week in Florida, Savannah was no closer to quelling her nervous energy than she was when she decided to bring her nephews on vacation with her. They had toured most of Disney World, spending the majority of their time at Epcot Center. She was feeling weary from the daily routine of spending the entire day at the park, walking from one exhibit to the next and riding through each of the presentations from different countries. She was relieved to be leaving, assured her nephews had enjoyed their stay. Spending this much time with them had never before been on the top of her agenda, but now she needed it. She needed it more than she had realized. She was a gynecologist and obstetrician by profession, but never felt the necessity to do anything more than deliver the little golden nuggets to their happy parents. Having a family of her own was something that was at the bottom of her eye chart in minute letters. These days, her eyesight was getting better though. Now she could see whom she wanted in her life, if only it weren't too late. She sighed and continued packing her luggage for the trip back to Washington, DC.

Savannah walked into her cabin and saw her brother standing on the deck. He looked contemplative, and initially she didn't want to disturb him, but, of course, his boys didn't share her reticence. Stephen had rounded the house, yelling for Hercules and then for his father. Savannah watched through the glass wall as Jefferson engulfed Stephen in his massive arms, Hercules caught between them. She smiled to herself at the loving scene and remembered how Stevie's conversation during the previous week often included his father, while Miles had been less inclusive. Miles had listened, though, when she talked about how wonderful Jefferson was to her when they were children and how he had taken care of her, albeit long distance, when they were older and away at different schools. Jefferson Junior was unimpressed by any of it, still harboring what Savannah thought were deep pains of resentment toward his brothers' willingness to give their father a chance to prove his love for them. Eventually, she thought, even Jefferson Junior would have to let go of some of the animosity that seemed to consume him.

"The boys tell me they had a great time," Jefferson said, to Savannah as he came into the cabin and hugged her.

"Uh, yes, they did," she said and returned his hug. Something in his face was different though. She leaned back in his embrace and smiled curiously. "What's this I see in your eyes?"

Jefferson snorted around a smile. "Relaxation. I've forgotten how necessary it is to the human condition."

Savannah wasn't convinced. She held on to Jefferson and cocked a doubtful eye at him. "Sure, and if you think I believe that, I've got some prime swampland I'll give you for a good price." She eyed him more closely. "You know, Jeff, if I didn't know better, I'd swear you look ten years younger."

Jefferson didn't think it showed that much in his demeanor, but obviously his last seven days with Dakota had given him a new lease on life. He remembered every minute with more than a healthy dose of physical reaction. Never would he have believed she was…

"Jeff?"

"Uh, yes," he answered, coming back to the present.

"What's with you? You seem positively stellar."

Jefferson grinned, but kept his own council. "Glad you're all home and safe."

"Safe? Why wouldn't we be safe?"

"Nothing, it's nothing."

Again, Savannah wasn't convinced. She had never seen stars in Jefferson's eyes before, but those dark pools held universes. She wanted to investigate further, but she had to leave. She was going to work the next day and needed time to relax at home before she went in to face her patients. She'd get back to her brother's all-too-apparent change later in the week. For now, she needed to get back to the city and relax.

Savannah walked into her town house and immediately knew someone else was in her home. The table in the dining room was set, candles were glowing in the darkened room, wine was chilling in an ice bucket, and soft music, her favorite, was playing in the background. A grin rimmed her lips. Then she heard someone moving around in her kitchen and smelled the aromas of tantalizing food. She was starving, but if her senses were right, what she hungered for—Nathan—was about to be satisfied.

It would not be the first time he had surprised her with a home-cooked meal and then a night of pampering and passion when she got home from a long day at work. Excitement tingling her body as she slipped out of her shoes and stripped down to the provocative teddy she was wearing under her clothes. She flipped out the light she had turned on when she came in and padded toward the kitchen. She couldn't help the grin that flushed her face.

He was back! He had gotten over their silly squabble and he was ready to pick up where they had left off. She closed her eyes and inhaled the tantalizing aromas. He was a helluva good cook—in bed. He made her sizzle. She entered the kitchen and saw the firm bottom of a man wearing a long robe, bending to search the refrigerator. She snuck up behind him, cupped him, and began exercising him unmercifully.

"God, I've missed you," she said, wrapping her arms around his waist to his front and laying her head against his back. She felt him hardening in her hand and pressed her body closer. "When did you get home? Never mind. Just make love to me. I need you now."

The man stood and turned in her embrace.

"The feeling is mutual. Here on the kitchen table or floor?" he said, grinning.

Savannah drew back, shocked. "*Jacob! What the hell?* How did you get in?"

"Foolish question, don't you think, Savannah? I own several corporations. One of them makes security systems. I simply flew one of my engineers in and he opened the door and turned off your security equipment, but that's such a boring topic. I'd rather go back to your first suggestion—kitchen table or the floor?"

"Out, Jacob!" she bellowed, pointing an arrow-straight arm, hand, and finger toward the front door. "Get out now or I'll call the police and have you arrested!"

Jacob laughed derisively. Then he leveled his gaze over her teddy-clad body. Wordlessly, he moved toward her, untying the sash and letting his robe fall to the floor. Savannah couldn't deny that the man was eye candy. She looked her fill, backed away, and started to leave the room, but too quickly, Jacob had her. With one hand, he held her neck and pulled her against him while with the other hand he ripped the teddy from her body. Like a deer caught in the headlights of an oncoming truck, Savannah froze as Jacob assaulted her body with light, mesmerizing kisses. She trembled involuntarily. With one hand, Jacob swept everything from her kitchen table onto the floor, laid her bare body on the cold marble, and spread her legs far apart. Then he stood and regarded her, his hands moving lightly over her, touching every inch.

Her body reacted to the exquisite pleasure and massiveness of his erection. She drew ragged breaths through gritted teeth. *No! No!* her mind was warning, but then Jacob found her weakness. He buried his head between her thighs. Electricity shot through her. Jacob knew every button to push to bring her to fruition. Over and over again, he made her scream in ecstasy. Her nails dug into his shoulders and tore into his long, silky hair, which only made him increase the tantalizing assault on her body. He pulled her to the edge of the table, hoisted her legs on his shoulders, and roughly entered her. Savannah arched her back, squeezed her eyes shut, and tried to visualize Nathan's face. Jacob aroused her beyond distraction, as he slowed his motion.

"Give in to me!" he demanded. "Give it *all* to me! Stop holding back!"

"No!" she shouted, but her words belied her body's convulsive orgasmic reactions. "I'm his! I belong to Nathan!"

"Not for long! Not ever again!" he shouted back, as he increased his motion, thrusting in and out of her faster and faster, harder and harder for what seemed like a lifetime. Then the air was crushed when he shouted his release. "You're mine! I'll never let you go! Not ever!"

Savannah didn't know what time it was when she woke, but she smelled the acrid smoke of Jacob's cigarillo. She lay perfectly still, trying to think how she could let herself succumb to him when she loved and wanted Nathan. She had let Jacob possess her all night before they both dropped off to sleep from pure exhaustion. Her conscience whipped her. How could she do this? Nathan was who she wanted, not Jacob!

Savannah started to rise and felt Jacob's hand on her arm.

"Where are you going?" he asked gruffly.

"To work," she said over her shoulder. She tried to jerk her arm away, but Jacob held on to her tightly.

"You're not working today. I've arranged for someone else to cover your patients. I've got other plans for you."

Savannah turned sharply and looked at Jacob. "You did *what?*" she bellowed. "How dare you! This is my career you're screwing with!"

"You don't need a career. As Mrs. Jacob Hawkins you'll have your hands full."

"Your *wife?*" she bellowed. "When hell freezes over!" She pulled away from him, unmindful of her nakedness, and stormed into the bathroom, slamming the door behind her.

The door flew opened just as fast as it had closed, banging loudly against the wall.

"Oh, you'll marry me alright!" Jacob said lowly, his body in the buff.

"*Fuck you, Jacob!*" She yanked on the shower and misty spray descended from two directions.

Jacob crossed the expanse between them and spun her around.

"I'm not asking you, Savannah. I'm telling you! Don't mistake me for that wimp Flack! He hasn't a clue who you are and he's not man enough to hold on to a woman like you!"

She yanked away from him. "Nobody tells me what to do, least of all you!" she flared. "As for Nathan, well he's more man than—"

"Don't you even *think* it, Savannah! He's through with you! It's over! You're just someone he used to know! Just like all the other men in your life! Just like the first night I met you with Roderick Baylor! There won't be any more Roderick or Nathan or any other men for that matter! I told you, you're mine!" he stormed, as he grabbed her and pulled her down to the fluffy bathmat on the floor. He took her fast, hard, and unrelentingly. Her cries of ecstasy were lost under his driving force. "You're going to beg me to marry you." He grinned, as he undulated his strong torso against her. He reached his orgasm and looked down into her blurry eyes, as his spasms subsided. He lowered to kiss her, but she turned her face away.

Jacob roughly uncoupled himself from her and then stood, glaring down at her. "You're going to want me and no other man! You can't help yourself. You're wild and untamed and more woman than I've ever had. You think I'm going to step out of the way for the likes of Nathan Flack? Forget it! May his soul burn in hell!"

Jacob's words sent a chill shooting up Savannah's spine. A finger-snap of fear began to grip her, erasing the euphoria.

"What do you mean 'may his soul burn in hell'?" She got to her feet.

"Nothing," he said almost as if he had said too much, but Savannah didn't believe him. He seemed to be hiding a secret.

"I asked you a question! What did you mean?"

Jacob snorted and turned to leave. Savannah grabbed his arm, digging her nails into his flesh. *"Answer me!"*

"You want something from me, you know how to get it," he said, the look in his eyes seemingly as cold ice. "Give yourself to *me*," he said, jabbing his thumb into his chest. "Beg *me* to marry you and I'll give you anything and everything that you want."

Savannah released him and took a step back. "Never," she said coldly. "We'll see," was his only retort.

Then he left the bathroom. Savannah stood for a moment rooted to her spot. *Was that a threat?* Was Jacob threatening Nathan? Threatening his life? Jacob Hawkins was a powerful man. He had connections everywhere, including some very unsavory characters. She stepped inside the octagonal shaped glass enclosure and lathered her body with a sponge and fragrant shower gel, as she thought of his words. She poured herbal shampoo in her hands and lathered her hair. The fragrant soap trickled down her face and body. She closed her eyes and turned her face up to the ceiling, waterfall spray.

No, Jacob couldn't do anything to hurt Nathan. Nathan is a diplomat, an ambassador. He is insulated and protected, she assured herself. *Still, what if—* she cut off her thought. *No, it would never happen. Certainly not over a sexual fling. He was just saying that to frighten me into submission; just over the thrill of it. To control me to get what he wanted...or was he?*

Later that day, Savannah was sitting in the doctors' lounge munching on an apple and carelessly flipping through a magazine. It had been a hellified day. First Jacob and now undoing the work her ten days of absence had caused. The doctors she had asked to cover for her weren't as thorough as she when it came to her patients. Several of them she had to recall for more tests, which made them nervous and fearful something was wrong with their pregnancies or previous test results. She spent over an hour reassuring one mother, who was having her first child in her late thirties, that all was well. Then her husband had come by unexpectedly to reassure himself his wife was well. He was only twenty-nine. After that, the morning had flown by and Savannah was looking forward to leaving early to get some rest.

As she thought about what she perceived as a threat to Nathan, she noticed the noon news and saw a picture of Nathan flash across the screen. Quickly, she leaped across the coffee table that separated her from the flat screen television and clicked the remote.

"…and sources close to the negotiations state the shift in locations is merely a precaution," the reporter was saying. *"More news at five and world news at six. In other local news…"*

Locations? Why would they shift locations? She flipped through the channels, looking for one of those all-news stations. She found one and her wait was not long. The first shot was of Nathan standing before a podium, answering questions asked by reporters. The voiceover by the announcer angered her. She wanted to hear Nathan's voice, as well as see him. He looked tired and a bit drawn, very much unlike himself.

"Hey, is that Nathan?" Chuck Montgomery asked, as he came into the lounge.

"Shhh!" Savannah said, waving her hand to quiet him.

"I assure you Ambassador J. Ashdon Logan has not involved himself in these negotiations…" Nathan was saying.

He must be tired, Savannah thought. *No one referred to Jefferson as J and his middle name is Alden, not Ashdon. Nathan knows that. What is wrong with him?* When the news clip ended, Savannah sat back in her seat. A chill edged up her spine. She recalled her argument with Jacob Hawkins that morning of what sounded suspiciously like a threat. He was very influential, but he couldn't affect world events…could he? Still something seemed wrong. Terribly wrong.

CHAPTER 25

Jefferson had paced in front of Dakota's cabin more times than he cared to mention, but still she hadn't returned. The boys were anxious to see her to tell her about their trip to Disney World. He knew that she was scheduled to join the Vice President's wife's, Mrs. Erron's, entourage for a few weeks. He read the online newspaper accounts of the Mrs. Erron's visit to Africa and saw the photo ops the press had plastered all over the front pages. Dakota wasn't in any of the photos he could see, even though the wives of other industrialists were prominently displayed. It had been weeks since he had seen her, touched her, loved her, and he needed her more than he wanted to admit.

***

Dakota strapped on her weapons and stood to connect her parachute cord to the zip line. "Coming up on the LZ, Sir, uh, I mean, Ma'am," one of the pilots called out. "We're at thirty thousand feet."

Dakota turned to her team, turned her baseball cap backward on her head, strapped on her helmet with a night vision shield, and stared at each one of them. She had trained these warriors to be the best team in the spec ops service of their country.

"Look around you!" she ordered. The men and women all looked at each other. "I want to see every one of you back when this mission is over! No fear because I'll be here!" she shouted. They all repeated her words and began their mantra sounding off.

"Viper! I'll be here!"

"Cougar! I'll be here!"

"Stinger! I'll be here!"

"Cobra Kahn! I'll be here!"

Each one of the thirty men and women; less than half of her team, hooked on and began to move forward toward the open door of the aircraft.

"LZ! LZ!" the pilot yelled.

The team flipped the helmet visor over their faces and began the nighttime helo jump into darkness over the landing zone. Dakota followed them down praying her body would not fail her.

***

"Mr. Ambassador, please hold for the President," a man's voice said over the satphone.

Shortly, a voice Jefferson recognized came on the line.

"Carl, what's the problem?" Jefferson asked.

"I need you at Camp David, Jeff. I know you'd want to be in on this."

"I'm on sabbatical, Carl. I thought we agreed I could take time to spend with my sons. We're trying to—"

"Jeff, it involves Flack. He's in trouble."

"Trouble? Aren't the negotiations going well?"

"Jeff, we can't discuss this over this line. I assure you this warrants your attention."

Jefferson felt the severity of the problem by the tone of the President's voice.

"I'll have to bring my sons. It's too late to find someone to take care of them."

"Fine, but please hurry, Jeff."

Jefferson closed his cell phone and looked at his boys playing basketball at the hoop he had constructed for them in the backyard. If he was right, there was no time to waste.

"Hey, guys, come on in. We're going for a little ride."

Within thirty minutes, Jefferson pulled his Land Cruiser up to the gates of Camp David, the Presidential retreat in western Maryland. He knew his SUV and its occupants were being electronically scanned. Then the gates opened and he was ushered forward. He knew where he was going. He had been there many times before in his years of civil service. None of the previous times seemed as urgent as this though.

The President's own two sons, who were eleven and fifteen, were at his side when Jefferson parked his vehicle. They exchanged pleasantries, made introductions, and then all of the boys were whisked away while the President guided Jefferson inside. They walked toward a large double door that two Marines opened as they approached. Immediately, Jefferson recognized the Joint Chiefs of Staff, the heads of every secret service agency and the head of the National Security Council. When he saw the head of The Nursery, Delta Dawn, a chill went up his spine. He turned and looked at the President.

"Flack, he's been taken hostage," Jefferson said more as a statement of fact than a question.

"We think so," the President said. "All of the details aren't clear at the moment and no one outside of this room can know about this."

"How did he signal there was a problem?" Jefferson asked.

"He called you J. Ashdon in a news conference."

"Then there is a problem. He and I discussed it when the first departure was delayed. We agreed if all was not well, he would use that name as his stress word instead of what he usually calls me. How long have they been captive?"

"We don't know and we don't know who's got them. From all outward appearances, things are normal, but every day, two or three of the party are missing from the daily press conferences. Never the same ones. Yesterday, their meeting location was changed to a private residence heavily fortified and, we understand, impenetrable."

"What are you doing about it?"

"I've sent in special agents. A crack, elite force to assess the situation."

"Assess? What do you mean by 'assess'?"

"Patience, Jefferson, we're doing all we can for now. We have a few aces up our sleeves."

"That can only mean one thing, Carl. You've got someone on the inside."

The President nodded in agreement. "I've ordered the Secret Service and State Department to step up security on all American Embassy personnel worldwide, including you and your family."

"Whoever they are, they want something, Carl. What is it?"

"You, Jeff. We think that they want you."

Later that night, as the boys prepared for bed, Jefferson sat alone on the deck, looking out over the dark night. He was deep in thought, his hands steepled before him. The night had gathered in around him, yet the moon was bright in the blue-black sky. Brief, thin clouds shifted over the stars, making them appear to be blinking off and on. Small, night creatures darted along the edge of the woods. He could make out the silhouettes of ducks and geese as they silently glided on the lake, ruffling the moonlight on the water. He shut his eyes to clear his head, inhaling the moist, forest earth, the pine tree, and wild flowers. He also sensed the heightened security around the cabin and in the woods. Yates was also there and ever vigilant.

"Dad, are you asleep?"

Jefferson's eyes shuttered open. "No, I'm not asleep. I was just resting my eyes."

Miles moved away from the door toward his father. "Why did the President want to see you?" Miles asked quietly, standing behind him.

Jefferson turned and looked over his shoulder at the boy. He had not heard him come out of the cabin. He reached his hand toward Miles, the boy took it, and came to stand next to Jefferson's chair.

"I guess you're too old to sit on your old man's lap, huh?" Jefferson asked, running his hand over Miles' slim, but firm shoulder.

"I'm not a baby," Miles said, shifting from one foot to the other.

"No, I guess you're not, son." Jefferson pulled the boy into his embrace and Miles returned the affection.

"Why, Dad?" Miles asked, his head resting on Jefferson's shoulder. "Why did the President call you?"

"Oh, nothing really important, son. Nothing for you to worry about." He rubbed Miles' back.

Miles shifted so that he could look into his father's eyes. "Dad, Roger told us something big was going on. His father had been in these secret meetings—"

"His father is the President of the United States. He's always in secret meetings. It's his job."

"You're treating me like a kid, Dad, and I don't like that," Miles said, pulling out of Jefferson's embrace. "The President wanted you for something very important, didn't he?"

Although Jefferson wanted to spare his son any worry or concern, he couldn't and wouldn't lie to him. "Yes, son, he did, but it will all work out just fine. I may have to go out of the country for a few days and—"

"You're leaving, Daddy?" Stephen asked, suddenly appearing by his brother's side. "You're leaving us?"

"No, son, just a short trip," Jefferson said, lifting Stephen into his lap and hugging him close. "A couple of days maybe and then I'll be back."

"Hercules and I want to go with you, Daddy," Stephen said, looking pleadingly up into his father's eyes. "We won't be any trouble, I promise."

Jefferson smiled. "I thought maybe you'd like to visit with your Aunt Savannah in Washington and keep her company while I'm away."

"No, Dad, Stevie and I want to go with you," Miles said.

"Don't beg him," Jefferson Junior scowled. "It's just an excuse. He's tired of us just like Grandfather said he would be."

"That's not true! He loves us!" Stephen fretted and buried his face in Jefferson's chest.

"Stevie is right. That's not true, son," Jefferson said, as calmly as he could. "I do love you—all of you," he said, looking directly at Jefferson Junior, "and I'm not making excuses to leave you again. I don't ever want us to be separated. I really wish I could take you with me, but this is very important."

"More important than us," Jefferson Junior scoffed.

"*Nothing* is more important to me than the three of you. I promise, this won't take long and then maybe we could go somewhere—Jamaica or something—for a few weeks. You'd like that, wouldn't you?" he asked the three boys.

All were silent.

After the boys were asleep, Jefferson remained on the deck, looking across the lake. *Where is she?*

CHAPTER 26

Dakota silently hand signaled for her team to move. They had been there outside the compound for three days, monitoring the movements and identifying each of the guards who surrounded the place. Security was tight, but her team was better than any precaution system. She personally picked and trained each one of the men and women she led. Many of them were from Native American tribes, outcasts who were lodged at a camp near the orphanage where they had all grown up. Isolated in the North Dakota outlands, it proved to be an ideal training facility.

They moved silently, but swiftly to her hand signals. As the rigorous training provided, they found a way into the compound and were about to make their move. Aerial photos gathered by camouflaged bird drones had tracked the daily movements around the perimeter, and her agent's signal—a patch just under the skin of his shoulder with a miniature receiver and transmitter—steered them to where the hostages were being held.

***

Bill Chandler winked at one of the guards who he pegged as gay as a blade. He had been the one who frisked Bill thoroughly—too thoroughly, Bill thought, at the time. When the hostages were permitted to go to the showers, this guard lasciviously eyed him. Bill knew the look all too well. On many undercover operations, he had truly been 'undercover' with a man or a woman. Frankly, it didn't matter to him which target he was assigned to get the intelligence from. He could get himself psyched up by just thinking about his former partner and then boss, Dakota. She truly had no knowledge of the effect she had on him or any of the men on her team. They would have followed her into hell both because most of them were half in love with her and all of them respected her skill and cunning. Now he was solo for this mission. What she taught him would be put to the test, again.

Bill knew the guard was watching as he lathered his body so he did it more slowly while sensuously stroking himself often to bring on an erection. He knew, sooner or later, the guard would approach him. He didn't have to wait long as the guard handed his automatic weapon to another guard and came into the open shower room with high walls and narrow windows at the top. Bill continued to lure the man and then turned toward him, eyeing him in the same suggestive manner. The guard took the bait. He'd be able to use this one, he thought.

Something above Bill's line of sight, at the window directly across from him, caught his eye when he looked up. Two eyes peered down at him. He would know those eyes anywhere. Then a penlight signal in Morse code flashed. He read the message as he continued to distract the guard. Bill signaled his responses by blinking his eyes. He was getting tired of holding off his release. Frankly, the man did nothing for him, but he could be used if it became necessary. Finally, Bill gave the man what he wanted and had been working so hard to achieve.

***

Jefferson was caught in a dilemma that tore at his gut. Several days, nearly a week had passed and still the President refused to let him go and retrieve the envoys in exchange for himself. He knew the President was waiting for the intelligence gathering teams to feed information on which to make a decision, but he had half a mind to journey to North Africa on his own without Presidential approval.

Then there were the children, his sons to consider. He could not just pack a bag and hop on a jet anymore. Since this situation had arisen, they were more quiet and introspective. He and his sons had come a long way in nearly two months, but they still had a long way to go to become a family and that's what he wanted—to be a family man again.

He thought of Dakota. She was on his mind a lot. He had no idea where she was or what she was doing, but he wanted desperately to see her, to hold her in his arms. He needed to be held, too, but only one person could make him feel again—Dakota Sinclair.

***

Dakota was pissed off. Usually it took a great deal to make her angry, but Bill knew every trick in the book and what was worse—she taught him, read him every chapter and verse. She wanted to bring him and the other hostages out of there, but Bill warned her off. *Too dangerous*, he signaled. *It's a trap. They want someone else. Bigger and more important.* He didn't know yet who. She and her team gathered the intelligence they needed and retreated without so much as a footprint left in the grass. They all retreated to the landing zone and were picked up by F-35B Joint Strike Fighters—the stealth harrier-jet helicopters—and whisked away under the radar back to safety.

When she returned to her temporary base of operation on the North African continent, she met with other top ranking officials to map out a strategy to implement if it became necessary to rescue the hostages by force. That would likely require a contingent of Marines. She and her people were SEAL and Mossad trained. They did their work with stealth, not brawn. While they were preparing several alternative plans, orders came down from headquarters that everyone would be at parade rest. Dakota didn't like the sound of that, but she knew her role there was tentative, at best. She was pulled off temporary medical leave and the Asian assignments she knew extremely well. She was only re-inserted in this mission because she was the best available person to handle her teams, some of whom were already deployed for the mission. Besides, Bill Chandler, her XO, Executive Officer, was involved. They had been a crack team for many years. She couldn't and wouldn't let him down now.

Dakota was in her temporary quarters when the door opened. She looked up from the intelligence report she was reading, immediately got to her feet, and came to attention.

"At ease, Wind Breeze," her mentor, friend, and trainer said.

"Yes, ma'am, Explorer One," Dakota said, accepting the hand offered to her for a shake. "It's been a while."

"It has, but I keep an eye on all of my Explorers, especially the ones who are still running black ops teams."

"I hope we have not disappointed you."

"No, you haven't. I'm very proud of the work that you've done over the years."

'*Over the years?*' Something began to register with Dakota. Why would Navy Admiral Stacy Greene Alexander be here in Northern Africa? Her command was in Japan. Then it dawned on her. "I'm being replaced, aren't I?"

"No," her mentor, friend, and former handler said, looking her in the eye. "This is your op from start to finish."

"Then why are you here? This is not your usual area."

"You're right, it isn't, and I think you know why I'm here."

She did know and the realization hurt in places that cut to her core. "Delta Dawn asked you to talk with me."

"No, I volunteered. I didn't have to be asked."

Her worst fears were coming true. She would be let go. Turned out of the only career she ever wanted, but maybe there was still time...

"I know what you're thinking, Dakota, but I've seen your medical records. Even if you hadn't had a serious injury during Operation: Afghani Sky, you would have been experiencing difficulty with stress fractures. Scouting more than fifty clicks a day in the Afghan mountains is grueling. According to your chart, you've been pushing yourself to get back your muscle tone, agility, and speed. You're still faster on foot than most of your team, but you're tearing down your body. You're too important an asset to Delta Dawn and The Nursery to risk you on ground insurgency. That's why he posted you to the Africa desk."

Dakota turned away from Stacy and looked out the window. "He's been planning this for some time, hasn't he?"

"Yes, he has. That's why he paired you with your second in command, Stallion. Together, you two can infiltrate many markets where others would have difficulty. As VP for CompuCorrect International, you have entree to the upper echelons of governments all over the African continent. As the wife of an industrialist, you have a natural entree into African corporations and other business entities to gather intelligence and stem the tide of cybercrimes and human trafficking. This assignment is where your skills and abilities are most needed at this time. From time to time, we may have to activate you for field duty."

Dakota turned to look at Stacy. "There are no other options? Perhaps as a stationary in Afghanistan? With my skin and hair color, I have passed for an Afghani woman. Or, I could cover my face. I can speak the language…" she subsided at Stacy's negative shake of her head.

"You're too beautiful to make that work. You'd constantly be fending off men and that would be dangerous. Even if we gave you the cover of a wife of a prominent Afghani man, the situation is too unstable under the current government regime." Stacy moved toward her, reached out, and took Dakota's hand. "You were still in college when you were tapped for covert operations by the CIA. They did so because of your athletic skill and your high intelligence quotient. Although you were certainly eligible, they convinced you not to take advantage of your opportunity to train for the U.S. Olympic track and field team. They didn't want your face to end up on every cereal box in America and in foreign counties. I picked you and eleven others out of over three hundred women to be the first to secretly train as SEALs and as Mossad operatives. You were in my first class, passed BUD/S without a sweat, but you twelve were not my only class. I'm still running the covert SEALs and Mossad training on an island in the Pacific. If you want to become one of my recruiters or trainers, I believe that can be arranged. It means living and working abroad, but say the word and I would speak to Delta on your behalf. He would be disappointed, because he needs you in overt tasks in Africa, but I could use your skills and abilities in finding new talent or training new recruits. The team you recruited and trained is the best at insurgency. However, we need more teams like them. Since your health dictates that you move on from there, you need to pick new leaders to take your place in the field, but who will still work under your command from HQ. Otherwise, the only options are as I have described. It's either take the Africa assignment, gathering intelligence or you're at a desk at Langley, interpreting data."

Dakota dropped Stacy's hand and turned away to look out the window, again. She was a loner. She didn't want to be responsible for scouting for new recruits or training them for tasks she still wanted to perform herself.

"You have some time to think about this, Dakota. Operation: Rescue is on hold for the time being. The hostages are not being harmed, so Delta wants to drill down more into who is behind this seizure. He is not satisfied this is a particular government takeover or even a fringe faction group, like Boca Raton or ISIS. Until he's satisfied with the intelligence he receives, he doesn't intend to send you in for an extraction.

"However, he does need you to resume your role as an envoy with the Vice President's wife's entourage. The press and news media have picked up on your absence and are asking questions about your whereabouts. You're being reinserted with the tour. Your cover story complete with pictures and video is you were in Jakarta working out some importation problems for CompuCorrect International's massive computer hardware shipment. Now you've resolved those transportation problems, you're free to join Mrs. Erron's tour." She handed a file to Dakota. "Your updates are in here. Review and destroy."

Dakota took the file and then looked into Stacy's eyes. "I don't want you to think I'm ungrateful for the opportunities I've been afforded, particularly the opportunity to train and work with you. I just didn't expect my career would come to such an abrupt halt. I don't know how you managed to go from covert to overt with such ease."

A Mona Lisa smile grew on Stacy's face. "His name is Benjamin Staton Alexander."

"Your husband?"

"Yes and our children. I can do without a career, but I can't do without my family."

"You're still ambitious though."

"Within reason. I've reached all of my professional goals because of my husband and family. I'm an admiral in the US Navy, a member of the Joint Chiefs of Staff, and the wife of the only man I ever loved. I have had a hand in getting more women, like you, into leadership roles and covert positions. It doesn't get any better than this. That's my life, but it's not yours. You have never been interested in climbing the ladder to higher office in the CIA or The Nursery, and that's fine. You're exactly where you want to be in your career—leading your special ops team's incursions. You've done excellent work and never failed to successfully complete your missions. Now, through no fault of your own, your missions have changed and you don't have the support system in place to help you transition to these new challenges. Take time over the next few weeks to think about what you want for the rest of your life."

***

As Admiral Alexander informed her, Dakota was inserted with the wife of the Vice President and press conferences were held primarily so, among other things, her cover story would be distributed far and wide. The group had done a number of public appearances during the week since she rejoined the entourage, and were scheduled for another American Embassy party. She was dressed and waiting with other wives to be introduced to the U.S. Ambassador and his wife when she felt a tug on her gown. She looked down into the upturned smiling face of Stevie Logan.

"Hi," he said, brightly.

Dakota quickly scanned the room and then stooped to his level. "Hi, yourself. Did your dog get lost again?"

"No," he giggled. "My daddy brought us," he said, grinning at her. "He had a talk with the President and then I asked him if Hercules and

I could come to Africa with him, too. Jay got really mad and said Daddy wanted to leave us again, but Miles said that wasn't true, so here we are."

Oh, God! Jefferson Logan is here? Standing, she did another quick scan and spotted him coming toward her with his sons at his sides.

"Ah, there you are, Stevie," he said, smiling at his son. "I thought we had an agreement about you wandering away?"

Stevie looked down and shifted from foot to foot. "Yes, sir," he said just above a whisper. Then he looked up at his father. "But I haven't seen Dakota, I mean Mrs. Chandler, in a long, long time, and she was just standing here with the other ladies and..." he trailed off when the women with Dakota chuckled.

"He is absolutely adorable," one of the women said. Then turning to Jefferson, she extended her hand. "Hello, Ambassador Logan. I don't think we have met. I'm Claudia Erron, the Vice President's wife."

"A pleasure to meet you, Mrs. Erron," he said then nodded a greeting to the other women in her entourage including Dakota.

"These handsome young men must be your sons," she said, regarding each boy.

"They are, yes," he said and introduced each one to Mrs. Erron and the other women with her. "And now they have met you, Mrs. Erron, Ambassador Hawkins, and his lovely bride, it's time for them to retire," he said meaningfully, looking at his boys.

They knew better than to protest in front of others, so the boys were led away by Yates and other guards.

Jefferson wanted nothing more than to get Dakota alone, but Mrs. Erron took his arm and moved toward Ambassador Hawkins while carrying on a lively conversation. Yet, Jeff kept a careful eye on Dakota. He had gone to a lot of trouble to instigate press and news media inquiries into her location without bringing attention to himself. Now he knew where she was, he wasn't about to let her out of his sight again.

Dakota dropped back in the line so she could move out of Jefferson's line-of-sight, and make a strategic escape, but no sooner had she accomplished that when another dilemma intruded.

"Dakota? Dakota Sinclair?"

Dakota turned and looked into the eyes of another former classmate from Spelman College, JaiHonnah Hawkins Baylor who was also Ambassador Jake Hawkins' daughter and Jacob Hawkins' sister. As she was brought into the warm embrace of one of the few former classmates who had befriended her, she found she couldn't extricate herself from reciprocating the hug.

"It's good to see you, JaiHonnah. It's been a long time."

"I'll say. You were a senior when I was a freshman. I lost track of you when you graduated. Then I recently read you are the Vice President for CompuCorrect International's Africa project and married Bill Chandler. I was really surprised. I know Bill very well. I really didn't expect him to marry. He and Vivian Alexander Montgomery were housemates and classmates during law school at Georgetown. Before Vivian became a judge, she and Bill were founding partners in their law firm. Vivian's brother, Kenneth Alexander, although now the California Lieutenant Governor, was the Executive Director of CompuCorrect, International, the company you work for. It's truly a small world. You may remember Vivian Alexander, too. We were classmates."

"Yes, I remember Vivian. I recently saw another of your classmates, Savannah Logan, in DC. We'll have to make time to talk, but I'm with Mrs. Erron's—"

"Ah, not to worry. I'll arrange for us to sit together during dinner so that we can catch up, okay?"

"Don't go to any trouble, Jai—"

"No trouble at all. We're here visiting with my father and Roderick's sister. Besides, I don't think you've met my husband, Roderick Baylor."

"Uh, no, I haven't. I did follow his career when he played professional basketball and I read that he was selected by your father to manage his company, BlackHawk Holding."

"Yes, Roderick and I are both picking up the slack for my father since he was named Ambassador to this country. Come on. The line is much shorter now. Let me introduce you to my father and my stepmother,

Kelley, who also happens to be my sister-in-law," JaiHonnah said, laughing. "Kelley Baylor Hawkins is one of Roderick's sisters. Talk about a small world."

Dakota didn't want to cause a scene by trying to extricate herself from JaiHonnah, so she permitted herself to be guided to Ambassador and Mrs. Jake Hawkins. She had no real interest in meeting the multi-billionaire, but she surmised she would have to come in contact with him at some point to fulfill her intelligence gathering missions in Africa. He was a surprisingly handsome man in his late fifties or early sixties and his wife, who appeared to be in her forties, was an arrestingly attractive woman. However, when Ambassador Hawkins' eyes landed on her, she felt something akin to a lightning bolt jolt to her nervous system. He took her hand and stared at her as if he knew her. She had never met him before, yet there was something familiar about him.

"Honey?" Kelley Baylor Hawkins inquired when she noticed her husband's intense expression.

"Dad?" JaiHonnah asked, concerned.

"When were you born? Who are your people? What is your name?" Ambassador Hawkins rapidly asked her, not relinquishing her hand.

Dakota was temporarily stunned, but tried to recover. "My name is Dakota Sinclair-Chandler, Mr. Ambassador. I grew up among the Arapaho."

"They are not your people," Ambassador Hawkins stated bluntly.

Surprised and concerned they were causing a scene, Dakota looked around furtively. *Where is Bill Chandler when I need him? Oh, he had to go get himself held hostage!* She fumed silently. She didn't know what to do in this situation. This seemed personal, not professional.

As if sensing her concern, the Ambassador instructed her, "Come with me."

Since he had not relinquished her hand, she had no other choice than to accompany him into a private salon in the embassy. Mrs. Hawkins and JaiHonnah followed. No sooner had the door closed behind them, it was opened by Adam Hawkins, the Ambassador's younger of two sons.

"What happened?" Adam asked, concerned.

Dakota looked at Adam and then JaiHonnah. They looked so much alike they could have been twins. She remembered that JaiHonnah won a Ms. Texas beauty contest and was the first runner up in a Ms. America contest. Adam didn't have a feminine characteristic in his countenance, but was incredibly handsome, with movie-star good looks. In his spare time, she remembered reading he liked to design, engineer, and race Formula One cars. Yet something about Adam and JaiHonnah standing side-by-side, starring at her and Ambassador Hawkins' penetrating scrutiny made her feel lightheaded.

"You're my daughter. You're my LaiLoni Skai," Jake Hawkins said with conviction. Tears gathered in his eyes, as he brought the hand that he had yet to relinquish to his lips for a kiss.

Dakota shook her head slowly in denial or disbelief, she didn't know which, but something in her gut told her she might be looking at her father. Other than her height, she didn't see any resemblance between them. However, given the resemblance she now recognized between herself, JaiHonnah, and Adam, and the unidentifiable and unsettling connection she felt to Jacob Hawkins during the reception at the Naval Observatory months ago, she could not dismiss the possibility out of hand. In the dense atmosphere, she heard JaiHonnah's and Adam's sharp intakes of breath.

After his initial statement, silence reigned in the salon. She needed to sit down before her legs gave out on her, but sheer tenacity kept her on her feet while everyone stared at her.

JaiHonnah took a picture from her purse and handed it to Dakota. "This is a picture of my mother, Skai Littlefeather Hawkins. She was Navajo. My grandmother, Kiavi Ramose Littlefeather, still lives on the Navajo Reservation near Shiprock, New Mexico. My mother died of breast cancer when we were very young."

Adam picked up the story. "Her and my father's second child, a baby daughter they named LaiLoni Skai, was kidnapped from the birthing clinic less than twenty-four hours after she was born. My parents never gave up hope of finding their daughter, our other sister."

Dakota took the picture of the woman and looked at a face that, except for a slight difference in coloration, could have been her mirror image. It was such a jolt to her system; she finally had to sit down on the closest flat surface she could reach. She continued to stare at the pictured image so much like her own. Jake Hawkins brought a chair and sat facing her, their knees touching. When she looked up at him, his face was still wet with tears.

"I know this is a lot for you to take in, but you are my daughter."

"I don't...I don't know what to say to you or what to think," Dakota said, trying desperately to get herself on solid ground again. When she looked at the picture again, she couldn't deny the possibility. "I don't have any recollection of my childhood before I was about four or five years old. I grew up in an orphanage in the Rocky Mountains."

"Shortly after you were taken, the federal authorities busted a national, black market, baby-stealing ring. One of the agents assigned to the case thought you were probably kidnapped by members of that ring, but they were never able to trace where you were taken. I was an oil-rig worker in Texas and couldn't afford the high cost of a fulltime private detective, but we tried to follow up every possible lead to find you. Later, when I could afford it, I kept a private security firm on retainer to protect my remaining three children and to continue the hunt for you."

"You seem so sure I'm your daughter, your LaiLoni Skai, and I can't deny I look a lot like the woman in this picture...your wife."

"Your mother. I am sure. If you'll submit to a DNA test, I will prove it to you, too."

Dakota looked around at all the warm, accepting faces, before nodding her head in silent agreement.

Ambassador Hawkins pulled a cell phone from his pocket and began issuing orders. In less than thirty minutes, a doctor had done a mouth swab and drawn her blood, Jake's blood and the blood of his son and daughter, Adam and JaiHonnah. Ambassador Hawkins oldest son, Jacob Junior was summoned to come to Africa without delay.

After the doctor left, Dakota looked up into Jake Hawkins' eyes. "What if the tests come back negative?"

"They won't. You are my daughter."

***

The embassy reception for the Vice President's wife and her entourage was in full swing when Dakota and the Hawkins family rejoined the festivities. Ambassador and Mrs. Hawkins had duties they could not avoid, even in the face of their soul-shattering personal revelations. Yet Dakota felt their eyes on her. Adam and JaiHonnah were her constant companions, taking every opportunity to touch or even to hug her; a situation that did not seem to go unnoticed by Jefferson Logan. His efforts to maneuver her away for a private conversation proved futile.

At the conclusion of the evening, Ambassador Hawkins arranged for her to join him and his family at his private residence, a decision that allowed no argument from her. He seemed concerned someone would take her away from him again. Little did the Ambassador know she could have provided her own security team if the situation had warranted. In the morning, there were channels she would tap to develop a dossier on the Hawkins and Baylor families. For the present, as she finally retired for the night and closed her eyes, she put herself into an REM sleep mode.

CHAPTER 27

Jefferson left the American Consulate Compound after insuring his sons were under Yates' supervision and enjoying a swim with the children of other American diplomats. He had been asked to join Ambassador Hawkins for breakfast at his private residence. When he entered Ambassador Hawkins' solarium, he expected to find Mrs. Hawkins and the Ambassador's children, Adam and JaiHonnah. He was surprised only the Ambassador was in attendance and the table set for two.

"Great to see you again, Jake," Jefferson said, extending his hand.

"I'm glad you could join me this morning on such short notice, Jeff. Please sit," he said, showing Jefferson to the breakfast table where two waiters held chairs for them. "You may serve now," Jake instructed. They ate and talked about general issues and politics until coffee was served, and the wait staff silently withdrew from the solarium.

"What is the abduction cell after, Jeff?" Jake asked bluntly.

Jefferson had known Jake Hawkins too long to hedge. He also knew Jake had the President's confidence; otherwise, he and his family would not have been cleared to leave the United States and travel via a private Adventurer Executive Airline jet to Africa. Therefore, he told Jake what he knew of the abduction and hostages.

"Whoever is behind this has not officially claimed the industrialists are hostages. They appear to be conducting talks as was previously arranged, including periodic news conferences. Nothing would seem to be amiss were it not for Nathan Flack's use of code stress words we agreed on to signal trouble."

"Yes, I've been read into the operation that went in to gather intelligence." He looked into Jefferson's eyes. "Apparently, this abduction cell is trying to lure you into these talks. There were countries that were not pleased with your decision to withdraw from these sessions."

"I know and I met with the representatives of those countries and Nathan to assure them Nathan had my full support and would be an acceptable substitute."

"Yet, you are here setting yourself up to be abducted in exchange for the hostages."

Jake's insight surprised Jefferson. "I can't afford to let those people suffer because of me."

"The President and I will not allow you to sacrifice yourself to bring Flack, his diplomatic team, and those industrialists home; particularly when it's unclear why this cell wants you."

"So what is to be done in the interim? Eventually the press and news media will pick up on the fact that not all of the team members are present at each press conference and they will start digging. That could prove dangerous to the captives."

"For now, an additional security detail has been assigned to continue to protect you and your family, including your sister. I know you have a former Israeli Mossad officer, you call Yates, protecting your sons, but two more layers of security have been added."

"You know about Yates?" Jefferson asked surprised.

"You saved his life years ago when, as a young man, he was captured in Iran. After intensive, secret negotiations, you walked him and the two Canadians you were sent in to get out of a hellacious Iranian prison onto a US helicopter that flew all of you to Bonn, Germany. Since Israel would not negotiate for the return of one of its own, Yates never returned to his homeland. He's been your shadow ever since."

"You're extremely well informed."

"With good reason. I can afford to buy extremely good intelligence without costing the US government one red cent. That's why the President made me a special envoy for the African Continent. Publically, I have to color within the lines by making nice with the various African countries and factions. Privately, I can afford to make changes where and when necessary. Right now, I have a legion working on this hostage problem."

"Why are you so involved in this, Jake? Egypt and other Arab countries are not your area of responsibility. As I understand it, you're accountable for the Southern African countries, the sub-Saharan."

"My son is, however."

"Your son?"

"Yes, eldest son, Jacob. You've met him. He's involved himself with your sister."

"Yes, of course, I've met him and I'm aware of his interest in Savannah, but I didn't think there was anything serious going on between them. Rather, it's my belief that she's in love with Nathan Flack."

"I'm aware of that, too. Jacob is in for a rude awakening where your sister is concerned. However, if anything happens to you or Nathan Flack, Savannah will be affected. For the time being, if Savannah is affected—"

"Then Jacob will be affected. Do you always keep such close scrutiny on your children and the people they come in contact with?"

"Yes, without fail and for good reason."

"Care to share? Your family appears to have turned out well. I have three sons that I am just now getting to know again."

"I lost one of my children to kidnapping nearly thirty-five years ago."

"I'm sorry, Jake. I had no idea. Now I understand why you're so vigilant."

"Vigilance didn't pay off as much as luck did."

"Luck? I don't understand."

"How well do you know Bill Chandler?"

Jefferson thought the question odd, but answered anyway. "I don't think anyone actually *knows* him. He's an extremely capable sports and entertainment lawyer, a businessman who owns and operates several companies, a movie and television actor and sometimes fashion model. He and DC Circuit Court Judge Vivian Alexander Montgomery are very close friends and have been since they met in their first year in law school at Georgetown. They were partners in her law firm, one of the most prestigious in the country, until she was appointed to the federal bench. He still is a partner, I believe, a founding member. He travels extensively, often with her, her husband, and family, but I don't know much about his family background other than he's a New Yorker, with parents and a sister who live in the Catskills."

"And his wife?"

"Wife?" Jefferson said with a derisive snort. "Questionable."

"How well do you know her?"

Jefferson was beginning to believe this line of inquiry was really getting far off the beaten track. "Dakota Sinclair? She's as much of an enigma as Bill Chandler. There's more to this than you're letting on, Jake. We were talking about your children and then—" Something suddenly registered with Jefferson and pieces of a puzzle began to fall into place. "Dakota Sinclair was an orphan who grew up in the Dakotas. She would be in her early-to-mid thirties. I understand your first wife was Native American. You said you lost a child to kidnapping about that long ago and luck paid off more than vigilance. Are you saying Dakota Sinclair is your kidnapped daughter?"

"Yes," Jake said, bluntly, nodding in the affirmative. "She is my daughter."

"That's why you spirited her and your family out of the ballroom last evening?"

"Yes, it is. She was in the receiving line when my younger daughter, JaiHonnah, spotted her. They were at Spelman at the same time and JaiHonnah was in the same class along with your sister, Savannah, and Vivian Alexander, but Jai didn't recognize the resemblance back then. They were friendly, JaiHonnah tells me, because they were both of Native and African American heritages, but the woman you call Dakota was a senior while Jai was a freshman. They weren't in the same class and only acquainted for eight months. The moment Jai brought her to me to be introduced, I knew. I took one look at her and saw my former wife's, Skai's, image stamped on Dakota's face. I lost Skai to breast cancer many years ago.

"The person you know as Dakota Sinclair-Chandler is my daughter, LaiLoni Skai Hawkins."

Jefferson was flabbergasted.

"I understand you've gotten to know her," Jake commented.

"She has a cabin near Camp David in the same area where my sister, Savannah, has a cabin. However, I first saw Dakota years ago at an American Embassy party in London. I saw her again more recently at an event in DC when the President announced my sabbatical. Your son, Jacob, was also there and sat at my table with her and Bill Chandler." He was surprised that Jacob didn't recognize the resemblance.

"You've spent a considerable amount of time with her before she joined Mrs. Erron's tour."

"Yes, I won't deny that. She needed…" he trailed off.

"Yes, the pinched nerve. I know about it."

"How did you find out?"

"As I said, I'm wealthy enough to buy anything I want. Since I found her, I've launched investigations into every aspect of her life."

"Does she know?"

"She will, but I have more information now than I did yesterday. My son, Jacob, has had your sister under constant surveillance."

"*What!* Why?" Jefferson asked, uncharacteristically showing anger. "How do you know this?"

"Why? That's easy. Jacob fancies himself in love with Savannah and he wants to rub JaiHonnah's husband's, my son-in-law's, nose in the fact he now has a woman Roderick once cared about. There's an ongoing rivalry that Jacob has instigated against Roderick since I selected Roderick to head my company instead of Jacob. Roderick is aware of it, but for the most part ignores it and Jacob's behavior. I imagine Jacob wants to dangle Savannah in front of Roderick often and continuously in the hope he will take the bait and try to have an affair with her. He doesn't understand what Roderick feels for my JaiHonnah. On the other hand, my son may be intrigued or even infatuated with your sister, but more than anything, he can't take no for an answer and she has said no to him many times. I can't blame him for that. He comes by it honestly. I don't take no for an answer either, especially where my children are concerned. You see, I make it my business to know everything about what's going on in their lives. My children are under close surveillance twenty-four-seven for security purposes as are my grandchildren and my wife. I lost my parents when I was fourteen years old and lived in an orphanage with my younger sister for a while. I lost my wife twenty years ago to breast cancer, and I lost thirty-five years of my daughter's life. I do not ever want to lose another person who is precious to me, if there is still breath in my body or a dime in my pocket.

"So you'll understand when I ask you, Jefferson, are you just having a short-term affair with my daughter or do you care for her?"

"Ask me that question a year from now and perhaps I'll be in a position to answer you," Jefferson answered diplomatically. He honestly didn't know the answer to the question at this point.

CHAPTER 28

Dakota was immersed in researching the Hawkins and Baylor families. She still couldn't quite wrap her head around the possibility she might actually be the daughter of Jacob Reese Hawkins, Senior, one of the wealthiest and most influential men in the world, but his story about his kidnapped daughter was factual. She really had to dig deep into CompuCorrect's secret databases to find much personal information on Jacob Hawkins. Most information she found was obtained during the vetting process before he was named as an ambassador.

He was born in the Louisiana Bayou, the son of an African-Cuban fisherman and a French Creole mother, both of whom died, leaving their children orphans. Jake Hawkins was an only son, but had a sister, Mavis, a nurse who was married to an Irish American, Alexander Lowry. They had six sons and one daughter. The Lowrys lived on Maryland's Eastern Shore. Like Jake's daughter, JaiHonnah, Mavis' daughter, Lizette Fiona Lowry, was also an architect. Al Lowry was also the head of a construction company and his sons worked for the family business and also headed their own individual businesses. Lowry Associates was a well-respected Maryland company focused on building unique homes, not commercial buildings. If what she uncovered was true, she had a living parent and stepmother, three siblings: Jacob Junior, Adam, and JaiHonnah, an Aunt Mavis, Uncle Alexander Lowry and seven first cousins. She had nephews and nieces, Roderick and JaiHonnah's children, and a living grandmother, Kiavi Ramose Littlefeather. Her birth name: LaiLoni Skai Hawkins.

In a sudden and unexpected way, she had family and an ancestry reaching back generations among the Navajo all the way back to Spain.

All her life she had wanted to be connected to her heritage, her people. Now, at potentially the worst possible time, her prayers were answered with more family than she could handle.

She needed more intel, but knew she couldn't reach out to her contact from inside the Ambassador's residence. Anything she tried to use to communicate would be picked up immediately by the web of listening devices she detected on her morning run around the interior compound perimeter. She had been looking for a way to make contact, but the place was too well guarded. Although it didn't appear to have over-the-top surveillance, she recognized the nearly imperceptible antenna arrays strategically placed throughout the compound.

There were armed guards, she noted, who paced her on her run, but never intruded on her exercise routine. She had a feeling, if her DNA proved to be a match to the Hawkins' family, Jake Hawkins would attempt to severely curtail her liberty. She regretted allowing the test, however, at the time she was so overcome by the possibilities that she was not thinking clearly about the ramifications. As it stood, she hadn't had much freedom since she entered the compound. Adam and JaiHonnah insisted on her joining them for breakfast. Admittedly, she enjoyed Roderick and JaiHonnah's six children: three girls and three boys, and JaiHonnah and Roderick were expecting again.

This was a lot of family to acclimate to in a short period of time, particularly because she had always been a loner. Yet she didn't want to get too close in case she had to find a way to extricate herself from them to continue her mission or embark on another aspect of her career. She still had decisions to make about the course her life would take after this immediate mission ended. She also didn't know what changes Delta would have to make if, in fact, she was a Hawkins.

Too many emotions were crowding her usually logical thoughts. First thing's first. She needed to construct her secure, undetectable satphone.

***

The moment she stepped out of her bedroom suite, Dakota sensed something was terribly wrong. She hadn't been an agent for fourteen years not to recognize the pungent scent of danger in the air. Silently, she moved through the hallway while daylight was just going to dusk. There was to be a family dinner in a couple of hours after the arrival of Jacob, Jake Hawkins' eldest male child. Ambassador Logan and his sons were invited to join them. She knew the Ambassador had arrived earlier because she saw his boys playing in a covered courtyard with Roderick and JaiHonnah's children and Hercules.

Now there was a sizzling stillness in the air, uncharacteristic of what she knew to be the rhythm and vibrancy of the household staff. She continued down a hallway, alert to any and every change in the air. As she reached a juncture, she stilled, barely breathing, going into a crouched position. Someone was to her left around the corner, moving as stealthily as she. He or she would expect to encounter someone standing up when they breached the bend in the hall. She would have the element of surprise from below.

She held her breath and sure enough, a face did appear, in the same crouched position. It was Yates, the former Mossad officer. His silent hand signals told her there were indeed five insurgents who had infiltrated the compound. He had been dispatched to find her and bring her to the safe room where the other family members were sequestered.

Her own Mossad hand signals told him she wasn't going to hide. If the rest of the family were secured, she would meet the threat head on. She was not surprised Yates agreed with her strategy.

Dakota knew her own elite team was in the vicinity, but since they were not on high alert status, it would take time for them to assemble and mount a coverage plan. She pressed the dot on her shoulder and silently stood with eyes locked with Yates. She had no weapons on her person except her skill and ability at hand-to-hand combat. Not expecting to have to fight inside the compound, nevertheless, she did have hardware secreted in her luggage.

She brought Yates back into her bedroom. While he stood guard inside the door, she opened her luggage and began to assemble the guns made of innocuous looking pieces of hard plastic and rubber bullets. Her arsenal of darts, spikes, knives, star-shaped discs and other Ninja weapons were also cleverly concealed, but easily obtained, if one knew what to look for.

When Yates signaled to cease movement, Dakota flipped a weapon to him and took up position behind the door. When the door swung open, a look through the crack alerted her that the insurgent was alone.

A quick maneuver had the man on his back on the floor and his weapon in Yates' capable hands. She sat astride him, knives pinning his open palms to the floor, and another knife at his jugular. The maneuver had only taken seconds to accomplish without a sound being uttered.

Without delay, she assessed the man was of western Asian ancestry with Somalian influences. Al-Qaeda, she surmised, but why they were in central Africa was a mystery. Moreover, why would they be targeting the home of an American Ambassador south of their usual territory? She pondered that thought for a few moments and concluded that perhaps they were mercenaries attempting to kidnap Jake Hawkins for ransom. After all, he was one of the wealthiest men in the world and Somalians had been hijacking ships for ransom for many years. She would have to give that theory further thought, but not now. If this man had been sent on a reconnaissance mission, others were likely doing the same thing in other parts of the mansion and compound. Sooner rather than later, this man would be missed.

She questioned him in several languages and dialects while searching his person, looking for anything that might give her greater insight into who the insurgents were and their mission. Until her team arrived, she would have to secure her captive. She didn't trust him though. He hadn't uttered a word in response to her questions even with her knives pinning his hands to the hardwood floor. Like her, he was a seasoned warrior, biding his time until he could strike at her and/or Yates to make his escape or sound an alarm. For sure, he would make that effort. Unless he was dead, she had no sure-fire way of containing him. He would be as resourceful as she. Though she had never been captured during any of her missions, she could read in his eyes his determination to break free.

Just a subtle movement of his arms under her knees alerted her to his working his arms and hands free of her knives a split second before his right hand came up from the floor. Her quick twist of his neck and his eyes went opaque.

She rose from him, retrieving her knives, as she stood, wiping his blood on the dead man's clothes.

Yates nodded at her, confirming she had no other choice. It was either kill or be killed. She had cheated death so many times, her brain refused to deal with the reality of what needed to be done.

One down, four to go.

In one part of her brain, she continued to calculate her team's response time while simultaneously stripping the man bare, thoroughly searching his body and clothing. She snapped a picture of his body, both front and back and another close up of his face in profile. She took a sample of his blood for DNA testing, mouth swabs, and fingerprints to be added to The Nursery's databases. Yates stood as sentry at the door while she worked efficiently and quickly. She found a bud, a listening device similar to a hearing aide in his right ear and a tiny, button-shaped device on his chest partially covered by his hair. She recognized the devices. The one on his chest was multifaceted and monitored his voice and heart rate. By now, the insurgents knew they were short one member and had probably dispatched others to this sector of the house. She and Yates had to move and move fast.

They secured the body, carving a space in the bottom of the king-sized bed's top mattress and then remade the bed. It would take a close inspection to determine a body was in that well-made bed.

They were out the door, down the hall, and around a corner when two more insurgents moved stealthily toward her room. They were in and out in a matter of seconds, attesting to the fact they had found nothing.

With weapon in hand, Yates hoisted her up on his shoulders as the insurgents traversed the hall toward them. She and Yates would have only a split second to subdue these two, but would not have the luxury of capture. They would have to use deadly force. Still, that would gain the upper hand and could then mount their own recon mission to capture the remaining two targets.

A nearly imperceptible breath of sound alerted Dakota her team had made better time than she had anticipated. They would shortly be reconnoitering egress spots to cause the least amount of noise that would alert anyone of their presence. For the time being, she and Yates still had two targets to subdue.

The impromptu plan worked as designed. While Yates dealt with the man to his right, she swooped down unexpectedly on his companion. As she took him down to the floor, a pain so severe, it took her breath away, shot from her knees through her body. She had no time to think of that at the moment, but she knew she would not bounce back easily from this new injury.

Once they secured the bodies out of sight, they returned to her room. She quickly wrapped her knees in Ace bandages and put on sweat pants to cover them up. She didn't want to give the enemy any slight advantage with the knowledge she wasn't one hundred percent.

Once again, with silent hand signals, Dakota alerted Yates that help had arrived, but would remain closeted until she made contact. She did so by a series of Morse code taps on her skin mole, giving her team their instructions. She knew her orders would be carried out to the letter without question or delay. She had thirty of the best operatives in The Nursery, all handpicked, and trained by her. She had never lost any of her operatives over the years of her service; though she had recommended team members to go on to lead their own teams just as Explorer One had done for her and as she had done for The Stallion, Bill Chandler. She had others who deserved to move on to head their own teams. First, she and her team had to survive this ordeal to make those recommendations.

***

Jeff Logan and Jake Hawkins huddled away from their families, concerned about what was taking place beyond their safe room.

Everyone was secure except for Jacob Junior and Dakota. It was one of the household staff who alerted Jake to the potential danger when he sighted a known Somalian terrorist chauffeuring Jacob Junior's car into the heavily guarded compound.

The family and friends were gathered together in preparation for the family meal when Jake received the warning and, acting quickly, shepherded everyone, including staff, into safe rooms throughout the compound. Their well-concealed, underground bunker provided an exit to the outside beyond the compound walls.

They had remained below ground, waiting to determine the fate of Dakota and Jacob Junior. Yates had volunteered to locate Jake's missing son and daughter while Jake and Jefferson remained behind, ready and able to defend their families.

Roderick Baylor, Adam Hawkins, and Kelley Baylor Hawkins were doing what they could to keep the children entertained while JaiHonnah rested to calm herself because of her pregnancy.

Jake sat at a console, monitoring the activities above ground. The insurgents had disabled his video cameras, but had not found all of his audio devices. He heard snippets of conversation in a dialect he had not understood, but Jefferson sat nearby wearing headphones while translating the conversations. What he heard he passed on to Jake. They looked into each other's eyes and knew their situation was grave. Communication with forces outside the compound would be impossible from so far underground. They were safe for now, but essentially cut off from the rest of the world. They needed to take the exit out of the bunker, but with his eldest son's and daughter's fate uncertain and Yates' condition unclear, they were unwilling to run away and leave them.

Jefferson could read the anguish on Jake Hawkins' face over the potential loss of his children, but he had the welfare of Adam, JaiHonnah, and his six grandchildren, his new bride, Kelley, and her brother, his son-in-law, Roderick, to contend with. Jefferson cast his eyes to his own three sons who were sitting with the six Baylor children, listening to Adam spin stories about his times racing Formula One cars in the Grand Prix and on other race tracks around the world. Stevie was nodding off, as were the twin seven-year-olds, Shelly and Shelby Baylor. Miles, at eleven years old, was more alert, but Jefferson Junior was keeping his eyes on Jeff like a heat-seeking missile. Jeff sensed his eldest son somehow knew the danger they were in. What he couldn't divine was how his son felt about what he understood. Was he frightened at the prospect of being taken hostage or was he going to be brave.

Jefferson thought of the ramifications, as he listened and continued to translate what little conversation he heard. Then the conversation abruptly ended in mid-sentence. Jefferson placed his hands on the headphones in the hope of hearing more, but there was only silence. He boosted the volume again in the hope of hearing more, but there was only white noise. He and Jake sat looking into each other's eyes while time passed.

Then a safe word came as a whisper in a voice that Jefferson recognized. It was Yates' voice using the safe word Alden, his father's first name and his middle. He and Yates had hastily chosen the word just as the siege had started. He was confident they could move safely to the surface. Yates would sacrifice his life or any other to protect Jefferson and, by connection, his sons.

Jake had heard the word, too, and at Jefferson's nod, had put the mechanism in gear to raise the elevator box to the surface. When the doors opened, Yates stood sentry armed to the teeth. In the center of the controlled chaos stood Dakota Sinclair, issuing orders as if she had been born to the leadership task. Their eyes met briefly, hers flat like a shark's eyes and unemotional, before she turned away, continuing her consult with those who were clearly under her command. Jake started toward her, but her warriors closed ranks, keeping him at bay. Jacob Junior sat away from the melee, guarded by two armed combatants who wore no insignia on their dark clothes. He looked up when his father came toward him and then stood. The guards did not prevent Jake from jerking his son into his arms for a long, fierce hug.

"Ambassador?" Dakota interrupted.

Jake turned and would have gathered her into his arms, too, but she held him off.

"I need to speak with you and Ambassador Logan...privately."

"My office—"

"No, I haven't had it cleared yet. Let's go to my room. I know that it's clear." She turned to Jacob Junior. "You, too, Jacob," she said in a tone that brokered no argument. Adam, Roderick, JaiHonnah, Kelley, and all of the children stayed behind under heavy protection.

He nodded and followed, escorted by the two guards. Once in her bedroom suite behind closed doors, the four stood regarding each other. Then Dakota took a deep breath to gather herself and spoke to Jacob Junior.

"Who is the target? Is it your father or Ambassador Logan?"

Jake narrowed his eyes, his brows bunched. "Why would Jacob know anything about any of this? I just summoned him here when we discovered who you are. He just arrived."

"Jacob?" Dakota said again, ignoring Jake's statements, as if he had said nothing at all. "Who are these flunkies after?"

Jacob looked at the woman who he now had no doubt was his younger sister and then at the disappointment he had every reason to expect would be in his father's eyes. Then he looked at Jefferson. "The target is Jefferson Logan," he said.

"Who is behind this?" Dakota asked.

"I believe it's Tyler Montrose."

"Why would he want Ambassador Logan taken captive or killed?"

"To keep him from retaining custody of his sons."

"Why would you be involved with this plot? What have his sons got to do with you?"

"His sons will inherit more than fifty-one percent of the Montrose empire. They hold title to four companies I want to solidify a deal with to hold more than fifty-one percent of BlackHawk."

"You would destroy our family for control of my company?" Jake asked incredulously.

"You gave our company away to Roderick without thinking of me or Adam."

"Roderick is your brother-in-law, your sister's husband, your nieces and nephews' father. He *is* family! Have you suffered from anything he or your sister have done with the company since they took over from me? Has your cut of the profits been less? Have you less control of your portion of company assets?

"No, you have not!" Jake thundered. "You are as much in control today, if not more, because of Roderick and JaiHonnah's leadership as you were when I named them as co-heads of the company. They are the chairpersons, but you are the President.

"Yet, you continue to try to discredit Roderick in my eyes, and to what purpose? I have loved you all of your life. I have built an empire and shared it equally with all of my children. You are the son of my beloved Skai. What more could you possible want or need that I have denied you?"

"Until today, you have never hugged me. Until today, I did not see in your eyes you loved me. Until today, you did not tell me you loved me.

"All of my life, since I can remember, you have searched for the child you lost. You paid little attention to me, the child you still had. You built an empire while my mother slowly died of cancer. She was always sad because LaiLoni Skai was lost and paid more attention to Adam and JaiHonnah when they were born than she did to me. I tried everything to gain your attention and respect, but you never noticed me among my siblings and then, when you decided to accept this post as Ambassador, when you should have handed over the leadership of BlackHawk to me, your eldest offspring, you passed it on to an outsider and your youngest child, your female daughter. How do you think that made me feel? I am the President of BlackHawk Global, but I am working for my baby sister and her husband."

"You saw that as somehow transferring my love for you to Roderick? Then you involve Savannah Logan because she and Roderick were once lovers?"

"That's what it was in the beginning. I took her away from Roderick, but he professed to be in love with JaiHonnah. Losing Savannah did not seem to make a difference to him. Then she had already moved on to

Nathan Flack. He became an obstacle in my desire to marry Savannah; to keep her constantly in Roderick's face so as to drive a wedge between Roderick and Jai. If Jai thought her husband still had feelings for Savannah, then she would leave him and you would, in turn, kick him out of the company."

At that moment, a knock sounded at the door.

"Come," Dakota called out. A big man with military bearing stepped into view. "Cougar," she said by way of granting permission to enter and approach. He came to her, handed a headset to her, and, turning his back to the others in the room, whispered into her ear. She then whispered back and placed the headset on her head when he left. She turned to Jacob. "What you have done can be construed as treason, Jacob. The intruders are Taliban sympathizers working in concert with al-Qaeda operatives who have now taken over the compound where the American industrialists have been held. What Montrose has instigated to eliminate Ambassador Logan has turned into an international incident of the most dangerous kind. America does not negotiate with terrorists, so the lives of those industrialists and the representatives of the Third World countries willing to negotiate on a trade agreement with America are now at grave risk."

Jefferson had stood listening to Jacob Hawkins speak of his sadness over his father's seeming disregard from his early childhood, but watching the dynamic Dakota Sinclair marshal the forces, that had clearly saved their lives, was mind-numbing. Her command of the situation elevated her to a new level in his admiration. For that, he would forever be thankful to her for protecting his sons, but beyond that, he recognized a warrior when he looked at her. She was magnificent in her ninja black with weapons barely concealed on her person.

Briefly, she looked at him as she pulled a slim, face microphone from the headset into place near her mouth and listened to something that was being transmitted to her. With her feet slightly apart and hands on her hips, a long, single, black plait down the center of her back, she spoke quietly into the microphone while gazing into near space. She began to pace with her hands still on her hips, but turning her back to Jake and Jacob, effectively dismissing them as her biological father and brother, while she dealt with issues obviously of more importance.

"Ambassador Logan?" Jacob said, redirecting his attention away from watching Dakota as she continued to pace.

Arms folded across his chest, he turned his head to look at the man who could have been the catalyst for his death and the reason his sons would be orphaned. He did not know Jacob Hawkins well and what he did know of the man now didn't deserve the pity he innately felt. He did not answer the man, but turned his head in Jacob's direction.

"I, uh, am sorry for my part in what could have happened to you, to your boys. I will do whatever I can to make amends."

"If anything happens to members of the delegation, nothing you say or do will be enough."

"I understand," he said and turned away. He went to sit in a chair by the window, the picture of desolation and defeat.

"Ambassador?" Dakota interrupted, "another security force has been ordered and should be in place within the hour. I and my team have been ordered to reenter the compound where al-Qaeda has taken over and reevaluate the situation—"

"You cannot do this!" Jake insisted boisterously, bringing Jacob to his feet to stand beside his father. "I will not allow it!"

"I can and I will," Dakota said without heat. "This is my operation and I've been given the green light to rescue the hostages."

"I cannot allow this! You are my daughter and I have just found you after thirty-five years!"

"The men and women who are being held captive are the sons and daughters of someone, too. Their lives are hanging in the balance, waiting for what I have trained and gained experience all of my adult, professional life to do. If there is time when I and my team have freed the hostages, I will find you. For now, considering what happened to other ambassadors in the past, the President is ordering you and your families to return stateside until this crisis is over."

"He's pulling us out?" Jefferson asked angrily.

She looked up into his eyes. "Yes. Your families are at risk here in Africa. The Vice President's wife and entourage are going wheels up as we speak. You and your families are to follow. The security team is clearing a secure route to an airstrip where your flights will land long enough to pick up you and your staff and take you directly to an undisclosed location."

"I'm supposed to go and leave you here?" Jefferson asked, speaking into the yawning silence.

She wanted to reach out and touch him. To erase the incredulous and fearful expression from his handsome and concerned face, but she held back. For her entire life, she had wanted to feel connected to someone and now she stood denying the need she read in her father's and her lover's eyes.

"This is as it must be. Your families, father, and Ambassador Logan, need you and I and my team have a mission to complete."

"Tyler Montrose will rue the day he set this plan into motion. I will make it my life's work to crush him into the dust!" said Jake, with fire in his eyes and conviction in his voice. "You come out of this without a scratch. Do you hear me, my daughter?" Jake demanded.

"That's always the plan. In the interim, I will send security forces to scan for listening devices in your residences.

"Ambassador, where did you get the Russet art?"

"Art? You want to know about a piece of art now?" he asked incredulously.

"Yes," she answered simply without breaking eye contact.

He didn't know why she asked, considering she had never been in his home, but her unwavering stare convinced him she had a purpose for the question. "It was a gift from my in-laws years ago. Why do you ask?"

"Do you have other such gifts from the Montrose family?"

"No, just that one piece."

"Arrange to have it given to my security team when they come. What you have is not an original. It is a copy and contains a listening device. For now that is all. You must leave to get to the airstrip."

"That's all? You can't just—"

"No fear because I'll be here," she said, repeating the mantra that she and her team used before each mission.

It galled Jefferson, but he knew she was right. He had to get his sons out of harm's way.

Before they left, the Logan boys flew to her and hugged her. She allowed the hugs and kisses and returned them in kind. Even Hercules got a good belly rub.

She watched Jefferson and her family as they were guided away and packed into the ground convoy. Then she circled two fingers in the air, signaling her team to gear up and get aboard the black, bat-winged, harrier jet copters standing by. Gun in hand, she stood on the skids from above and watched the convoy's progress to the airstrip. When they were secure and off the ground, she signaled for her pilots to get underway to their target to begin the rescue operation.

***

Weeks had passed since Dakota last saw Jefferson and his boys in Africa. She and her full team were on high alert outside the compound, steadily digging their way underground into where the hostages were being kept. They could not chance a full-scale attack via air because al-Qaeda had every member covered in separate locations throughout the compound. The slightest alarm and the industrialists and statesmen and women would be killed.

High-level talks were ongoing between the Russians and Syrians as proxies for the release of the hostages while Dakota and her team continued to tunnel in from four directions. They were already inside the compound, but needed to use water cannons to break through the concrete walls to gain silent entry to the underground bunkers. They would enter *en masse* and silently take out each guard, shepherd the hostages to the exit points, and, hopefully, accomplish this under the cover of darkness until all were free.

Her team practiced their plan for two weeks at a similar compound less than ten clicks from the target location. They were ready and, if their timing was accurate, they could be in and out without a shot fired in less than one hour. Timing was crucial because the guards reported in to a central command every hour. To be successful, they had to accomplish their task within that timeframe.

She didn't allow herself time to think about the man who was her father or the influence he could bring to bear and affect her career. She was not immune to his need to get to know her or to her own need to get to know her family. There were so many years she had to catch up on.

Also, if her missed period was any indication, she was nearly eight weeks pregnant with Jefferson Logan's child. This probability put a completely different light on the possible career options she wanted. She would never leave a child of hers to grow up feeling unloved or unwanted as apparently Jacob Hawkins had felt. She would be a full-time parent, an experience she never contemplated.

Her mentor and trainer had borne children and married, changing her role from warrior to diplomat. That was not a role Dakota had aspired to. She had been in clandestine black ops for her entire adult career. A field operative's life was lived out of a small duffle bag on the world stage. This, she realized, was not a way to raise a child.

Her life would no longer be her own. She would have to tell Jefferson about her pregnancy. He would have no doubt about the legitimacy of her claim to his paternity. He was shocked to find out, in the throes of their intimacy, she was still a virgin at thirty-five, but by then it was entirely too late. Though they made love several times that night, neither had uttered the words 'I love you'.

"We're in, Wind Breeze," her XO for this mission, Slade, aka Cobra Khan, announced, bringing her out of her reverie. She was stretched out on her bunk, but moved swiftly to the ops center. She would pass the word up the chain to Delta they would be ready to move in the early morning hours before dawn. She already had her stealth-harrier jet copters ready to move once they got to the pick-up area. Hopefully, all the captives would be in shape to make the escape. She would leave no one behind.

CHAPTER 29

Thank you, Sylvia," Jefferson said to Vivian and Kenneth Alexander's mother when she passed a refreshing glass of real mint-flavored iced tea to him. He was sitting on the screened lanai of the Alexander home in Goodwill, Summer County, South Carolina, looking out at the pool where his sons frolicked with Bernard and Sylvia Alexanders' grandchildren. When the group from Africa landed at Shaw Air Force Base, Kenneth Alexander met the flight and brought him, Yates, and his sons to his parents' home while Jake and his family continued on to a different undisclosed location.

Though Jake had offered him and his boys refuge with him and his family, Jefferson could not, in good conscience, accept. Jake Hawkins' son, Jacob, would be there and Jake had declared Tyler Montrose would pay for what he had done, involving his son in a plan that could find him tried and convicted of treason. Jefferson wanted no part of that. He had his sister's and sons' welfare and safety to contend with.

"Your boys seem to be enjoying themselves," Dr. Bernard Alexander, Vivian and Kenneth's father, commented.

"They're not the only ones. Savannah and I are both very appreciative of your hospitality and the time we've been here. It's so much like the life we had in Georgia before we lost our parents. You've reminded us of how happy we were living in a small, tight-knit community. We appreciate Kenneth and JeNelle for letting us stay in their summer home while they are in California. The accommodations are perfect."

"We're glad to have you. In fact, I wanted an opportunity to talk with you about an idea I have."

"Oh, what's that?"

"Do you mind leaving Yates, your sister, and your sons and visiting the local school with me?"

"I don't mind at all," he said, rising from his chair. He caught Yates' attention, who nodded in acknowledgement.

They drove to the campus of Summer County Academy and went inside.

"This is a fine school," Jefferson commented, as they traversed the wide halls with beautiful murals on the walls and ceiling and went into the school's main atrium-enclosed office.

"It is, yes, and I've worked very hard over the years to bring it to where it is today."

"You've done quite a job, it seems."

"I've done what came next and that's what I'm doing now. I want to offer you the opportunity to take this school to the next level."

Jefferson was stunned. "I don't understand. You want me to take over for you?"

"I do, yes. You have a global view of the world that I lack. I've read all of your books and papers and you see the world from a different point of view than I can. That's the view our students need. In the next generation, the children will need to know how to compete on a global basis. My duties as state senator don't allow me the quality time I would need to lead this school to the next level, but someone with your skill and ability could do this and make it a success."

It was certainly an intriguing idea, Jefferson thought, one that would allow him quality time to spend with his sons in a close-knit community. He already liked Summer County. It had the kind of enriched lifestyle that could be good for his boys. As dean of the school, he could insure his boys had the kind of education that would prepare them for life's challenges.

There was land he had seen that would be an ideal building site for a home, and, if Kenneth's home and others were any indication, artisans in this community took pride in their craft and workmanship.

There was really nothing holding him in Washington. With custody of his sons, he couldn't leave at a moment's notice and travel to some developing crisis somewhere in the world. Fatherhood had come to mean more to him than his career ever had. In fact, he initially planned to move back to Georgia after he and Felicia married so he could teach. Dr. Alexander was offering him an opportunity to do what he always wanted: to teach and help shape the minds of another generation.

"I will not reject the opportunity, Bernard. This could be just the very thing I need, but I have to discuss it with my sons, and, if they are in agreement, I will have to clear up some important issues before I can give you a definitive answer."

"I understand. I know the safety of your children is paramount in your mind. I can assure you that you and your family will be safe here."

"I believe you. I do feel comfortable here and I don't like the idea of keeping my sons sequestered while the hostage situation is ongoing." For more reasons than Nathan's safety and the safety of the other hostages, he worried about Dakota. Though she had demonstrated her ability to take care of herself, he had feelings for her that would not go away. He desperately wanted an opportunity to see her again and to talk with her. For the time being, he had to take care of his boys' welfare and keep them out of Tyler Montrose's clutches.

The FBI was investigating Jacob Hawkins' claims that Tyler had instigated the hostage taking to lure him into a trap to be assassinated. He did not trust Jacob, but he had no reason to mistrust his word on this score. He had finally consulted with his attorney about his sons' inheritance and found that what Jacob claimed was true. His sons' interest in Montrose Global was the controlling interest dictated by Tyler Montrose's father. He bequeathed his controlling interest in the monolithic company to his first grandchild. That child was Felicia and, although she was deceased, her interest transferred to her sons, specifically to Jefferson Junior, and control rested with him as their custodial parent and guardian until they each reached a certain age.

Now Jefferson understood why Tyler fought him so viciously and vigorously for years over the custody of Jefferson Junior, Miles, and Stephen. It was all about controlling interest in Montrose Global. His sons had it and Tyler wanted it.

Jefferson didn't care one iota about the money, but he believed once his boys were old enough to sign over their interests in the company, Tyler would have them do so. Then, considering the lengths Tyler went to in order to have him murdered, it wasn't a stretch that his sons might meet with some fatal accident that also took their lives. At that point, with no other heirs, the boys' future inheritance would revert to Tyler Montrose in its entirety.

His boys were in as much danger as he was. Since very few people knew where they were, Jefferson felt relatively safe in the Alexander's Goodwill home with Yates' expanded role to protect his sons.

CHAPTER 30

The air in the rounded tunnel was moist to the point of sticky heat. The huge whirling scythe on the nose of the bullet-shaped cone cut through the soil like butter leaving a rounded tube tall enough for an average height person to walk through, but the amount of water needed to cut through the concrete left them slogging in ankle-deep sludge.

With stealth, they entered the lowest level of several outbuildings on bare feet with night vision goggles and full head and facemasks in place. Ants crawling across a desert made more noise than they did. Hand signals were unnecessary; they knew exactly what they were required to do and executed each task with precision and covertness. They were among the most elite teams in The Nursery, an acronym for a worldwide security force known to only a precious few, created by the G8. As they predicted, this was the hardest part of the night for the al-Qaeda guards to be at their best and acutely alert. That fact made it a relatively easy task for the rescuers to spray a little mist, called Devil's Breath, in the air that put each guard instantly to sleep. DNA was extracted, fingerprints gathered, and pictures taken to enhance The Nursery's database of criminals and terrorists. Finally, tracking devices were injected under the captors' armpits and a spray applied to the center of their backs that could never be washed away. Each was then gagged and hog-tied to insure they would not interfere with the liberation of the hostages as the rescue continued.

Each hostage was awakened and passed to a waiting escort who took him or her back to one of the escape tunnels. When Dakota subdued Bill Chandler's guard, she found her former partner and XO wide-awake and grinning at her.

Bill Chandler knew the drill and had felt the subtle vibrations from the scythe for weeks. It was only a matter of time before he knew the exact night they would be liberated and was prepared for their arrival. He assisted with the rescue of Nathan Flack and the remaining hostages. As the sleeping guards were unshackled and ungagged, it was as if the rescuers were never there. Dakota and Bill were the last to leave before new brick walls were erected to cover their escape. As the scythe retracted, the soil previously displaced and compacted collapsed, filling the void.

Well away from the al-Qaeda compound, Bill silently shook hands with his teammates and proceeded to lock and load their expensive, secret equipment for transport. Nothing would be left behind to indicate how the escape was executed or by whom. They took pride in moving like ghosts through any operation without taking a life, if at all possible.

When the androgynous-looking rescuers reached their extraction checkpoint with their charges in tow, their faces and skin were still completely covered. The former captives, except Bill and Nathan, would remember little if anything of the escape. A timed-released substance in the bottled water they were given would induce a short-term memory loss. They would wake up in The Hague, Netherlands, to continue their talks at the Peace Palace under heightened security as if nothing untoward had taken place.

Some might remember the escape eventually, but most would recall it as a dream. Better living through a chemical haze. The operative word being living.

"Wheels up in five, Wind Breeze," Dakota's XO informed.

"Copy that," she acknowledged. She stood with her head down, hands in her BDU pockets, shifting her weight from one booted foot to the other.

Bill Chandler stood before her, his hands also in his pockets, looking at the top of his former partner's still covered head. "So, we're getting a divorce, huh?"

Dakota smirked at his glib remark, looked up into his too-handsome face, and squared her shoulders. "You never call. You don't write. You rarely even e-mail or send a text. What's a wife to think? And, where were you when I needed you in Africa? Nowhere around. Instead, you were hanging out around here in the lap of luxury, having all of your needs and desires attended to—something I can't un-see. I had to handle that little skirmish with a civilian Mossad officer. And then, I have to get all dressed up to come and find you? You're not good husband material."

"I would have stuck it out if you had kept me supplied with powdered sheets."

"I could not afford the high thread-count silk you prefer."

"Sir?" her XO again informed.

Bill and Dakota looked into each other's eyes, and then, with a nod and mutual flippant salute, they began backing away from each other before they turned and walked to their separate aircraft. There was an acknowledgement that, after many years as partners, they might never work together or even see each other again. He was first headed to complete the talks as his assignment dictated. Then Bill had his own team of sandbaggers to find and train into a crack team just as Dakota had once trained him.

However, Dakota's future was now far less certain. When she was again in the country, she would first confirm whether she was, indeed, pregnant, and, if so, what she needed to do next.

***

Six months later, Dakota, now better known as LaiLoni Skai Hawkins, sat in a rocking chair on the wide, deep veranda of Hawk House. The busy BlackHawk ranch surrounded her. Her father and stepmother returned from their last five months in Africa only a few days ago. In the time she had been at the ranch, her grandmother, Kiavi Littlefeather, often came to visit her for extended periods.

LaiLoni learned on her visits to the Navajo Reservation that Kiavi was a noted author of children's fiction and a shrewd businesswoman. Her husband, Keanu, was murdered to keep the Navajo people from establishing ownership of their land and the mineral rights. She learned she was the great granddaughter of Ra and Kove, the great, great granddaughter of Matisse, the Spaniard and Minnel, the Apache. Her history went back through the generations to Spanish nobility and also to the Mayans, Toltec, and Aztecs among her mother's people.

Her Aunt Mavis, her father's only sister, told her that her ancestry on the Hawkins side was rooted in the Louisiana Bayou country near New Orleans. Their history included escaped slaves who lived free and undetected in the swamp for many generations until the late 1800s. After a hurricane that devastated Louisiana generations later, Jake and Mavis escaped a brutal orphanage after the death of their parents and were picked up hitchhiking on a back road going west by Ezra Neal, a young, single oil field worker on his way to work the oil fields near Houston, Texas. Years later, they were all still together when, as a result of a work-related accident, an eighteen-year-old Jake Hawkins met a twenty-one-year-old nurse, Skye Littlefeather, and fell in love.

The insurance company paid the claim for the accident, but became suspicious of Jake's claim to be older than he actually was. Before a full-scale investigation could be launched, Jake and Ezra packed up and moved again, heading west with Mavis and a very pregnant Skai Hawkins.

On their way, many miles outside of San Antonio, they passed a government sign advertising the tax sale of a dilapidated ranch. Jake used his insurance money to buy the place for pennies on the dollar. When Jake and Ezra discovered oil on the property, Jake's multibillion-dollar career was launched. With nothing more than a sixth-grade education and the Midas touch, he created Hawkinstown, a community with a population in the thousands, for the people he employed to work his ranch and the various industries the land supported.

LaiLoni Skye was fascinated by the stories she heard from her newfound family members. Stories she would pass on to her daughter, she thought, as she rubbed her very round abdomen.

Jake came out onto the veranda in a pair of well-worn jeans and a white T-shirt. His feet were bare. He sat down in the rocking chair next to hers and extended his hand palm up. She took his big, meaty paw, and squeezed gently, interlocking their fingers. He took every opportunity to touch her whenever she was near. It was a connection and comfort for both of them.

"What you studdin', dahlin?" he asked.

"Nothing, really, Jake. The doctors said I could get some exercise since the surgery was successful. I just came back from a long walk over to watch Adam working on his cars."

"He'll soon be out on the Formula One race car circuit for the next six months. He's sticking close to home until this new little Hawkins shows up."

"I told him he didn't need to do that. All of you should just go about your business as if I wasn't here."

"Been too many years that you *weren't* with us. My Skai came to me in a vision and told me you would be returned to us. That was the day your sister married Roderick Baylor. That day, Skai released me to fall in love again with Roderick's sister, Kelley. Now, she kept her word because here you are where you should have been with us for the past thirty-five years." He squeezed her hand again. "Are you sad, LaiLoni?"

"No, not sad. A bit concerned about Jacob."

"Your brother has to take whatever punishment he is due. He has Vivian Montgomery's law partners representing him. I suspect now that Tyler Montrose is in prison at Gitmo, things will go better for him. Jacob didn't actually participate in the kidnapping plan, but he gained knowledge of what Montrose was up to after the fact and took no action to inform the authorities."

"Fortunately, no one was harmed. The talks are successfully concluding in The Hague. Nathan Flack is being hailed as a hero for what he has accomplished."

"Another month, maybe two, and the US will have new accords with previously waring Asian and Arab factions. Now that both of your missions and surgery were successfully completed, what are you going to do about Jeff Logan? You haven't called him to tell him about…What is it, LaiLoni?"

"Hold that thought, Jake. We will have to continue this conversation later. My water just broke."

CHAPTER 31

Nathan Flack walked off the State Department's aircraft chatting with Deputy Secretary of State, Kayla Hill. The attractive woman had joined the talks when the participants arrived in the Netherlands. She proved herself invaluable to the logistical process and security detail. She handled the daily press conferences, insuring each country or company representatives received ample coverage and face time with the media. She always worked behind the scenes, handling the most minute details. He understood why Ms. Hill was in the top echelon of the State Department's hierarchy. She was simply that good.

She guided him and the American industrialists backstage of the packed conference room where he would deliver a prepared statement and answer a few questions. Then he would head over to the White House to meet with the President, Joint Chiefs, and the Secretary of State. He had no doubt others would be in attendance, but he was bone tired and in want of a few quiet weeks at some undisclosed location in the tropics. He knew that was only wishful thinking. He would be directed to be on the media circuit for as long as their success was the top story in the press. Perhaps he and Gail could get together for a long weekend. At the first opportunity, he would have Mrs. Hilton look into secluded accommodations. He had heard that Plaza de Masquerada was among the best locations to decompress. It was a highly secure, exclusive tropical island retreat in the Pacific. That's the kind of downtime he would need. He would find out more about it.

As he waited for the cue that the press conference would begin, he thought about how he and Savannah would get away for long periods of time to her cabin in the Maryland mountains. Those days were precious memories to him now. He would always regret he and Savannah could not make their relationship work.

"Ready, Mr. Ambassador?" Ms. Hill asked.

"Yes," he said, snapping out of his reverie and preparing to meet the press and news media.

The Vice President was before the cameras doing the introductions, listing his background, achievements and what these new accords meant for the future stability of the United States and its economy. Then he heard his name announced amid the rousing applause. He walked on stage to a blizzard of flashing bulbs and high-powered camera lights. The industrialists trailed him onto the stage and arranged themselves behind him, all smiles for the press conference cameras.

He began his remarks when the melee decreased to a minimum. The energy in the room was electric. The press and news media, Fifth Estate wolf pack, waited impatiently for him to complete his remarks. As soon as he did, questions flew at him tumbling over one another. He took several minutes answering questions, mindful of the tight schedule he had for the rest of the day.

Bill Chandler was drafted to be the spokesperson for and by the other industrialists. He made brief comments and took questions. The man was the consummate professional and his presence commanded everyone's attention, Nathan thought.

He shook hands with Bill and the others forced to take time to pose with the Vice President. Shortly, Ms. Hill ended the press conference and had him and the Vice President in the motorcade from Andrews AFB, with flashing lights, headed for the White House. There were briefing sessions for the rest of the afternoon through dinner. After dinner, he was finally able to go to his office at the State Department where Mrs. Hilton warmly greeted him.

They talked for nearly an hour. She brought him up to date on other business that was held in abeyance, pending his return.

"I know you're tired, Nathan, but you need to read this," she said, handing a red-jacketed file to him.

He took the file and began to read. He became so incensed he began to pace as he continued to read. Finally, he looked up at his Executive Assistant in disbelief.

"Gail Conway was a plant?"

"Yes," she confirmed. "I had a security background check run on her the day she came to the office. The report came back whistle clean—too clean for my comfort, so I had the Secret Service drill down into her history and do an update. Though she claimed to have been born and raised in Minnesota, there were no high school yearbooks with her picture in it. The Gail Conway whose picture did appear in the yearbook could not have been the one who you met in that accident. Facial recognition confirmed my suspicions. The FBI took over the case and she was picked up on a silent warrant along with Tyler Montrose and several others. Somehow, she escaped custody. The authorities are investigating."

He shook his head in disappointment. He was glad they were never intimate. He would have no lingering regrets about what he thought they might have developed. He returned the file to Mrs. Hilton and continued to pace, grabbing his neck with both hands.

"You're tired, child, and probably jet lagged, too. Why don't you let your security team take you to a hotel so you can get some rest?'

"You're right, Sadie, I am tired, but I want to sleep in my own bed tonight. It's after midnight and you should be at home with your husband."

"He's waiting for me downstairs. I'll see you in the morning."

"Rest well, Sadie. My apologies to Bert for keeping you so late."

"He's a Marine. He understands. Goodnight."

The security team dropped him off at the front door of the Watergate Complex. He was dog-tired when he entered his condo, but not too tired to smell the scent of cooked food or to notice the candles burning around the room or the sight of Savannah asleep on one of the living room sofas.

He sat down on a coffee table across from her to observe her for a while. Nothing about the past months served to erase her from his mind and heart. He doubted anything ever would. Trying to distance himself from his love for her was fruitless. So, he set about shutting down the kitchen, blowing out the candles, and lifting Savannah in his arms to carry her to his bed.

He slept with her tucked into his right side and then woke later in the morning violently aroused. Savannah was somewhere under the covers between his open thighs, giving his phallus one helluva welcome home.

Much later, he and Savannah, sexually sated and freshly showered, sat across from each other eating for brunch the meal she had arranged for the night before. When the meal was nearly over, Savannah got down on bended knee, between his legs. Initially, he thought she was going to give him a repeat of her early morning gift. Instead, she produced a small, dark blue velvet box, which she opened. Inside was a titanium wedding band.

"Nathan Jerome Flack, you answer each and every one of my desires and—"

He didn't let her finish before he took her face in his palms and kissed her with all the passion he possessed.

"Yes," he said between kisses. He slipped the wedding band on his finger and said, "Yes, Savannah Alicia Logan, I will marry you."

CHAPTER 32

Dakota quietly closed the car door and strapped into the driver's seat. She checked the back seat once more before she started the SUV and drove away from the airport. Her father insisted she take one of his jets to Columbia, South Carolina, and wait while she tended to her next task. He wasn't fooling her, however. She knew he was having her watched and allowed it because of the years of separation from her he endured. They still had their battles; primarily because she refused to let him keep her under his watchful eyes or accept what her entire family insisted was her rightful share of the BlackHawk conglomerate. Wealth like that never was important to her. She had resources enough to take care of her needs. The stipend she received as a "deactivated" operative was sufficient.

The scenery she passed was surprisingly lush after she transitioned off the highway to the back roads. She let down her window and took a deep breath of the pine and honeysuckle scented air. Grey, ringlet Spanish moss draped the trees and swayed in the gentle breeze. The trees overhanging the road created a cathedral-like appearance, shading the graceful curves and bends. The countryside seemed almost mystical. She slowed when she approached pillars on the roadside that read: WELCOME HOME. It was a particularly glorious day.

***

Jefferson barely made it into the lanai's back door of his new, six-bedroom, four-thousand-square-foot, ranch-style home before Jefferson "Jay" Junior hit him again with another barrage from his water cannon.

Stevie and Miles already caught him off guard, as he was kneeling to test the water in the swimming pool, and pushed him in. Fortunately, he was wearing shorts and a T-shirt for his impromptu dunking. They were laughing uproariously until he climbed out of the pool and chased them around the acre of grassy yard with a much bigger Hercules barking and enjoying the chase. He had no sooner pitched Stevie and Miles into the pool and started after Jay when he got hit by Jay's water cannon. He was soaked to the skin and making a strategic retreat.

He and his sons made good progress toward becoming a family. When they were summoned to testify about the harrowing experience in Africa and about what they knew of their grandfather's underhanded dealings, they stepped up to the task. He didn't shelter them from the seriousness of what their grandfather attempted to do and the reasons for it. He permitted them to watch through a one-way mirror while the FBI, CIA, and other agencies interrogated their grandfather. Tyler was just as belligerent and arrogant, calling his grandsons names Jefferson regretted they heard. It was necessary, however, to have them witness, firsthand, their grandfather's duplicity.

Halfway through the interrogation, when Jefferson Junior, with tears in his eyes, rushed into his arms, nothing could have been more gratifying. Nor could anything have solidified his relationship with his sons better. The Court had no choice but to grant Jefferson's custody petition with no strings attached. Now their days together in Summer County, South Carolina, were filled with a growing closeness, fun, and new discoveries.

The Summer County Academy they attended, where he was now the Dean, challenged them scholastically and energized them intellectually. Jeff learned his first-born had a desire to be a fireman, while Miles was fascinated with all things electronic. Stevie was very artistic with both paper and pen and molding clay. However, Stevie was talented in a number of areas, Jefferson learned. It was a challenge to keep up with his varied interests. One of those interests was Roderick and JaiHonnah's twin daughters, Shelly and Shelby Baylor. They were in touch via Skype daily. Go figure.

In Goodwill, the boys were left pretty much to freely roam. Yates was still ever present, but not intrusive. The boys regarded Yates much as they did their Aunt Savannah; he was a member of the family.

His boys were excellent horsemen, Jeff learned, so he purchased horses and other livestock for their sixty-acre spread. The boys liked to ride their horses to school with other students. Sometimes Jefferson would ride with them. Farm life in this community seemed to suit him and his boys and was reminiscent of Jefferson's early childhood experiences living with his parents in Georgia.

On his way to his bedroom to change his sopping-wet clothes, he detoured to answer the front doorbell. When he opened it, there stood Dakota Sinclair.

He tried every way he could to find her over the past months, even appealing to her father and to the President, but all avenues to her location were closed to him. Nevertheless, he was not giving up hope of finding her. She was never far from his thoughts. Given what he witnessed of her leadership role in Africa, he recognized wherever she might be she would likely be sacrificing her life for her country. He understood that level of dedication to duty and wished for her sake and his she would keep herself safe.

At the moment, she was in serious danger of his loving her to death and never letting her go. Heedless of his drenched condition, he snatched her into his arms, his mouth covering hers in a blink of an eye. He heard her answering moan as her arms banded around him. Then with his eyes closed in silent prayer, he held her tightly and breathed her in.

"I'm in love with you, Dakota. Helplessly in love with you. So if that marriage to Bill was, as I suspected, a farce, you've got to put me out of my misery and marry me."

She looked up into his eyes, hers sparkling. "First, I have someone I want you to meet," she said and guided him through the still open front door to the SUV in his circular driveway. She opened the back door, revealing a sleeping, six-week-old, baby girl.

"This is Francine Sinclair Logan, your daughter."

Jefferson was momentarily stunned speechless, as he looked from the beautiful baby to the woman he loved. He kissed Dakota again, more tenderly this time, a grin engulfing his face. He reached, with trembling hands, to unlatch the restraints on the carrier until he had his daughter in his arms. He didn't realize tears were leaking from his closed eyes until Miles asked why he was crying. He had buried his face in his daughter's small body, unaware Yates and his sons silently stood by.

Later that night, Jefferson sat on his bed in the master bedroom and peered into the crib that Mrs. Alexander, Vivian's mother, brought by at his request. Dakota was stretched out on the bed behind him, watching him watch their daughter sleep.

"Did you know my mother's name was Francine?" he asked.

"I did, yes. I read a dossier on you. According to what I found, you were apparently a very closely-knit family. I thought giving your daughter her grandmother's name would please you."

"It does, very much, but so do you. You are going to marry me on Saturday, right?"

Dakota chuckled. "For the umpteenth time, yes, Jefferson, I will marry you. Jake is arranging to bring the family here to avoid the slip of any information to the press and news media. It will be a very discrete event with just your family and mine here in your home."

"As Shakespeare said, *Discretion is the better part of valor.*"

"You will have to be patient with me. I have never been in love before."

"Neither have I. So we will learn together."

"Never fear because I'll always be here."

ABOUT THE AUTHOR

Ann Jeffries is a native of Washington, DC. As an only child, she enjoyed the benefits of a private school education at Allen in Asheville, North Carolina, and a public education at the University of Maryland. Ann began writing fiction for her own amusement.